# tortured

*new york times* bestselling author
# NICOLE WILLIAMS

*For all of you who are suffering in silence.*
*Your voice is so much stronger than you know.*
*The world is waiting to hear it.*
*You are not alone.*

# prologue

Whenever he had to leave, it was torture. You'd think I'd get used to it, but I didn't—each time got harder. This one might have felt especially brutal because of how long he'd be gone. A year. We'd done weeks, we'd done months, but we'd never done the full year.

Being with someone in the military, I knew I'd have to get used to it. The separation. The worry. The loneliness. The feeling that I was trying to catch my breath for however long he was gone.

It was a way of life. And he was my life. So I'd just have to figure it out.

"I'm never going to look at dog tags the same way again." Brecken's mouth turned up as his eyes roamed over me splayed across the backseat as he tucked in his T-shirt. He twisted his wrist, his gaze moving to his watch. A crease folded into his forehead. "But I'm going to need those back before I climb onto that bus. Something about military regulations. Not wandering around enemy territory without them. Those marines are sticklers for the rules."

He was trying to make me feel better—trying to get me to smile—but little could lift my spirits other than finding out he didn't have to leave for the Middle East for twelve long months.

"You don't *need* them. Not really."

"Why's that?"

"Because you only need them if you're planning on dying, and so help me god, I'm not taking these off my neck if you have plans for some kind of a hero's death." My hand curled almost defensively around the metal tags hanging against my bare skin as I focused on the way the cool metal warmed in my hand. The way it seemed to come to life in my hold.

"I'm not planning on dying over there. I'm not *going* to die," he corrected the moment my eyebrow started to lift. "But I do have plans of scoring some gnarly war wound so I have a story to tell our grandkids one day and can hang one of those Purple Hearts off my chest."

I flattened my face as best as I could, even though it was kind of impossible with the way he was grinning at me as he wrestled his jeans back into place. "Not funny."

"Come on. It'll make me look tough."

"You already look tough. Too tough," I added as I scanned him for the millionth time since he'd arrived back in Medford for a week-long vacation before shipping out. Whenever I looked at him, I didn't just see the good-looking guy others did—I saw every good memory from my past. I saw every good memory that would be formed in the future. Brecken had been a part of my life since I was eight, and he was as much a part of me as I was.

"Nah, I need one of those big, angry-looking scars running across my chest. Or one of those bullet hole scars on my thigh. Something real tough like that."

"And why do you need your dog tags for that?" My fingers tightened around the thin metal ovals, refusing to let them go as if I hoped in doing so, he couldn't go either.

"Blood transfusion. Medics are going to need to know my blood type when they're trying to patch up my unconscious body."

"Unconscious body?"

He nodded all solemn-like. "I can't be one of those guys who earns his Purple Heart by getting a scratch on some barbed wire. I need to lose a quart or two of blood, maybe even code on the operating table. Something worthy of that medal."

The thought of Brecken marching through a hostile country with a rifle in his hands, with god only knew what aimed his way, made me feel weak with worry. The thought of him fighting for his life in some marine medical tent about took whatever was left of my sanity.

I must not have been doing a good job hiding my emotions, because his face broke when he saw my eyes, his arms opening toward me. "It's going to be okay, Camryn. I'm going to be okay. We're going to be okay. The year will fly by, and before we know it, we'll be getting married and buying a little house as close to the beach as we can afford. Okay?"

His arms wound around me, swallowing my body, and I let him tuck me close to him. I'd never known the feeling of being safe until Brecken Connolly's arms had shown me the meaning.

My hand planted in the middle of his chest, feeling his heartbeat vibrate against my palm. "Why can't we just get married now? Why can't I join the marines and go with you, wherever that is, so we can be together?"

His laugh was muffled from his mouth being pressed against my temple. "Well, you can't join the marines and my unit because the military's under this impression that us marines of the male species become distracted and one-track minded when the women we love are marching beside us. They're convinced the only things on our minds are protecting you, flirting with you, or screwing you."

Quietly, I counted off on my fingers, "Protecting, flirting, screwing ..." Then I nodded. "Damn, they sure have you pegged."

Brecken's fingers brushed up and down the bend of my waist. "And we can't get married right now because you've got two more months of high school to finish before you earn that nifty diploma thing." He kept going, undeterred by my grumble. "And I need to save some money to give you a proper ring and wedding. I'm not doing the courthouse thing with cheap silver bands. Not for you. You deserve the best."

My head tucked beneath his chin as I let him hold me in the backseat of his aunt's old Corsica. The only good thing I could say about the car—which was a coin toss if it would start any given day—was that it had a decent-sized backseat that Brecken and I had made more than ample use of. Growing up in a strict household with my dad as Brecken grew up in the packed household a few houses down, privacy had been in short supply for both of us. Thankfully, his aunt was willing to lend Brecken her car whenever she could, like today, when I'd just made love to the only boy I'd ever loved for the last time for the next year.

My fingers curled into his chest as I willed time to freeze. "I have the best."

Brecken grunted like he doubted that, his head lifting to check out the windshield. We were parked way back in the bus depot lot. His bus would be leaving for the long drive back to Camp Pendleton in a few short minutes.

"Besides, you already got me a ring." I raised my left hand in front of him, rolling my fingers so he could see the adjustable birthstone ring on my finger.

He shook his head. "I won that for you at an arcade when we were ten."

"It cost you twelve hundred tickets too. You saved up all summer to get that many tickets."

His fingers touched the ring, twisting it around with a small smile on his face. "And it probably has the street value of a nickel. Not exactly the kind of wedding ring I want my wife to have."

I found myself staring at the ring with him. The gold paint had started chipping off the thin band years ago, but the small pink birthstone still sparkled when the light hit it just right. "Well, it's priceless to me. I don't care what the street value is. Or how many tickets it cost."

"Even so, I'm getting you a nice ring. With all of the hazard pay I'll earn this year, you'd better start working that left ring finger out so it can bear the weight of the diamond I'll be dropping on it."

I was glad he couldn't see my face, because he hated knowing how worried I was about him. He said hazard pay like a sales rep mentioned a bonus, but I heard it for what it really was—the government giving you a little more money for the likelihood of losing your life increasing.

"One more year. That's it. Then we'll be able to be together like we've always planned. Away from here." Brecken's arms loosened around me. We didn't have much longer. "Away from these people."

An uneven exhale came from him, the muscles in his arms twitching. I knew who he was talking about without him going into detail. Neither of our lives had been charmed or particularly easy, but mine had been worse. Being raised by a single dad who was so strict he made a monk's life seem carefree, I'd had an unusual upbringing. Brecken only knew what I let him know about it, which was barely half of the reality.

"I don't like leaving you alone with him," he said, his voice a note lower. "If things get hard again, just leave. Move in with my insane family or a hotel or anywhere. Don't let him hurt you. Words or fists. He does it again"—Brecken's hands curled into balls as his back stiffened—"I'll kill him. I swear I will."

"He won't," I said instantly, in my most convincing voice. "He's working on all that. Not drinking as much." I made sure to hold his stare to sell as much conviction as I was capable.

My dad wasn't just a strict man. He was a sad one, a lonely one. After my mom left, he'd turned into someone else, almost like she'd taken everything that had been good about him and stuffed it in that small suitcase too. Since I was the only one around and bore a striking resemblance to my mom, I'd taken the brunt of my dad's grief. In the form of cutting words and, occasionally, outstretched palms.

Brecken had been walking down the sidewalk one day when he saw my dad strike me across the cheek for attempting to leave the house in a skirt he described as "fitting for a whore." Brecken had only been thirteen, but he'd taken my dad down, managing to land a few punches before I could pull him off.

My dad stopped hitting me after that. At least where anyone passing by could see.

Not that I needed to tell Brecken that now. Though I guessed it would get him to stay a while longer … if only to be charged with murder and thrown into prison for the next twenty to thirty years.

Suddenly, that year didn't seem so bad.

"He won't," I reiterated, when Brecken continued to give me that penetrating stare, like he was capable of finding a lie if I was hiding one.

Both of his brows lifted. "He better not."

"If anything happens, I'll crash at your family's place, I swear."

Sitting up, he pulled his wallet out of his back pocket. "With fourteen people sharing twelve hundred square feet of space, good luck finding a quiet spot to do your homework." He pulled every bill out of his wallet. Even the last crumbled dollar. "Take this, hide it from your dad, and use it if you need to. That's enough to get you a week or so at a hotel that isn't a dump, and as soon as I get my next paycheck, I'll send more."

My head was shaking as I tried to stuff the money back into his wallet. He'd already closed it and was sliding it back into his pocket though. "I'll be fine."

Brecken's gaze dropped to the money in my hand. "Yeah, I know."

"Brecken."

"Camryn," he mimicked.

"I'm not taking the last dollar in your wallet."

"Why not?" he asked, making a face. "I'd give you the shirt off my back, the air in my lungs, the last drop of blood in my veins. The last dollar's a cakewalk compared to, you know, dying of suffocation or bleeding out." He winked as he folded my fingers around the wad of money in my hand, then he leaned down to pull on his boots. He was moving quickly, glancing in the direction of the buses like he was making sure his wasn't pulling away from the curb yet.

"Do you want to walk with me to the bus?" His focus stayed on cinching up his last boot as he waited for my answer.

He already knew it though. Good-byes weren't my forte. Especially not the kind where I had to wave good-bye to the man I loved as he prepared to head into the middle of a war zone for the next year. Good-bye came with a whole different context when you said it to a marine.

"I know, Blue Bird. I know." He sighed, his eyes narrowing at the weathered floorboards before he reached for the dog tags still hanging around my neck.

I didn't make any move to lift my head or slide my hair aside to make it easier for him. As long as those tags were on my neck instead of his, he was safe. He was alive.

"I'm not going to die over there," he whispered, pulling the tags over his head. They clinked together as they fell against his chest. "I'm coming back to you."

My throat was burning from trying to keep myself from crying. "You can't promise that."

He reached for the blanket that had fallen on the floor and gently tucked it around my still-naked body. It was strange how I'd forgotten I was naked until he'd taken his tags off of me. Now though, I felt bare. Exposed. Vulnerable. My dress was somewhere around, even though I didn't see it. We'd barely managed to make it to the parking lot before falling into the backseat together.

"Yes I can," he said, his thumb tracing my collarbone before tucking the other corner around my shoulder. "Have I ever broken a promise to you?" He angled himself so he was in front of me, so I was forced to look him in the eyes.

"This is different. You can't know for sure."

"I'm going to enjoy watching you eat those words when I'm standing in front of that pretty face in twelve months, Blue Bird."

I pulled the blanket tighter around me. "You know I don't like it when you call me that when I'm mad at you."

"You're mad? At me?" He blinked. "Why?"

"You know why." My eyes automatically moved toward the line of buses.

"To set the record straight, it's the marine corps sending me to Iraq. Not me by personal choice."

"No, but you made the personal choice to join the marine corps."

"Yeah, because I didn't want to spend the next twenty years pumping gas at the Qwik Mart." His hand curled around the back of the front seat. "We've talked about this, Camryn. I'm not cut out for college, and I sure as shit am not going to spend my life working a minimum-wage part-time job and stuck in Medford. The marines is a chance at a real life. A career where I can be promoted and provide for a family and get a chance to kick a little ass every once in a while." He leaned forward to kiss my forehead. Then my lips. "This is the ticket to that life we've been talking about for years. But it comes with a price." His mouth covered mine again, this time a bit longer. "I'll be okay. I'll make it back."

My eyes closed so I could focus on the taste of him left behind on my mouth. "You're always the first to charge into anything. You don't hang back. You don't like the shadows. You like being the one who cast those shadows."

When my eyes finally opened, I found his dark blue ones inches away from mine. His light hair, buzzed short so he was all ready for deployment, the few freckles scattered across the bridge of his nose, the way his jaw tightened when he stared at me, those were the things I'd remember when I'd lay awake at night, wondering where he was. If he was safe. If he was thinking about me. As long as I held on to a part of him, he could never really leave me.

"I'm coming home to you," he said like a solemn vow. "It might be in more than one piece, but I'm coming home to you."

I tucked his tags inside his shirt. They'd become cold again. "A thousand pieces, I don't care. Just come home."

His smile was almost as forced as mine as he leaned in, pulling me into his arms one last time. He held me for a minute, one hand secured around my neck, the other around my back, rocking me against him. Then he kissed me one last time. "Gotta go, Blue Bird. The Middle East isn't going to settle itself down."

As he threw open the back door to go around to the trunk to grab his bag, I leaned across the seat. He was leaving. For what felt like forever. "Yeah, don't think you're single-handedly responsible for tackling that agenda either."

Throwing the bag over his shoulder, he crouched beside me. This smile wasn't contrived. It was real. Perfect. "I'll see you soon."

"Soon?"

His hand formed around my cheek as his thumb traced the seam of my lips. "Sounds better than *see you in a year*, right?" Tucking his thumb into his mouth, tasting my lips on it, he gave me a wicked smirk before shoving to a stand and starting toward the buses. "I'm coming back for you, Camryn Blue Gardner, so you'd better be waiting for me, or I'll just have to come find you and remind you why you fell crazy in love with me."

Tucking the blanket around myself, I slid out of the car, leaning over the open door. "I'm not going anywhere. I'll be waiting."

He'd started to jog backward. "Waiting as in a few days until some other guy makes his play?"

My eyes rolled as I gave him a look. Brecken and I'd been together since I was fifteen and he was seventeen. Even before that, we'd been inseparable, no one able to come between us.

I cupped my hand around my mouth. "Waiting as in forever."

"I won't keep you waiting that long. Just long enough." He was shouting now, the rumbling buses muffling his voice.

"Long enough for what?" I yelled back.

Even with this much distance between us, I didn't miss it. The look in his eyes. The tip of his smile. "For you to agree to marry me the moment I get back."

The breeze played with my hair, sending it away from him, like forces out of our control were already pulling us apart. "I will!"

He paused just below the bus steps, his eyes consuming me from a hundred yards away. "It's, I do, Blue Bird. *I do*." He grinned and handed his bag off to the person stuffing them into one of the outside compartments. Then his hands cupped around his mouth, and he dropped his head back. "I do, too!"

His voice echoed across the parking lot, earning the attention of more than just me.

That was it. He climbed the stairs, turned the corner, and disappeared inside the bus. I wouldn't see him for a year. I might not see him ever …

My jaw tensed as I put a stop to that train of thought. Wedding vows and rings were the last things on my mind as his bus lurched away from the curb.

"Just come back to me," I whispered to no one. "Just come back."

# one

Graduation day. It was probably the most overrated, underwhelming milestone in a person's life. All this buildup, years of school to get there, only to be handed some piece of paper while faking a smile as someone snapped a photo.

My view might have been jaded since Brecken wasn't there to experience it with me. His graduation two years ago had seemed like a much bigger deal, way more worth celebrating, but that was probably because we'd been together. Instead, all I'd had in the crowd was my dad, who instead of clapping when I was awarded my diploma, slouched deeper into his seat and stared around like he was looking for where the booze was being served.

Oh, well. I could cross that mile marker off my list and move on to the next. Whatever that was. I'd been so focused on getting through each day, I hadn't spent a lot of time thinking about what came next. At least other than being with Brecken. Did I want to go to college? Did I want to go straight to work? What did I even want to do? Those were questions I needed to work on filling in the answers to, but they could wait another day. Tonight, I was planning on eating my weight in onion rings and milkshakes.

Half of the graduating class had wound up at the local burger joint to celebrate, and the other half had wound up out at Miller's Point, kegs and condoms galore. That had never been my scene, not that it would have mattered if it was. My dad was as against underage drinking as he was sex outside of marriage. What could I say? My old man served his moral agenda with a hefty side of hypocrisy.

"Picture to mark the occasion?" Crew Graves slid into the half foot of booth beside me, holding his phone in front of us as he threw his arm around me and leaned in.

I didn't miss how, across the table, Gina and Sierra's attention went from each other to the boy snapping a picture beside me. Crew was "that guy" of our graduating class. At least that was how I'd heard him described, not that I held that opinion personally. Like Brecken, I'd pretty much grown up with Crew. He lived down the block with his parents, so the three of us had been friends until it became obvious that Brecken and I were becoming more than just friends. Crew eased back after that, but I still counted him as a friend. Brecken did too. Crew was a little hardcore, one of those guys who went from cold to hot after one bad call from a ref or someone shouldering by him in the hall, by accident or otherwise. Good guy, just one whose temper ran on the hot end of the scale.

After snapping a couple of shots, Crew lowered his phone and didn't make any move to go back to the table he'd come from, where the rest of the football guys were belching their way through the school anthem.

"Brecken still kicking ass?" he asked, seeming ignorant to the gaping stares of the girls across the table from us.

Which had me fighting a smile. I supposed Crew was cute in his own right, a little too "cute" for me, but I understood why girls' heads turned when he passed.

"Always," I answered with a nod, breaking a few of my fresh onion rings apart so they'd cool down faster. The grease was still popping across the batter.

"Miss him?"

"Always," I said with a sigh.

"Hey, two months are already down. Ten more to go. You've got this." Crew nudged me, snagging a butter knife from across the table to cut the rest of my onion rings in half so I didn't have to keep burning my fingers.

"I know that's supposed to make me feel better, but two months have felt like two years. I don't want to think about getting through another ten."

The noise in the diner was deafening, so Crew had to lean in closer to hear me. For some reason, I found myself almost uncomfortable with having him so close. Brecken was the only guy I'd ever been close to, the first one I'd held hands with, the one I'd lost my virginity to, and having another guy so close felt awkward. Like someone was trying to shove me into a pair of shoes that didn't fit.

I slid more into the booth, which only smashed me up against Damon. He was a nice guy, but one who didn't seem to believe in personal hygiene.

In the midst of my scooting and shifting, the collar of my dress got pulled a ways down my shoulder. Crew's eyes dodged there. "Damn, Camryn. What did you do to yourself? Charge into McKenzie without wearing shoulder pads?" Crew tossed a wadded up napkin at his former teammate, Todd McKenzie, who was tipping the scale closer to four hundred than three hundred.

"Last day of gym class. Ran into a volleyball pole." The answer came instantly, easily, as I shrugged. "Couldn't leave high school without one last accident in gym."

Crew chuckled, reaching for the bottle of ketchup for me. "Coordination is not your ally. Maybe in your next life."

"Maybe," I mumbled, squeezing a stream of ketchup over my onion rings.

"So he's doing good though over there? Keeping his head down and staying toward the back?" When I scooted my tray of onion rings, offering Crew one, he tossed one in his mouth.

"Yeah, right," I said with a snort. "He's already been promoted to lance corporal and is leading a firing squad. You know Brecken. He doesn't know how to keep his head down. Or stay in the back."

Crew nodded as he chewed, giving me a sympathetic smile. Brecken was who he was. I couldn't change that. I didn't want to change that. I just wished I could roll him up in bulletproof bubble wrap.

"So what's your plan after this? High school chapter is officially over. What's the next one?" Crew blocked a French fry that had gone off course and was flying toward my face. After smearing it in a glob of ketchup, he fired it back at Watson.

This place was mayhem. I couldn't believe we hadn't been kicked out yet—Miller's Point was probably tamer than the scene in the diner.

"Once Brecken's back," I shouted above the noise, "I'm going to be moving out to Oceanside where he is."

Crew threw his arms out when Watson spun around with a pissed look. When he saw who'd thrown the fry, he wiped the ketchup smear off his cheek and took a seat again.

"What's your dad going to say about that?" Crew asked, glancing at the television hanging in the corner absently.

I shrugged. "He can't say anything because we'll be married."

Crew's head twisted my way, his mouth falling open a little. "Wow. Really? Eighteen and married?"

I gave another shrug, dragging half of an onion ring through some ketchup. "He's who I want to be with. What does it matter how long we wait or don't wait to get married?" I paused, making sure the shoulder of my dress hadn't twisted out of place again. "We're going to be together either way."

Crew was quiet for a minute. At least his words were. His thoughts, not so much. "Okay, so other than marrying Connolly and moving to California, what's your plan?"

Since Gina and Sienna were still staring at us, I offered them some of my onion rings. No takers. "I don't know yet. Haven't really gotten there yet."

It had taken me thirty minutes to figure out what dress I wanted to wear today. Big life decisions were out of my mental scope right now. With Brecken gone, I just felt kind of … lost. Like my North Star had been pulled out of the night sky, throwing off my whole course.

"Nothing? No idea what you might want to do?"

"I don't know, I guess I'd kind of like to be a teacher." I stuffed an onion ring into my mouth to give myself a minute. Brecken knew that I was considering teaching, but it wasn't something I'd ever shared with anyone else. Mainly because where we came from, kids were happy to get a job at the local grocery store where they might be eligible for benefits after putting in a couple of years. It was a working-class bunch that did what they had to, not what they wanted to. "Kindergarten, first grade. I love being around kids, but the thought of four more years of school is nauseating right now. I don't know."

"Four years is a long time, especially if you're getting married so young and will probably start popping out babies." Crew twisted his graduation cap around so his tassel was hanging down the back of his neck.

"I didn't say anything about babies."

"Yeah, but it'll happen," he said, all matter-of-fact.

That made me twist in my seat and give him a not-so-sweet look. "What makes you say that?"

"Because you just said you love kids." His shoulders lifted beneath the shiny blue graduation gown. "And Brecken loves you, so he'll go along with whatever you want."

I wasn't sure how to answer that, so I went with your garden-variety shrug.

"My point is, don't go to school for four years, rack up thousands in school loans, only to become a stay-at-home mom in a few years."

My gaze wandered to the television. News. Whenever I flipped it on, I had to flip it right back off. It was usually about some place or some people getting blown up, and I didn't need that in my life right now. "I didn't say I was planning on being a stay-at-home mom."

"You're not going to be one?" His dark eyes told me they knew better.

"I don't know. Again, haven't gotten that far." My appetite for fried food and milkshakes vanished, so I scooted the rest of my plate in front of Crew. "By the way, 1950 called. It said it wanted its assigned gender roles back. Oh, and don't forget to include the black-and-white television."

Crew laughed as he worked on my onion rings. "Okay, okay, I'm old-fashioned. I like the idea of bringing home the bacon so my wife can stay home and be with the kids. If she wanted to," he added when my mouth started to drop.

"That's not old-fashioned," I said, blinking at him. "That's primordial."

Something flashed in his eyes, his smile faltering for only a moment. Then he laughed it off.

"What exactly do you have planned for bacon-bringing?" I asked, scooting a little closer to Damon.

"I'm going to apply to the police academy." He sat up taller in the booth. "I might not be fighting terrorists on foreign soil, but I'll be doing my part to take down bad guys on the home front."

I clapped, making an impressed face. "I can totally see you doing that."

"Girls love a guy in uniform." His eyes settled on mine for one moment too long. "Or so I've heard."

I was back to staring at the television as a distraction when someone burst from the booth in front of me, blocking my view.

"Hey, Pilinski! Turn the volume up!" Wilson shouted as he shoved out of the booth. "Those terrorists bastards got some of our guys. My brother's in the army over there. Turn it the fuck up!" Wilson stormed toward the television as fast as his body would take him, but Pilinski had already dialed up the volume.

The diner went quiet as the Breaking News banner flashed across the screen.

I recognized the two news anchors talking on the screen. I even heard the words they were saying, but those words wouldn't take root. They wouldn't process.

"Those cock suckers!" Wilson drove his meaty fist into the wall beside the television. The cooks from the kitchen had even paused to stick their heads out to see what was going on. "They took four of them. Four of our marines."

My throat collapsed in on itself, making it impossible to breathe. When I swayed in my seat, Crew's arm reached out to steady me, but I was shoving against him to get out of the booth. I needed to know. I needed to hear. I needed to see his name, because I already knew. I could feel it deep inside.

"I'm sure it's not Brecken. There are probably thousands of marines over there right now," Crew said, following me through the crowd of silent bodies.

What I didn't say was that I knew it was. Of course it was. If a marine had been taken captive, it would be Brecken Connolly because there was no way in hell he'd let one of his brothers or sisters be taken instead. It was what I loved about him. It was also what made it hard to love him.

Wilson was stationed directly in front of the TV when I made my way to him. As soon as he saw me, he cleared some space for me to be up front.

"It's not him," Wilson said, nudging me lightly. "Even if it is, I pity those fools who thought taking Brecken Connolly prisoner was a good idea. Pity those fools," he repeated, more to himself than to me.

Crossing my arms, I slid closer so I could hear what the newscasters were saying. When the images flashed across the screen a moment later, I realized I didn't need to hear the words to understand what had happened. My heart took off when I saw the recording of four marines on their knees, burlap sacks tied over their heads, a couple of them looking like they were barely able to stay kneeling. It was a poorly made tape, the foreign words barely discernable in the background. The four marines had been lined up in some dark room that looked more cave-like than manmade.

People around me started to whisper. A few girls from my class wiped their eyes as the newscasters' voices spoke in the background. Something about this marine squad being captured, demands being made, negotiations in the works, but I didn't really hear any of it.

All I did was stare at the screen, where those four bodies hovered seemingly right in front of me. He was right there. In arm's reach. Half a world away, in hostile hands, in the worst kind of situation a marine could ever imagine finding themselves in, there he was. Right in front of me.

As the reporters listed off the names of the POWs, my heart stopped beating. I never felt it restart. Two privates, Garcia and Armstrong. One private first class, McVay, *Kristen* McVay. Finally, the squad leader—Lance Corporal Brecken Connolly.

For one collective moment, I felt the whole diner stop breathing with me. I felt everyone experience the same measure of sorrow settling into my insides.

For one instant, they knew my pain and shared it with me.

"He'll be okay. He'll make it out of there." Crew's arm came around me, his hand rubbing at the outside of my arm like he was trying to stimulate my circulation.

That was when whoever was filming the video panned in close, to where another enemy soldier was holding up the tags around each marine's neck to confirm who they'd captured. Brecken's tags were covered in dried blood, no hint of silver left to shine through.

My tears had always felt warm on my cheeks, but these ones felt cold.

"He'll make it back," Crew repeated as the diner started to come out of their fog, curses and outrage stabbing the silence.

A dozen different protests were on my lips right then. POWs didn't make it back from over there. Public beheadings had become all the rage. The country he'd been captured in didn't abide by the Geneva Convention and the so-called Rules of War. A dozen more protests followed the first batch.

But as I stared at that screen, I reached out my hand until it was touching the spot where Brecken was kneeling, and I nodded. "I know he will."

# *two*

I watched the person I loved die.

I witnessed his murder.

It might have been through the filter of a television screen, but I watched the life of the person I loved most in the world leave this world. I watched his blood paint the ground beneath him. I watched as his head was severed from his body.

I watched Brecken die.

Even though he'd been the one who had lost his life that day, I'd lost mine as well. Six years later, I still hadn't recovered it. Brecken was part of me. Still as much a part of me as I was.

At first, I couldn't sleep. When I tried, I'd wake up screaming, the image of his murder so vibrant in my mind, it was as though I'd been inches in front of him. I had the smells that went with the scene, the sounds, the sensations. I must have been there with him, in spirit or subconscious or some similar explanation. If nothing else, that gave me comfort when little else did.

They held him for a month after the capture. Doing whatever they did, getting what information they wanted, not getting whatever information they wanted … then they disposed of him, like a student dumped a textbook when the class was over and its use expired. Like a human life was worth so little. Like that human soul wasn't everything to another human soul.

It was a living nightmare. One a person could never wake up from. One that had become as much a part of me as Brecken had been, almost like the horror of his death had filled the places the peace and happiness of his life had filled within me.

The execution made national news, and the country erupted with a unified cry for justice.

For all of two weeks.

Then people moved on to the next headline, the next outrage, the next soapbox they'd stand upon and do absolutely shit about.

The country had moved on years ago, but for me, moving on wasn't an option. I was stuck. Tied to him. Bound to his fate. That had always been the way of Brecken and me, and it went on even in death. Some connections went beyond the norm, the explainable, and that was how we had been.

When the war department showed up on the front porch of the house Brecken had grown up in, I'd managed to convince the man that I was his cousin. He seemed content enough with that, leaving me with the few personal effects they had of Brecken's before he drove off like he couldn't put Lance Corporal Connolly behind him fast enough. When his aunt got home later that night after work, I gave her everything. Except for one thing. His tags. Those I kept. Those I wore for months, not even taking them off to climb into the shower.

I remembered sliding them out of the small manila folder they'd been in. How cold they'd felt in my hand. How clean and sterile they'd looked, contrasted to the last way I'd seen them on the television. They still smelled of the alcohol someone must have used to clean them before passing them on to the hands of the next of kin.

His tags I kept for myself. The medals and accolades I left for his family. I didn't need any of that to remember the hero he was—I'd figured that out the day Brecken had thrown himself at my dad before he could strike me again.

Today's grocery shopping has taken me longer than usual thanks to my mind wandering. The first couple of years, my mind strayed constantly, but I'd gotten better at blocking some of that out. For some reason, today, I felt like I was back at the beginning. Back at Day One of Life Without Him.

However, an eighteen-year-old's responsibilities were entirely different than a twenty-four-year-old's. I had a schedule to keep and responsibilities to tend to. I couldn't throw the covers over my head and pretend the world didn't exist anymore, because I'd learned the world would come looking for me if I tried to hide.

As I weighed the apples to make sure I wouldn't go over the budgeted grocery funds in the envelope stuffed in my purse, I overheard a conversation going on at one of the nearby checkout stands. Gus's Groceries was a small, locally run shop, quiet enough a person could hear what was being said all the way across the store if they wanted to.

After putting an apple back, I twisted a tie around the rest in the bag and steered my cart up front. It was already two, and I needed to be back by three in order to have enough time to get everything ready for the evening.

"Oh my god, I know! I just heard." Jenn Douglass was checking out, chatting with Teresa, the checker who'd been there since I was a little girl.

I made my way into line and started loading my groceries onto the belt.

"Can you believe it? It's a miracle." Teresa shook her head as she weighed a bag of grapes.

"After all this time. Finding him. *Alive*." Jenn was staring out the row of windows like she was seeing something I wasn't.

"Can you imagine what that poor man's been through?" Teresa said, and both of them shared a sigh.

Neither of them had noticed me, or if they had, didn't feel the need to include me in their conversation. I didn't usually listen in on other people's conversations, but this one I couldn't tune out. This one I couldn't ignore. They could have been talking about anybody. Anyone. But something inside me was telling me this wasn't about just anybody. This wasn't some random someone they were talking about.

"They're having some big homecoming for him. It's been all over the news," Teresa continued as she finished ringing up the last couple of items in Jenn's order. "I heard the city council is working to put on a homecoming here for him too."

My throat was so tight right then, as if someone had wrapped their hand around it and was crushing it. I couldn't speak. All I could do was listen. Guess. Assume. *Hope*.

My life was so different now though. A shadow of what it had been.

When I placed my bag of oranges on the belt, Jenn and Teresa noticed me. Their heads twisted, smiles pulling into place right away. Teresa's eyes dropped to my hand, one side of her face pinching.

"A first attempt at a cartwheel in a decade. A *failed* attempt," I added with a smile, lifting the wrist brace strapped around my left hand.

Teresa's smile changed to a more forced variety. "How many times do I need to tell you, Camryn? Be care-ful," she emphasized slowly, making eye contact. "Cartwheels are dangerous."

The way she said it, the way her eyes looked as she did, I knew what she was really telling me. Though I pretended I didn't.

"Did you hear the news?" Jenn angled toward me as she swiped her card through the reader. It took a couple of moments, but then something registered on her face. It morphed from curiosity to regret.

The hope inside me started to spread. Jenn had graduated a year ahead of me, one after Brecken. She knew about us. She knew the way things had been between us. Her eyes dropped to my left hand like Teresa's had.

"Did I hear what news?" I managed to force out in a voice that sounded like I was choking on gravel.

Jenn's teeth sank into her bottom lip, chewing on it as she exchanged a look with Teresa, who just lifted her hands.

"If she hasn't heard yet, she's going to. News spreads like wildfire in a community like this. Better coming from you than …" Teresa handed Jenn her receipt, her pause stretching. "Than someone else."

"Jenn?" I didn't realize my hands were shaking until the box of generic corn flakes fell out of them.

She mustered up a smile. It was a sad one. The kind a person gave to someone they were embracing at a funeral. "It's Brecken. They found him alive."

My knees wobbled, making me have to grab the magazine rack for support. "What?" I didn't realize I'd said it until Jenn answered.

"They found Brecken." Her voice sounded like it was coming down an endless tunnel, almost indiscernible. "He's coming home."

An entire century passed me by right then as I replayed those words in my head. Even though the clock on the wall revealed barely a minute had passed, I knew better. I felt ancient when I came back to life. Or came back to the present.

"Camryn? You okay, sweetheart?" Teresa started to slide out from behind the register. "You need to sit down?"

"God, I'm sorry. I should have thought about what I was saying—who I was saying it to." Jenn slung her purse over her shoulder, her gaze fixed on my left hand like it was about to make her cry.

"He died." The whisper floated from my lips. "I watched it. They killed him. I was there."

Teresa and Jenn exchanged a look as Teresa slid up beside me, picking up the fallen box of cereal and dropping an arm around my waist. It enveloped me, her hand managing to wind all the way around to my stomach. "You're wasting away on me, Camryn. Do me a favor and eat some of this food you're in here every Tuesday afternoon buying, okay?"

I nodded absently, concentrating on staying on my feet.

"I know, we all thought he was gone. The whole world did. We all watched that—" Teresa stopped herself as she finished unloading what was left in my cart. "The news just broke a few hours ago, but it sounds like the person they executed was someone else they'd dressed up in Brecken's fatigues."

My mind went back to the image of him kneeling, frail-looking, head hidden by another burlap bag. Could that person really not have been him?

"They're sure?" My hand curled around the cart, my knuckles turning white.

Teresa nodded slowly, her hand giving mine a soft squeeze. "I saw it on the news. I saw *him*. It's Brecken."

Jenn was still lingering at the end of the checkout stand, like she wasn't sure if she should stay or go, working her lip still. I didn't miss the way she lifted her eyes to the ceiling as she wiped at her eyes, like she was trying to keep tears from falling.

"It's been six years. Six years," I repeated. "Where's he been? All this time? Where was he?"

Teresa rolled my empty cart up a ways so she could ring up my items. She was having a hard time looking me in the eyes. "They had him in some old underground military barracks on the border of Iraq."

The grocery store started to revolve. "He's been a prisoner this whole time? They've had him for six years?"

Teresa didn't answer as she rang up my first items. Jenn did though—that first tear finally slipped free.

"Why? What have they been doing to him? What did they need from him?" The words that had evaded me minutes ago came spilling out like a volcano erupting. "Why the hell would they film his execution if they were planning on keeping him alive all of this time? Why would they do that to someone? Why would that do that to me?"

Jenn had given up wiping her eyes, electing to just let the tears fall while Teresa focused on bagging my groceries. "I don't want to pretend to think I know the answers to those questions, Camryn."

"Is he okay?" I croaked, feeling every extreme a person could experience all at once. Clammy hot to ice cold. About to pass out to never feeling so awake. Floating to falling. Weeping to laughing.

"The news didn't have a lot of details yet. This is all just coming to light."

My head shook. "Did he *look* all right?" I glanced at Jenn since she was the one who'd said she'd seen him on the news.

Jenn's gaze drifted to Teresa, as though she needed her help to answer my question.

"It's been six years," Teresa said, the corners of her eyes creasing. "A lot's happened."

Six years incarcerated by an enemy not known for their mercy. My stomach churned.

"He's changed, we've all changed—" Teresa's eyes drifted back to my left hand.

I pulled at the sleeve of my sweater to cover more of the wrist brace. It seemed ridiculously trivial to be concerned over something as little as that when we were discussing Brecken and what he'd been through.

"But he still looks like Brecken Connolly. He's still part of that boy we all remember. Coming back as a man we'll have to get to know."

# three

The entire bag of carrots was peeled. I'd only needed three for dinner tonight. Chock that peeling marathon up to my mind reeling and my life feeling like it had fallen out of orbit. This morning when I woke up, everything had been normal, expected, and ten hours later, nothing felt right. I had to check four different drawers to find my measuring cups even though they'd been in the same one for the past few years. I'd walked smack into the side of the hall table that had been resting in the same place since last summer.

The world outside hadn't changed. But the world inside me had.

Brecken.

He was …

Alive.

*Alive.*

He was …

Safe.

He was …

Coming home.

My emotions had run the full gamut since leaving Gus's this afternoon. From crying tears of joy in the car to weeping tears of devastation when I realized that while I'd found comfort in knowing, for the past six years, he was resting in peace, he'd instead been in the hands of enemy interrogators, enduring anything but peace.

Worry as I unloaded the groceries.

Relief as I started the laundry.

Anxiety as I ironed shirts.

Excitement as I checked the mail.

Hopefulness as I started dinner.

Hopelessness as I set the table.

Emotions were a strange thing. How they could propel you forward one moment, only to bury you in an unmarked grave the next. I wasn't sure what mine's intentions were for me—to bring me back to life or complete the process of finishing me.

While dinner finished cooking, I moved into the living room, checking the time. I had another half hour at least. All afternoon, I'd kept the television off, the newspaper folded on the entryway table. I wanted to let myself get comfortable with the realization that Brecken was alive before I let the world fill in the details I both wanted to know and wanted nothing to do with.

Crossing my arms, I stared at the blank screen. Clicking it on felt as though I were opening Pandora's Box. I didn't know what I'd find when I did but accepted that once that door was open, it couldn't be closed. There was no going back.

Shuffling closer, I grabbed the remote, punched a couple of buttons, then dropped to the carpet a few feet in front of the television. Sitting across the room on the sofa felt wrong. It felt right being right there, a few feet in front of the screen, on my knees.

The first news channel I scrolled to had the story going. The second one too. The same could be said for the others. Brecken Connolly had captured the attention of the nation again. I wondered how long it would last this time. Two weeks for being executed on live television. How many for coming back from the supposed dead?

My hips sank to the floor as I watched the broadcast, my eyes refusing to blink. I kept the volume low, like the newscasters were sharing with me a secret that couldn't be spoken too loudly or else.

Or else what? The same men who'd held him prisoner for six years would come back to get him? The same life that had held me prisoner for the same amount of time would suddenly set me free?

The broadcasters only knew so much at this point, but people were already speculating which super anchor might get the exclusive story from Lance Corporal Connolly, which publishing house would print the biography. They were almost talking about him like he was a commodity, a card to be played, instead of a human being.

There were a few photos of the underground barracks he'd been kept in, along with names and pictures of the SEAL Team responsible for finding and rescuing him. From the sounds of it, they hadn't been looking for POWs in those barracks. They'd been looking for a high-profile enemy soldier whose policy on brutality was unmatched.

They hadn't found that man, but they'd found another. Nothing was mentioned about the other three POWs who had been captured, but the nation had believed them dead as well.

It wasn't until I saw him that I started to cry. Not the same wet sobs I'd broken into in the car earlier, but careful, almost measured tears. Each one I felt. Each one felt like a silent echo of the scream thundering inside me.

The first image I saw of him was the photo he'd had taken straight out of basic training. Buzzed head, tough face, alive eyes. It was the same picture I'd had on my nightstand.

The second was a photo someone had snapped of him on a stretcher as he was being carried out of the barracks by the SEAL Team. Long hair. Weak face. Dead eyes.

He barely looked like the same person. The rest of his body was covered in blankets, so all I could see was his face, but that was enough. I didn't want to imagine what his body looked like if his face was unrecognizable. His eyes were sunken, his skin so pale it was almost transparent. The dark splotches on his cheeks and forehead could have been bruises or shadows.

More tears. One for him. One for me. For him. For me. Endless tears. For what had been. For what could have been. For what could never be again.

Tears for six years of hell. His. Mine. Tears for the however many years of hell to come. For him. For me.

Tears for hoping his stint in perdition ended sooner than mine.

Time became irrelevant as I sat there staring at the face of a man I thought had left this life years ago. I didn't hear the car. I didn't hear the door. I didn't hear the footsteps.

"You heard the news."

I did hear the voice. His voice was hard to ignore.

My eyes still glued to the television, I nodded. I should have turned it off. I should have wiped my eyes. I should have gotten up.

I couldn't do any of that.

"I heard," I answered in a voice that was more robotic than human.

The footsteps tapped closer. "Isn't it great?"

Taking a moment to consider my answer, I swallowed. I decided agreeing with him was the best option. "Yeah, it is."

He'd said he'd be here later, I thought as I checked the clock on the wall. Instead, I discovered he was actually fifteen minutes later than I'd expected him.

"Are you happy you get to see him again?" His voice gave nothing away. Which, from my experience, gave everything away.

Putting my answer together in my head first, I forced myself to glance over my shoulder. He was loosening his tie, sliding off his watch, his expression a tomb of emotion.

"I'm happy he's alive," I replied, putting on a smile when he glanced at me.

"Do you want to go to the homecoming party next weekend? It's all anyone is talking about." He moved to the edge of the area rug, looking down at me in a familiar way. His jaw twitched when the basic training picture of Brecken flashed up onto the screen again.

That was when I turned off the television. "Do you?"

"Of course." A shrug as he wandered onto the carpet and moved behind me. "We were friends. All of us. *Good* friends."

My hands twisted in my lap. "After everything he's been through, he probably doesn't even remember me."

"I highly doubt that." He squatted behind me, his bent legs coming around me, trapping me inside them.

"Why?" I tipped my head to the side as he slid a sheet of my hair aside.

"Because you're unforgettable." Nuzzling my neck, his mouth covered the skin below my ear. He sucked at it, his tongue tasting before his teeth nipped at me.

I flinched, but his legs held me where I was as his mouth pulled away.

"How's that wrist?" he asked, gently lifting my injured hand in front of us.

"Better," I answered, closing my eyes as his other hand skimmed beneath my sweater, moving up.

"No more cartwheels for you," he whispered like it was an order as his hand reached my breast. He groaned as he kneaded it, pressing his erection into my back. "You need to take care of yourself. Or I'll have to."

His other hand tightened around my wrist just barely, but it was enough to make me wince. It was so sensitive, even to the lightest touch.

"Dinner's almost ready," I managed to get out as he let go of my wrist to work my skirt up my body.

"Dinner can wait," Crew rasped, pushing me to the floor as he rolled over me, freeing himself from his slacks. "Your husband can't."

*four*

"Camryn, what's taking so long?" Crew's voice echoed up the stairs, seeping beneath our bedroom door. "How many dresses are you going to try on before you decide on one?"

"Just getting my shoes!" I hollered back, standing in front of the full-length mirror hanging on the back of the door. There was a crack running down it from a couple of years ago, but it still served its purpose.

Contrary to what Crew thought I'd been doing, I'd been standing here for the past ten minutes, staring in the mirror and trying to remember the girl I'd been before. The one from six years ago. The one who could smile without thinking about it first, the one whose light eyes popped against the contrast of her olive skin, the one who could look herself in the eye to see who she really was.

Ten minutes in front of that mirror, and I still hadn't been able to look myself in the eyes. I wasn't sure I'd ever be able to. Not with the guilt I bore. Not with the skeletons. Not with the secrets. People who liked themselves could look themselves in the eye in the mirror. People who didn't could barely stand to look at any part of themselves in the mirror.

"Camryn, really!" Crew's voice was impatient, for more reasons than my seeming inability to pick an outfit.

Today was the day of the homecoming celebration. The day he'd be back. The day I'd see him for the first time, with my own eyes, his own eyes looking back.

"Coming!" I shouted, stuffing the tags curled in my fist into the pocket of my denim jacket before I threw it on. I kept Brecken's dog tags hidden in a soap box in the back of my bathroom cabinet, but every once in a while, I pulled them out. When I needed comfort. When I needed clarity.

When I needed to give them back to their owner.

Throwing the door open, I rushed as fast as I trusted myself to move down the stairs in my wedge sandals. Grace had been in short supply the day I'd been created, and I was already accident-prone enough without galloping down a steep set of wooden stairs in three-inch heels.

"Whoa. Look at you." Crew was waiting at the bottom of the stairs, his eyes scanning me as I approached. "I haven't seen that dress in a while."

I glanced down, holding out the skirt like it was no big deal. "Hot summer day. Seemed like a good day for white."

Crew continued to inspect the dress like he was reading some story written on its layers. "Is that why you're wearing a jacket? Because it's such a hot day fitting for a skimpy white dress?"

My brows came together as I looked down to make sure I'd put on the dress I thought I had. It was a simple linen summer dress. Knee-length, no cleavage showing, not cut close enough to hug the body. It was strapless, but the denim jacket took care of that perceived "skimpy" component.

"Do you think I should change?" I asked, not really caring since it would give me an excuse to stall for another five minutes.

"No. We're already late and this thing is practically taking place out our front door. That will have to work." Crew was messing with his tie, shifting in place, almost looking nervous, which was unusual for him. This was a big day for more than just myself.

"It's just a dress." I took his arm and gave it a light squeeze. "It doesn't mean anything other than it was the first one I touched when I reached into the closet."

"And it's just the first day Brecken Connolly is back in arm's reach." He masked his harsh words with a soft smile as we moved toward the door.

"Crew …"

"I know, I know. I'm the one you chose. The one you married." He held the door open for me. "But can you blame a guy for being a little anxious about his wife coming face to face with her first love, the same guy who's been deemed a national hero?"

I matched my smile to his, brushing his chest as I passed by. "No, I guess not."

"I'm feeling a little territorial. Especially with you in that dress." He closed the door behind us, following me, but I was frozen on the top step.

Tangle Root Road, the street we'd all grown up on, had been closed off for the day, so a spread of tables, chairs, food, and people could celebrate the return of a hero. Red, white, and blue streamers, balloons, and ribbons were stretching all up and down the block. An endless cluster of round tables surrounded by handfuls of chairs were dotted down the road, the rectangular food tables stationed in the center of it all.

As if that wasn't enough, the people. My god, it looked like everyone in Medford had shown up for the homecoming. Kids were running up and down the sidewalks, friends with drinks in hand shared stories, and women bustled around the food tables, shooing flies and the brave child trying to sneak a drumstick.

"Looks like it's going to be one hell of a party. Too bad I have to leave early for my shift." Crew took my hand, winding my arm through his, and started down the steps. I went with him.

"I'll make sure to save you some food," I promised, even though I knew he was talking more about the other part of the feast—the drinks.

"Forget the food. You just make sure to crawl into bed in this dress so I have a nice present to come home to tomorrow morning." Crew's hand drifted behind me, skimming beneath the hem of my dress. Then he spanked my butt hard enough to make me flinch. "Panties gone."

He was waiting for some kind of confirmation from me, so I managed a smile and made sure everything was back in place when we made it to the sidewalk.

It was like the news of Brecken's return had turned him into an insatiable organism that couldn't get enough sex. There hadn't been a night in the past two weeks when I hadn't been awakened by him grunting above me, his powerful thrusts knocking the headboard against the wall until the drywall had cracked. In the morning, he'd bend me over the bathroom sink after crawling out of the shower. On his days off, he'd grab me as I was walking by and coax me to my knees in front of him, pulling at the roots of my hair as he took his pleasure with the acquiescence of my mouth. He couldn't get enough of my body. He couldn't spend enough of himself inside my body. He needed the reassurance that I was his, and all I could do was give it to him. Because there wasn't another alternative.

"What time is it?" Crew asked as we moved from the sidewalk onto the street.

A few of the neighbors waved when they saw us. Everyone knew Crew on the block, and everyone loved him.

"A little past three, I think," I said, focusing on breathing as I scanned the crowd. He wasn't supposed to arrive until around four, but still, I could feel something charging in the air.

"Damn it. So much for draining a couple of beers before my shift. With my luck, it would probably be the same night the chief decided to do a random piss test on us." Crew shook his head, clapping one of our neighbors on the back when he held out a beer for him as we passed.

"Probably not the best idea to drink before you have to go to work. Especially when that works involves a gun and bad guys." I said it in a teasing tone, but Crew must not have picked up on it.

"I'll drink when I choose. I'm a grown man. I don't need your commentary on it."

My hand fell away from his elbow. I knew he was stressed about everything, but damn, he was already taking it out on me with his dick. He didn't need to act like an actual dick too.

"I'm going to check with Lisa to see if she needs any more help with the food. Will you check on—"

"Yeah. On it," he practically snapped, already moving toward the Johnsons' yard, where a herd of kids were running through a sprinkler.

Doing my best to put Crew's mood behind me, I moved through the crowd. A few of the other detectives and officers' wives were milling around, clustered together, but I didn't know any of them very well. Crew hung out with the guys all the time, but he wasn't as interested in the couples' date nights. When I waved at the wives, a couple of them waved back while a couple of others looked like they were trying to place me.

"Look at you. Aren't you a sight for sore eyes?" Teresa, the checker from Gus's, was going around the salad table, sliding serving utensils into the endless variety of dishes.

"It's nothing. Just an old dress I needed to dust the cobwebs off of." I swept the front of the skirt with my hands.

"Cobwebs or not, I'm sure one lance corporal won't complain."

"Teresa!"

"What? He probably hasn't seen a woman in half a decade. I know you're married and off the market, but a man can look." She winked and waved one of the serving spoons at me. "And he'll be lookin'."

"That's what Crew said too." I sighed, grabbing a few spoons to help.

"Jealous?"

"What do you think?"

Teresa kept moving down the table. "Has he lifted his leg and marked you yet?"

My nose wrinkled. "Not that I'm aware of?"

"Then he's not in the blind jealous category, so that's not so bad."

When I stuffed a spoon into one of the coleslaws, I noticed something on my forearm. Unrolling the cuffs of the jacket, I kept moving down the line.

"What about you? Nervous?"

My breath came out all at once. "Blind nervous category."

Teresa laughed, wiping her hands on her apron when she reached the end of the table. "Have you peed on yourself yet?"

My forehead creased. "No?"

"Then that's not so bad." With a wave, she bustled into the crowd like she was on a mission.

Teresa, Lisa, a few other ladies, and I had been responsible for putting the food together. I hadn't planned on volunteering for any part of the party—because I knew how Crew felt about it, as much as he tried to disguise it—but when Lisa called me up one night, begging me to put together a list of Brecken's favorite foods, I got sucked into it. Brecken's family had long ago moved out of the house they'd rented when we'd all grown up, and no one knew how to get ahold of them anymore, so the task of putting together Brecken's favorites fell at my feet. Who else knew him better than I had? The girl who'd almost married him. Before marrying one of his friends.

God, how was I going to explain that? How was he going to take that?

Would he even care? He'd spent six years in an Iraqi prison. I doubted his thoughts had been consumed by me and getting married when he got out of there. Survival. That had been on his mind. Not me.

I knew enough about POWs to know he'd come back cracked in places that had been whole before. The point of those camps was to break the body to ultimately break the mind. From what I'd heard, they'd done their damnedest to break his body. How far had they made it into his mind? Part of the way? Halfway? All the way?

I'd find out soon. Either way, whoever he was today, whatever was left of him from yesterday, I'd find out.

I heard his arrival before I saw it. The hoots of children, the buzz of voices, the drum of shoes on asphalt, the echo of hands applauding. While everyone moved toward the black sedan that had just rolled up at the end of the block, my feet melted into the street, the courage I'd broken from my reserves with them.

The crowd converged around the car like a swarm, voices cheering, hands still clapping, kids thrusting little flags into the bright blue sky.

It was too much for me. Stimulation overload. I couldn't imagine how he felt. If he felt anything. My hand covered my stomach as the crowd erupted in a surge of noise as I could just make out a head break above the herd. It wasn't buzzed like it had been before, but it wasn't as long as it had been in that picture of his rescue.

I knew it was Brecken. It might have only been the top couple inches of his head, but I knew. He'd always stood above any crowd, for more reasons than just his height.

He didn't move for a while, probably unable to thanks to the swarm circling him, vying for photos, handshakes, and autographs. My heart ached right then, enough to make me gasp. I hadn't realized it still resided in my chest until that moment. I was certain it had flown off to Iraq with him,

but now it was back, hurting in my chest like it was struggling for life.

I stood there for I didn't know how long, waiting. For
what, I didn't know but waiting just the same. The crowd
finally dispersed, though it was only thanks to a couple of
uniformed police officers making a hole just big enough for
Brecken to emerge from.

My lungs collapsed when I saw him. All of him. Nothing between us. No cameras. No screens. No frames of
glass. He looked exactly as I remembered—that was the first
thought I had as he broke through the crowd.

A moment later, I took off the glasses of my youth and
first love and realized he didn't look anything like I remembered.

The fundamentals were still there: same height, same
shade of brownish-blond hair, same blue eyes, but that appeared to be all that was the same.

When he took a couple more steps, I realized he was
walking with a limp. He was trying to hide it, but he favored
his right leg with every step. His gaze wandered for a minute, staring at the houses lining the street like he was trying
to remember them. When he made it to the gray one beside
me, his focus changed.

One hundred feet back, hundreds of people gathered
around him, a lifetime of consequences circling me, when
his eyes found mine, I felt life rush into every vein. Energy
charged into every nerve ending, power surfaced in every
muscle fiber. Like I was present for my own resurrection, I
felt him bring me back to life, one broken step at a time.

His eyes never wavered. His trajectory never varied. He
moved toward me like he was taking the final steps in a six-
year journey to get here.

I didn't notice the figure approaching from the corner of my eye. I didn't hear him coming either. His hand ensnaring mine was hard to miss though.

My chest felt like it was petrifying when I witnessed the look that cast over Brecken's face right then. His feet stopped moving, his body freezing as his eyes roamed from where my hand was encased inside another's, up to see who it was beside me.

It was quick. It was fleeting. But I didn't miss it. The look that settled into Brecken's face when he saw Crew beside me, holding my hand, his wedding band catching the light of the sun. Apparently there had been something left to break in Brecken Connolly, because I witnessed it shatter right there on the street we used to race our bikes down as kids. The same street where he'd pulled me into the shadows to kiss me until we both felt the world fall away beneath our feet.

In that moment or two it took him to recover, I felt a lifetime pass. A lifetime I'd planned on and had to run a knife across.

When he started moving again, his steps were heavier, like he was dragging something behind him. The whole time though, his eyes never looked away from mine. It was like he wanted me to see. Wanted me to know.

The crowd stayed back a ways, some of them trying to focus on something other than the ghost moving toward me.

Beside me, Crew broke the spell. "Fuck me. That's what six years in an Iraqi prison camp will do to a soldier." A low whistle echoed from his lips as he watched Brecken approach.

The closer Brecken got, the more I felt the ground beneath me firm up, so I was standing on it instead of sinking through it. The closer he got, the stronger I felt. Maybe that was because I knew that to get through this, I couldn't fake strength this time—I'd need the real thing. The same kind that had gotten him through the past six years, I guessed.

Brecken stopped a ways in front of us, staring through the distance between us with a furrowed brow. I would have said something—I should have said something—but my throat was clogged with a ball of emotion. The same rainbow of emotion I'd been warring with ever since finding out the first boy I loved was still alive.

He wasn't in his fancy marine clothes like he'd worn at the celebration in Washington. Instead, he was in a long-sleeve dress shirt and pair of slacks. I couldn't help noticing that we were the only people in long sleeves out here in the sweltering heat. The only people looking like they were trying to hide, or actually hiding, something. It was so strange to see him with hair longer than a fraction of an inch. His aunt had started cutting it short when he was in grade school as a means of keeping it simple, and the marines had cut it shorter.

He was thin. Even though his clothes tried to disguise it, he'd lost probably thirty to forty pounds of the bulk he'd been carrying around ever since puberty, when the rest of the boys would have killed to have a muscle bulge, or moderately display, in their bicep. He still stood tall, though his shoulders seemed to fold forward more than before, his skin a shade of alabaster only a person who'd seen little, if any, of the sun in years could attain, and his eyes … they were hazy, cloudy almost. Still blue, still able to look right through me, but changed. Different. Like someone else was looking at me behind those eyes.

"God, this is awkward." Crew cleared his throat as the silence dragged on between the three of us. Stepping aside, he lifted an arm at me. "Hug her, man. It's okay."

Brecken's jaw worked when Crew motioned at me. When Brecken's eyes reached mine, there was a question in them. I answered it by moving closer, my arms already falling open, tears already raining down on the inside. He limped forward a step, then another to meet me, his own arms opening, welcoming me. As I stepped into the border of his embrace, I felt the heaviness of the past, the guilt of my mistakes, slip away. His arms didn't feel the same as they formed around me, but the feeling that came with them felt exactly the same.

Home.

Peace.

Safety.

*Love*.

My arms slipped up under his, hooking beneath them like I needed to find a good hold so I didn't slip away. I hadn't meant for my head to loll onto his shoulder, but it became too heavy to hold up. His head stacked beside mine, his chin tucking behind the side of my neck. Behind us, I heard more clapping, some cheering, and what I guessed were probably some hushed whispers shared over raised brows. Plenty of people in town knew about Brecken's and my past, but everyone knew I was married to Crew Graves, police detective and all-around upstanding guy.

I might have been able to hug the returning hero, my old boyfriend, this once, but it wouldn't be deemed so acceptable again. I'd have to be careful hugging, touching, even talking to Brecken. Crew wouldn't like it. The town would gossip about it.

This embrace would have to be it. A hello and a good-bye. A greeting and a farewell. My life didn't have the luxury of choice or room for mistakes. I'd made enough of those already in my twenty-four years of life.

When my arms tightened around him, sensing the end, his mouth moved outside of my ear as his fingers splayed across my back, pulling me closer. "Hey, Blue Bird." His voice was lower, his words raspier than before. "Sorry it took me so long to make it back."

My back shook from the sob I kept buried inside. I'd experienced pain and I knew peace, but I'd never experienced them together before. At the same time. Like they were bound to one another. Connected by some invisible force.

The pain was staggering, having Brecken in my arms but out of my grasp. The peace was staggering, having Brecken back when I'd accepted his loss years ago.

Crew's hand dropped to my shoulder. He wasn't pulling me away, but his grip was tight enough to give the hint. Inhaling Brecken one last time, I slowly stepped back. His arms didn't let me go at first, but then all at once, they gave up, falling away.

"God, this is unreal. You here. A damn Lazarus." Crew slung his arm behind my neck when I fell back beside him.

Brecken stood there, finally looking at Crew. His expression was vacant. His eyes void.

"What do you say, Connolly? You and me. Case of beer. Shooting the shit?" Crew lifted his chin toward our front porch. "Planning our revenge on those SOBs who had you the past six years?"

Brecken didn't seem to hear him, or chose not to. Instead his focus stayed on me, appraising me like he was staring at an apparition. As if he couldn't tell if I was real or not.

"Sound like a plan, man?" Crew continued.

Brecken nodded, still staring at me in a way that was starting to make me uncomfortable. If only because I could tell it was making Crew uncomfortable.

"I'm staring. Sorry." Brecken swallowed, shifting in place. He didn't stop staring though. "You're still the most beautiful thing around, Camryn Gardner."

The corners of my mouth lifted, trying to decide if a blush or a bow was more fitting for that compliment. No one had ever looked at me the way he did—like I really was the most beautiful thing in creation. Brecken's eyes matched his words, instead of contradicting them like other guys I'd encountered.

Crew stepped a bit in front of me. "Graves. It's Camryn Graves now."

Crew's statement, his verbal and non-verbal one, didn't diffuse Brecken's stare. "Of course it is. Sorry," he added, like the apology was trained in him.

"You'll get used to it," Crew said, slipping the bend of his arm around my neck a little harder.

"Maybe." Brecken glanced at the ring circling my ring finger.

My fingers curled into my palm. A different ring had occupied that finger when he'd seen me last.

Only a moment of awkward silence had a chance to take root before an eruption of noise came from one of the yards. One of the neighbor moms came marching straight for us, a small someone in tow behind her. What was it this time?

"Keenan just pushed another little boy down for no reason," Gina announced when she was in front of us, waiting like she was expecting a drawn-out explanation and apology from me. She clearly didn't realize or care that the hometown hero was two feet away.

Instinctively, I took Keenan's hand from Gina, pulling him away from her. Gina and her husband had a few kids and parented like they were running a reform school. Kneeling so I was at eye level with him, I didn't miss the way Brecken was looking between the little boy and me.

"Why did you push that boy down?" I asked.

He was only five—or five and one quarter if you asked him—but he knew to look someone in the eye when he answered them. "He pushed down Maddie." His voice was more matter-of-fact than defensive, his eyes darting over to the yard where some other little boy was wailing like he'd just had his arm broken.

Crew stepped in, looking down at Keenan with raised brows. "You don't push people down because they pushed someone else."

Keenan's forehead creased. "But he pushed her down. For no reason. Because he's a big bully."

"Keenan"—Crew crossed his arms, looking the picture of stern—"you can't hurt a person for hurting another person."

Keenan was about to respond, strong-willed to the end, when someone else beat him to it. "Sure, you can." Brecken moved up behind me, studying Keenan. "I don't care how old he is. If a boy pushes down a girl, he deserves it right back."

Keenan blinked at Brecken, taking him in. Gina, who was still lingering like she was waiting to make sure a suitable punishment was dished out, finally realized who was here with us. I went with keeping my mouth closed, since I wouldn't contradict Brecken. I felt the same way.

"Not exactly what they teach in those parenting books," Crew said, as if he'd read any of them.

"They should." Brecken lifted his shoulders. "I don't want my sons thinking it's okay to watch a girl be mistreated and do nothing about it. You see something that isn't right, you step in. He did the right thing."

Keenan was now gaping at Brecken like he was some brand of Marvel superhero. I stayed where I was, crouching in front of him, waiting.

Crew thanked Gina for bringing "the situation" to our attention, gave her arm a quick squeeze, then stepped closer to Brecken. "Look at that, stating your opinions and shit, you still have that mind everyone's been speculating you lost in captivity."

My breath caught. I'd guessed things would get messy between the three of us eventually. Just not ten minutes into our reunion.

Brecken tapped his temple a few times, not blinking as he returned Crew's stare. "Don't let me fool you."

Silence.

Silence.

Then a chuckle. Forced. I had plenty of experience with Crew's artificial emotions.

"Hi. I'm Keenan." He stepped around me, moving toward Brecken like he wasn't the least bit intimidated. "You're the one we're having the party for? The soldier everyone's calling a hero?"

I glanced behind me, focusing on keeping my expression flat.

Brecken stared at Keenan and was quiet for a moment. "To be a hero, you need to do something heroic. All I did was survive." He glanced at the ground, the skin between his brows creasing. "I'm a survivor. Not a hero."

Keenan's head tipped. "But they said you helped that soldier escape. That girl soldier."

My eyebrows came together. I'd stayed away from the news as much as possible since Brecken's return. Clearly, someone else had not.

"That makes me human, not a hero." Brecken's hands balled as he swallowed. "And she didn't escape. None of them did."

Keenan slid a step closer. "Only you?"

Brecken's head nodded mechanically. "The last marine standing."

"Keenan, that's enough questions." Crew put his hands on his shoulders, pulling him back.

"No, it's okay. I've been answering questions for days now. I don't mind."

Crew held Keenan against him. "Well, I do mind. I'll decide what's best for my son. Whether that comes to pushing others down or asking questions that aren't age appropriate."

Brecken didn't hear Crew past the first half of his reply. He was looking at Keenan with new eyes as the reality of who this child really was sank in.

I rose up, trying to stand as tall as I could stretch myself. "*Our* son," I said, glancing at Crew before ending on Brecken.

"Your son?" It was a whisper, but loud enough for all of us to hear as he stared between the three of us.

"Who did you think I was, silly?" Keenan giggled, reaching for my hand.

The creases in Brecken's forehead went deeper. "I don't know."

"Hey, it's okay." Crew reached out to pat Brecken's arm, but Brecken went rigid and stepped away before he could. Crew exchanged a look with me, one that wasn't subtle—one that read, *how messed up is this guy?* "You've been through a lot. Give yourself some time to adjust back into society."

Brecken's eyes moved between the three of us. "I'm not sure I can."

**"D**id I wait just long enough?" I asked, creeping behind the rusted chain-link fence overgrown with weeds and just about every variety of creeping plant imaginable.

Rolling to a pause, I waited for his answer. He'd clearly come here because he wanted to be alone, but people at the party were starting to wonder where he was. Crew had left for work and Keenan was playing with Julie's grandsons at her place. After that mess of a reunion, I needed to speak to Brecken alone. To explain. To at least *try* to explain.

Brecken glanced up from where he was sitting on the same alley curb the two of us had spent countless hours on in another life. "You waited long enough. Sorry I disappeared on you." Something flashed in his eyes, something that implied he was talking about more than our present situation.

"I saved you some food. It was going fast." Ducking the rest of the way beneath the curled chain link, I angled the weighed down plate so he could see.

"Thanks." He scooted over, patting the curb beside him. "And I saved you a seat."

As I walked toward him, he met me with that same stare from back on the street. That same unblinking, reverent look, like he was trying to distinguish between reality and a dream.

"Staring again." He sighed, his eyes shifting in another direction. "Sorry. *Again*."

My footsteps seemed muffled as I walked. Almost like I didn't exist here in this small corner of the world. "It's okay. I don't mind."

He huffed. "Why would you mind some guy you haven't seen in years gaping at you, right?" His eyes narrowed on the crumbling brick wall behind me.

A few more steps put me in front of him. "Actually, it's kind of nice to be gaped at every once in a while."

When he noticed my smile, his formed as well. Brecken had all kinds of smiles, one for every emotion, ones for different occasions. This one took me back to the first summer we were a couple, the nights he'd lure me down to the river to skinny-dip or make out or whatever else he had in mind.

"I'll work on it," he said eventually, "but I won't beat myself up if it takes me a while to get it under check."

"Works for me."

"Wait. Switch." Brecken rose when I started to take a seat beside him. "My hearing's better on this side" Half a smile formed as he settled on my other side, keeping some space between us. But not much. When he saw the look on my face, he tapped his other ear. "Perforated eardrum. Years ago."

I wasn't sure what to say. How did a person have a conversation about torture on a concrete curb while holding a plate of barbecued chicken?

"I brought you your favorites," I said eventually, holding out the plate I'd made for him.

He took the plate, staring at the heaps of food. "I don't remember what my favorites used to be. At least food-related favorites." He glanced at me from the side, another hidden message in his voice.

"Barbecued chicken—wings and legs—baked beans, potato salad, sweet rolls." My hand swept across his plate. "Those *used* to be your favorites anyway. I'm not sure if they still are, but only one way to find out."

After staring at the plate for another minute, he picked up a leg, turned it over a few times, then tore off a bite. As he chewed, he dug his fork into a couple of the salads and added that into the mix. His brows lifted as he finished chewing.

"Well, damn," he said, tearing off a chunk of a roll. "My favorites."

"Some things never change." As I went to nudge him, I stopped short. From the way he'd flinched away from Crew earlier, I guessed he wasn't quite ready for that kind of human interaction—the taps and touches he wasn't expecting. Not that anyone could blame him.

"Most things do though." Brecken took another bite of chicken then set down his plate.

My hands came together as I stared at the brick wall with him. He was right. Most things changed. Nothing could stay the same forever.

"This is so …" His eyes narrowed.

"Strange?" I suggested immediately. "Awkward? Surreal?"

He seemed to consider those before shaking his head. "Nice."

"Nice?"

"I wasn't sure I'd see you again. And now I have." His head turned toward me. "There's nothing strange or awkward about being with you. Even after everything."

My eyes darted toward the opening in the chain-link fence. It was practically invisible to someone who wasn't looking for it, but still, I didn't want anyone to find Brecken and me out here, alone. People were already talking after our public reunion on the street.

"So you're a mom? A wife?" He clasped his hands in front of him, his voice level.

"I am," I answered, making myself look away from the fence. It was fine. No one was going to find us here.

"How's that?"

"Harder than I thought it would be."

"Well, you married Crew Graves. What were you expecting?" He smiled as he said it, his tone teasing.

Still, tears started to fall. That was the moment they decided they were done being dammed up. That was when I finally felt safe enough to let myself show what I was feeling. My head fell into the cradle of my hands, and I let myself cry. I let myself exorcise the emotions I'd been tormented by over the past two weeks. The past six years.

"Oh, shit." Brecken scooted closer. "God, I'm sorry. I didn't mean it like that. To make you cry." His arm came around my back, seeming to thaw into me as he tucked my body closer to his. For whatever reason, he didn't seem to have any problem touching me. Being touched was different, but giving it seemed okay. "Just don't pay any attention to anything I say. I've spent years being screamed at in a language I didn't understand, or in solitary confinement. I'm inept in all forms of communication at the present moment."

"I'm sorry, Brecken," I sobbed, sounding like I was choking on a watermelon. "I'm sorry for what happened. You must hate me. I'm sorry I'm not … I didn't …"

When I was lost for words, he found some for me. "That you're not in love with me anymore? That you didn't wait for me?" He spoke slowly, clearly. Instead of loosening, his arm cinched a bit tighter. "Blue Bird, please. I died. You had every right to move on with your life. To live it. I asked you to wait for a year, not into our next lives."

My head was shaking, tears still streaming.

"I died," he said, a finality in his voice.

"You're right here," I squeaked.

"The whole world believed I was dead. You had to move on. You had every right to. I could never be angry at you for that. I could never hate you for living your life."

My head just kept shaking. He was trying to make me feel better, which only made me feel worse. I was guilty of so much more than moving on with my life.

"I'm happy you're happy. Whether that's with me or him or whoever." His other hand slid my hair behind my ear, not letting me hide my tears from him. "That's what I wanted for you. Happiness. However you found it."

Happiness. I'd had glimpses of it, moments I felt it stir when Keenan was tucked in at night, safe and serene, but the concept was a prank to me. The dangled carrot. The smoke and mirror. It wasn't real. A person might be fooled into believing otherwise for a while, but it didn't last.

Happiness was for fools. Survival was for the rest of us.

I took a breath, calming myself. "What about you? Are you happy?"

Once he saw the worst of the tears were over, his arm returned to his side, his eyes to the brick wall. "I don't think I remember what happy feels like."

I found myself staring at his hands. Like the rest of him, they looked the same, but at the same time, they were entirely different. Fingers that had once been straight appeared crooked, almost bony-looking. His fingernails were dull, a few of them bruised, a couple missing. That those small parts of his body looked like they'd been through so much sent a tremble down my back as I tried to wrap my mind around what he'd endured.

"I'm so sorry." My words came out all broken, but I kept going. "For what happened. For what you must have gone through. I can't imagine …"

"Don't try." His voice pierced the air, his eyes losing focus. "Don't try to imagine. And don't feel sorry for me. I made it back. I survived."

I shifted when I found my hand reaching for him. There were more than a million reasons to not touch him. "Were there times you ever just wanted to give up?"

"Never." His jaw worked.

"Not once?"

"Not once. I knew I had to get back. To get back to you." His eyes slid toward me. "I made you a promise."

My hand smoothed my dress across my knees. "Thank you for keeping it."

"I always will," he said with a shrug, like it was a curse and, at the same time, all he knew. He picked up his fork again, stabbing at the plate he'd barely touched. "Catch me up on six years. You're married and have a son. What else have I missed?"

I couldn't see the look on his face, but his voice gave nothing away.

"Your family moved a few years ago," I said, not sure how to sum up a lifetime in a few paragraphs.

"Yeah, Texas. I've talked to them already, and they all seem good. Still crazy, but good." He worked half a smile into position.

"See? Some things never change."

"But most things still do." He rose from his seat after a moment, moving toward the opposite wall. "What about your dad?"

His question caught me off guard. I was prepared to talk about Brecken, not myself. I needed to talk about him, not myself. "He died. Almost four years ago. It was a heart attack." It all came out in one breath, leaving me breathless at the end of it.

Across the corridor from me, Brecken was quiet, his back toward me.

"It's okay. I'm fine," I added.

"No, it's not that." His head shook stiffly. "I'm just trying not to show my relief. I know I'm supposed to give condolences or say I'm sorry, but I can't."

My hands tied together in my lap. "He's gone."

"I thought about you while I was over there. All the time." He picked through the tangle of ivy choking the brick. "I worried about you a lot too."

My eyes narrowed. "You worried about *me*?"

"I worried about you being here, alone, with your dad. If you were still living in the same house. If he'd gone back to hurting you." He moved down the wall, searching through the web of ivy. "I was desperate to get back to you to make sure you were okay. And now I can see that you are. You got out of that house, away from that man, years ago. You're safe." He exhaled, his shoulders relaxing. "I'm not supposed to feel relief that your dad died, but damned if I don't."

What I wanted to reply with unsettled me, so I rose from my seat and cleared my throat. "I should get back. Crew had to leave for his shift, and I should check on Keenan to make sure he's not pushing down any more bullies."

Brecken nodded, still searching. "You're raising him right, you know?" He looked over his shoulder, his eyes connecting with mine. "Evil is nothing more than the result of good turning its head. Don't teach your son to look the other way."

My throat bobbed. Brecken might have looked like half the man people remembered him as, but to me, right now, he was twice the man I remembered. "I won't." I moved to the opening in the fence. "It's in his blood."

Before I ducked through it, I heard Brecken make a noise. When I glanced back, I found him clearing a patch of the wall he'd just uncovered, ripping vines of ivy away. I'd forgotten about the initials he'd carved into one of the bricks the summer before his senior year.

He stared at it for a minute, his brows furrowed. "Some marks can be hidden." He ripped another ribbon of ivy, his eyes finding mine. The cloudiness in them receded for a moment. "But they never disappear. They go too deep to be erased."

# Six

"Unbelievable," Crew muttered again as he glanced out our living room windows again, adjusting his tie. "The house right next door. How's that for subtlety? Not that Connolly ever knew the meaning of subtle."

I was in the kitchen, making Crew's lunch for his shift. He liked roast beef on rye sandwiches, the same kind my dad had preferred. I couldn't stand the taste of either, and the smell twisted my stomach as I rushed to stuff it into the baggie.

"How's him moving back here such a big shock?" I asked, watching Crew glare out the window at the house beside us that had been empty for months. Not anymore.

"The house right next to the woman he was planning on marrying?" Crew's neck rolled, cracking. "The shock is him spending six years in an Iraqi prison and still having whatever balls he must have left to think he can just move in on my territory."

"It was the only house for sale on the block. It wasn't like he had some evil scheme to live right next to us." When Crew's head twisted back, a warning drawn onto his forehead, I drew a smile to the surface. "I'm sure he's not trying to move in on your territory. He's just trying to get back to his old life the best he can."

Crew's dark brow arched. "His old life you played the starring role in."

Instead of confirming or denying it, which would be a trap either way, I went back to packing his lunch. It had been a couple of weeks since the homecoming party, and I hadn't heard a single thing from Brecken since I'd left him staring at our initials on that brick wall. Rumor was that he'd been through an endless stream of debriefings back in Washington, but I didn't know if any of that was true. Wherever he'd been, whatever he'd been doing, he was back. Like he'd never left. Moving into the house next door.

The longer Crew stood at the window, the redder his face went. Thankfully he was going to work tonight. He clearly needed to distance himself from what was happening.

"What happened to grabbing a couple of beers and catching up? You two used to be friends, you know?" I said, tucking a napkin into the paper bag.

"And then I married his girl. He doesn't want to be my friend. And with the way he's clearly planning on making his play to win you back, I sure as shit don't want to be his friend either."

"He's not trying to win me back," I said, stepping into the living room and setting his lunch on the table next to his briefcase.

"What makes you so sure? Because this looks like trying to win you back." Crew's arm flailed at the window as if Brecken was standing right outside it with my name tattooed on his chest.

"Because I can't be won back." I checked the time. Ten minutes. Crew was a man of habit and left for his shifts on the dot. "I'm with you."

"I know that. You know that. But he clearly doesn't."

"He's been through a lot. I'm sure the last thing on his mind is rekindling some flame with his high school girl-friend." I rolled down the sleeves of my sweater as I approached him.

"He hasn't been close to a woman in six years. Believe me when I say rekindling whatever he can with you so he can shove his dick somewhere inside you is on his mind."

"Crew—" My gaze flashed up the stairs, making sure Keenan wasn't lingering up there in silence like he sometimes did when we were having a "talk."

"Six years. That's enough to make a man desperate enough to do just about anything to get off."

"Sex? You really think that's all that's on his mind right now?" My arms folded as I stopped a few steps away from him.

"What do you think's on your hero's mind? Affection? Redemption?" Crew huffed, not blinking as he stared out the window.

"Stop calling him that."

"What? Your hero?" Crew's tone was sarcastic even though his expression was serious. "That's what he is, isn't it? What he's always been? The guy who stepped in to save you from whatever you needed saving from? The one you went to when you needed something?" His head shook as he pointed out the window at Brecken, who was carrying a box up the walkway slowly, like it was a chore. One of the guys helping him move in whisked by him with a bigger box, his pace ten times that of Brecken's. "Some fucking hero you've got right there, Camryn. Some fucking hero." Crew's hand snapped out from his side, capturing my wrist. "What's he got to save you from now?"

I swallowed, letting Crew drag me closer. "Nothing."

"That's right. You don't need him anymore. You've got me. To save you. To give you what you need." Crew's pinkie traced a line down the inside of my wrist. "To take care of you."

My soft smile held, despite everything inside me starting to rattle. Something was coming. I could feel it, like a wild animal could sense a storm coming. It was a survival mechanism for those beasts of nature, just as mine had been honed to keep me alive.

Crew tugged me closer as his head moved toward mine, his mouth settling beside my ear. "Get on your knees."

The words were whispered, but they made me recoil like he'd shouted them at me.

"Crew …" My eyes flitted up the stairs then to the window.

He slid the curtain open as far as it would go and flicked on another lamp behind me. "Come on, baby," he crooned, his eyes darkening as he reached for his zipper. "You know I don't like having to ask twice."

I could feel my pulse throbbing in my wrist. "You've got to leave for work soon."

"You know I never last long when you put my dick into that filthy mouth of yours. Just thinking about you working me over has my balls pulling up." Crew's hand wound behind my neck, his fingers tying into my ponytail. "You make me ask twice, I'll expect twice the reward. Both times will have you on your knees though, where you do your best work."

"Keenan's upstairs. He's awake." I gave a little wince when he pulled at my ponytail.

"He's building with his Legos. The house could catch on fire and he wouldn't notice. Besides, he wouldn't object to having a little brother or sister running around. A kid needs a sibling or else they turn into a self-entitled brat." Crew's hand trailed down my back as he pressed himself into me. He rubbed his erection against me, breathing heavily as he adjusted our position in the window.

"There are a bunch of guys out there. Not just Brecken." My voice was shaking, not from what Crew had in mind but from who he was hoping would see it. I was used to the sex, from the rough to the incessant, but this was a first. Having an audience did the opposite of turning me on.

"So they'll have some fresh material when they wrap their fists around their dicks tonight. Consider it a public service." His hand drove inside the back of my jeans, his fingers digging into me. His breaths were coming hard and uneven, like they did right before he came. His hand thrust deeper, until his fingers were invading me. "Baby needs a little foreplay, it feels like. My cock in your mouth ought to be just the ticket. I know how much it turns you on when you get me off with your mouth."

His fingers drove deeper into me, making me flinch in pain. Even though Brecken had been gone for the past two weeks, we couldn't turn on the TV or radio without hearing about him. The more we heard of him, the more Crew sought the release only sex could give him. It seemed to provide him the only relief he had these days, temporary as it was.

I'd been sore for weeks now, and even though I could have said something to him, I knew how much he needed it.

He was easier to live with at least. Some soreness and interrupted sleep were small prices to pay.

However, *this,* what he was proposing? No. Just no.

His hand finally slid out of my jeans, grabbing the waist to pull me against him. "You're going to make me ask twice, aren't you?" His eyes sparked as a familiar smile spread.

I found my eyes moving toward the window when I should have kept them on Crew. Brecken was still struggling up the walkway, his focus on the task at hand, instead of what was taking place in the window next door. In that moment, I couldn't help feeling like I was the prisoner now, forced to play a role to stay alive.

"Mom? Is dinner ready?" Keenan's voice sounded at the same time his bedroom door whined open.

I jumped, sliding away from the window. Crew let me go, his eyes fixing on the house next door again.

"Almost!" I cleared my throat when I heard my voice. It sounded exactly like I'd been caught doing exactly what we'd just about done. "Wash your hands and come down. You can help me set the table."

"Night, Keenan. Be a good boy. Watch over your mom for me, will ya?" Crew's brow lifted at me as he drew the curtain closed before leaving the window.

"Okay, Dad!" Keenan said as the sound of a faucet blasted on.

"Have a good night." I handed Crew his briefcase and lunch.

His eyes roamed me. "You owe me."

"I'll make it up to you," I promised. *Just not beside any open windows.*

"Now there's a promise that makes a man eager to get home to his wife." Crew pulled open the door. "Be good." He closed it behind him, failing to detail what the *or else* component of his voice entailed.

Not that I needed to ask for details. I knew what would happen if I let Brecken back into my life the way Crew was so concerned about—destruction.

As I wandered into the kitchen, I tried forgetting about what had just about happened. What Crew had suggested. I knew he was going through a lot right now, and Crew had always bottled things up, but what he'd just suggested went way beyond the scope of what I'd come to expect.

Since Brecken was clearly going to be our neighbor, Crew would have to accept that and figure out some way to calm his insecurities that I was going to run off with him. I was trying hard to be understanding, given the whole situation, but my understanding had about run its limit.

I'd finished chopping the lettuce and tomatoes and still hadn't seen or heard from Keenan the Starving yet. He must have gotten distracted by his Legos after washing his hands.

"Keenan!" I called as I rounded out of the kitchen.

"Yeah?"

He wasn't upstairs; he was in the living room, propped in front of the window I'd just been by. He'd pulled the curtain open halfway and was standing there, staring out the window.

"What are you doing?" I asked, walking his way.

"Watching Mr. Connolly." His shoulders lifted. "I was watching him move in up in my bedroom too, but there's a better view from this window."

"You've been watching him this whole time?" He'd been up in his room ever since we'd gotten back from the park this afternoon.

He shrugged. "I like him."

My hand dropped on Keenan's head when I stopped behind him. I stared out the window with him, taking in the scene. "What do you like so much?"

"I don't know." His shoulders lifted. "I just do."

The moving van was gone now. Everyone was gone besides Brecken, who was unpacking a few things on his porch. He looked different from when I'd seen him last. He'd put on a little weight, gotten some color on his face, his movements weren't so pained looking. He was transforming back into the man I remembered, the one I'd fallen in love with sometime between youth and adulthood.

"Yeah, me too." Rumpling his hair, I made myself turn away from the window. "I'm going to finish up dinner."

I took my time finishing up the rest, needing a few minutes to gather myself. I'd needed more and more of that lately. Time to regather, recompose, re-*something*. It was because of him, of course—his return, his coming back from the grave. But it also had to do with me and feeling something inside me come back to life. I'd thought it had died with him. I couldn't name it, but I could feel it.

When I heard Keenan clomp into the kitchen, I forced myself out of my haze.

"We should invite him over for dinner," he announced, starting to set the table. I didn't miss him laying out all three place mats.

"Why's that?"

"It's dinnertime." He folded three napkins as well. "And I've watched him burn three different things now."

My eyes lifted to the living room window. Brecken wasn't on the porch anymore. "He's burned three things?"

"Earlier today, it was a grilled cheese sandwich, and then a can of soup. I didn't know you could burn soup." Keenan's forehead creased as he set down the forks. "Tonight, he burned some eggs. I'm afraid he's going to starve if we don't help him."

I turned off the burners on the stove. In the household Brecken had grown up in, it was a fend-for-oneself mentality. He'd learned to cook because it was essential if he wanted to eat. Nothing fancy, but he'd known the basics from the time he'd been in middle school.

"He burned soup?" I said.

Keenan motioned at our stove. "The pan started smoking. The fire alarm went off and everything. He didn't like that. He tore it down and smashed it against the wall and threw it in the garbage. I want to do that when ours goes off." Keenan sighed, as though if he'd been born Hulk, life would be so much easier.

Chewing on the inside of my cheek, I considered my options. I wasn't sure I had multiple ones, but it was nice to think I did. It had been a while since I'd had more than one of them.

"We should at least take some food over to him. You're always telling me to do the right thing, Mom." Keenan sighed, blinking at me. "Making sure Mr. Connolly doesn't die of hunger is the right thing."

"You can't die of hunger from missing one meal."

"Yeah, but he's going to miss two if we don't do something. That's enough to kill a person." Keenan's dark blue eyes stared right through me, totally serious. I supposed that to a young boy, missing two meals in a row would seem like a life-or-death situation.

"Okay, fine. We'll invite Mr. Connolly over for dinner." Reaching for the lids, I covered the pans to keep everything warm. "But I'm not sure he'll want to come over."

"Oh, I'm sure he will."

"Are you?"

Keenan's head bobbed. "He likes you."

"We used to be good friends."

"Are you still friends?"

I paused, thinking. "We'll always be friends." Moving past Keenan, I gave him another affectionate pat. For being so young, he picked up on things most adults were blind to. He got that from me, I guessed, though his father had some of that too. "I'll go invite him over, but you stay here. We don't need to guilt him into dinner."

Keenan slid into his chair, his eyes bright as though Brecken was as good as our dinner guest.

"I'll be right back," I said as I moved for the front door.

I wasn't sure how I'd explain this to Crew. He wouldn't like it obviously, but he would have to wrap his mind around the reality of us all being neighbors eventually. Brecken did not need for his old friends to turn their backs on him right now—he needed to know they were there if he needed them. He needed to know they cared. Whatever Crew's response would be to finding out I'd invited Brecken to dinner, I'd just have to chance it. The consequences of ignoring him when he needed me seemed far more severe.

Walking to the house next door felt strange. It had been empty for so long, I'd gotten used to ignoring its presence. But now, someone I knew was living inside it.

Several piles of boxes were stacked on the porch, a couple of them open but not unpacked. It was like he'd started but hadn't known where to go from there.

My finger hovered over the doorbell, unable to press it. I was standing in front of his door, about to invite him over for dinner. The man whose death I'd grieved years ago was behind this door, alive. I'd had weeks to get used to the idea, but certain moments hit me harder than others.

My finger finally made the rest of the journey. When the doorbell rang, I didn't hear any movement coming from inside. I waited a minute and still no sound, but just as I was about to leave, the door opened. Not a crack, not some of the way. It opened as far as it would go.

Brecken looked surprised to see me at first, blinking a couple of times. Then his expression cleared and he stared at me like he'd been waiting for me.

"Hi, neighbor." His smile was natural, appraising me in a way that made certain body functions betray me.

"Hi, yourself," I greeted back. "Hungry?"

The skin between his brows pinched. "What makes you assume that?"

"The fact that you somehow managed to burn soup."

"You spying on me?" The corner of his mouth twitched.

"I had a tiny detective do my dirty work for me. He just gave me the full report." I took a few steps back when he came out the door. Not because I wanted to, but because I had to. "He also asked that I invite the marine everyone's talking about over to our house for dinner, so if you say no, I have to tell him his hero just turned him down."

"You used to be above the whole guilt trip thing."

"And then I became a parent," I said, only part joking. "You find your moral code shrinks when you're forced to accept what you'd do to keep your child safe."

"So you're saying I have a choice when it comes to dinner tonight? As long as that choice involves a yes?" He was managing to maintain a straight face, which I wasn't.

I started down the stairs. "You're quick."

He was already following me, moving down the steps one at a time. "Sorry I didn't warn you before moving in right next door. It all kind of came together all at once."

"You don't have to check with the neighborhood to get approval to buy a house."

"I don't care about what the rest of the neighborhood thinks, just what you think."

I smiled over my shoulder at him. "I think I'm glad to have a neighbor I can bum a cup of sugar from when I need one."

"Guess I'd better stock up on sugar then." He shouldered up beside me, tucking his hands into his front pockets. "Does that mean I can come knocking on your door when I need to get some?"

My feet stopped. "You need to *get ... some*?"

"Yeah." He shrugged, stilling with me. "Some sugar?"

When I noticed the corners of his mouth twitch, I settled a hand on my hip. "You think you're funny, don't you?"

"I know I'm funny. There's a difference." He chuckled and kept moving across the yards with me.

"You might want to give Crew some time to adjust to your presence before you show up asking for some of his wife's sugar. As a fair warning."

He smiled at the ground, trying to make his limp less obvious. "What's Crew's deal with me? He's the one who married my girl. If anyone should be pissed, it would be me."

I wasn't going to argue his point. "But you're not?" When he looked at me, I added, "Pissed?"

"Do I look like I am?"

I took him in, not sure what exactly he looked like. "No," I said at last, "you don't."

"I take it from that fair warning that Crew won't be joining us around the dinner table tonight?" His footsteps were loud, solid sounding, as we climbed the stairs.

"He's at work."

"Does he know you were planning on inviting me over?" The look in his eyes told me he didn't care. When I shook my head, he came to a stop as my hand touched the doorknob. "So we're straight, I don't care what you choose to tell Crew or not tell him."

"I'm not trying to hide this from him."

Brecken's gaze cut to the spot where Crew parked his cruiser. "Is that why you keep checking the driveway every two seconds?"

"Things with Crew and me are more complicated than you and I were."

"When I hear people use the word complicated to describe their relationship, you know what I think?" When I made no attempt to answer, he stepped toward me. "What word are they really afraid to use?"

My face didn't change, but he saw the shift in my eyes. I could maybe still fool Crew, but Brecken had known me too long for me to expect the same with him. Even with the years apart, he was still calling me out the way he used to when I tried to pretend I didn't know what he was talking about.

"About how much longer do you think we'll stand here staring at each other in silence? Ballpark idea."

Giving him a look, I opened the door. "You started it."

"But you and me"—he waved his finger between us—"we're not finished."

When I noticed who was jogging down the sidewalk, I motioned him inside. Gina Meyers loved to gossip almost as much as she loved to feel the burn. Tonight's "workout" attire included black, Spandex shorts, and a bright coral sports bra that provided yoga support, not sprinting support. But then, maybe that was the whole idea, at least if one took a gander through the inner workings of Gina's mind.

"Are you trying to attach a double meaning to everything you say to me? Or is it purely coincidental?"

Brecken stepped aside, his eyes wandering the house as I sealed the door closed behind us. "More along the lines of intentional."

"He didn't come, did he?" A voice sighed from the kitchen, the same tone he used whenever Crew had to cancel a promised fishing day or joining us at the park.

Usually, I had to console him. This was a nice change.

"Was I not supposed to? Because your mom made it seem like I didn't have a choice." Brecken nudged me as we moved through the family room. He took in every little thing, from the family photos to the chair Crew lounged at in front of the television. He studied it all like there was some deeper meaning I wasn't aware of.

The moment we landed in the kitchen, Brecken's eyes locked on Keenan. Same story the other way around.

"Oh, wow. You did come." Keenan looked like he was trying to crawl out of his seat, but his body wouldn't let him.

"Save the wows. I'm the neighbor who manages to burn soup remember? Definitely doesn't inspire a wow rating." Brecken waved at Keenan, shifting after a minute as Keenan continued to gape across the kitchen at him.

"Keenan," I said, giving him the Mom Look, "it's not polite to stare. Especially at dinner guests who were too nice to say no."

"I only agreed so we could form a free sugar trade." Brecken shot a smirk at me as I moved toward the stove. "I'm just here for the sugar."

Keenan giggled as though he were in on the joke, still gawking at Brecken without taking a darn break to blink.

"And it's okay with the staring thing. I have my own issues when it comes to staring at certain people"—his attention stayed on Keenan, but I felt his focus shift to me—"and I know there's a lot to stare at when a person looks at me, so it's okay. I don't mind, and I'm going to have to get used to it. You can help me with that."

"He's not staring at you because of that. He's staring at you because … tell him, Keenan," I said, collecting the plates to dish up dinner.

"Because you are, like, my favorite superhero ever." Keenan's legs swung from the chair as he went on. "You're just like Captain America. Except you're real, and he's not."

Brecken came up behind one of the chairs around the table. "Captain America defeated the bad guys. Kind of the other way around in my situation."

"Let the boy have his real-life hero." I set the plates on the counter and tore the film off the pack of taco shells. "Please?"

"Shouldn't that be his dad?" he asked, coming around the table like he was planning on helping me.

"Was yours your dad?"

"Maybe. If I would have seen him after the age of five."

"It's fine. His dad can be his hero too. There's no rule that says a person can only have one hero." When Brecken paused beside me, holding out his hands in a gesture of willingness to help, I motioned at the chair across from mine. "I've got this. Just take a seat. Relax for a few minutes while I get everything dished."

"I spent years relaxing."

"Relaxing?"

Brecken motioned his hand back and forth. "Physically similar. Mentally not."

I was staring at the hand he'd lifted, unable to keep from wondering what he'd experienced if that one exposed part of his body looked as though it had suffered so much. I had to focus on stirring the taco meat so he wouldn't notice my eyes glaze over.

"You could get our drinks if you want," I said, starting to assemble the tacos.

He started for the fridge. "What'll it be, Keenan?"

"Soda!" When he noticed me looking at him, he tried again. "Milk, please."

"Yeah, that look used to do the same thing to me too. Don't feel bad." Brecken tipped his chin at Keenan as he pulled out the gallon of milk. "Camryn?"

"I'll just have some water. *Please*," I added when Keenan gave me the look this time.

"Water? All the choices in the world and you pick water?" Brecken motioned inside the fridge like the options were endless, when really there were about half a dozen, mostly Keenan's. "I can't tell you what I would have done for a Coke a few years ago."

"Fine, you've made your point. I'll have … Soda!" I exclaimed in as best a Keenan rendition as I could. "And since tonight's special, you can have soda too."

Keenan let out a whoop while Brecken exchanged the milk for the two-liter of Coke.

"Why's tonight special?" Keenan asked once his celebration hoot had ended.

I glanced at Brecken pulling three glasses from the cupboard, like he knew his way around. Or was at least pretending he did until he really knew. "Because we're getting to have our first dinner together"—I smiled at my son—"with our new neighbor."

"Thank you for being so 'neighborly.'" Brecken tipped the glass he was setting in front of Keenan. "I don't think I had anything left to burn in my kitchen."

Keenan was already taking a gulp of his soda. "Do you like tacos?"

"Crunchy shell? Meaty? Cheesy?" Brecken asked as if he wasn't sure he'd remembered them correctly, going back to grab the other two glasses.

Keenan set down his glass, his eyes widening. "Don't you know what tacos are?" The kid lived for tacos and was unable to comprehend how anyone else didn't feel the same.

"I haven't eaten a taco in years."

As Brecken set his and my glasses down, I set Keenan's plate in front of him.

"But it's coming back to me now," he said, glancing at Keenan's plate.

"Why do you walk like that?" Keenan asked as Brecken moved toward his chair.

"Keenan ..." My eyes found his and I shook my head.

Brecken didn't notice. "I broke my leg a while ago, and it didn't heal the way it was supposed to."

"How did you break your leg?"

There was a few moments pause of silence. Then the sound of Brecken settling into his chair. "I don't remember."

"Did it hurt?"

I'd stopped in the middle of making a taco. Keenan knew what had happened to Brecken in a context appropriate for a young child, which wasn't much. He knew Brecken had been in the military, captured by the enemy, and held prisoner for a long time before being rescued. That was the extent of it. He didn't know, or need to know, what could or did happen during that stretch of time.

"I don't remember," Brecken answered at last, his voice sounding distant.

"You don't remember how you broke your leg or if it hurt?" Keenan was back to gaping at him like he was some otherworldly being.

Brecken's shoulder lifted. "Bad memory."

"But you remember Mom." Keenan pointed at me as I approached the table with two plates in hand.

Brecken's eyes found mine, his expression softening like he'd just let out a deep breath. "My memory's not *that* bad."

Keenan smiled, which always made me smile.

"Wow. I think your mom's trying to tell me something." Brecken motioned at his plate I'd set in front of him.

"I am," I answered, trying not to laugh at how absurd that many tacos looked on one plate. "Eat."

"I should give you my plate instead. You need it more than I do from the looks of it." His eyes skimmed over me, the corners of my mouth dropping.

"I think he's trying to tell me something too," I pretended to whisper at Keenan, who was crunching into his first taco.

"I am," Brecken said, placing a couple from his plate onto mine. "Eat." He waved at my plate, then at me. "Between the two of us, we've dropped an entire grown adult. But at least I have a good excuse."

I grabbed the salsa from the fridge, lingering like I was looking for something else. "And what makes you assume I don't?"

"I'm not assuming anything about your life. But I'm all ears if you want to explain any of it to me."

Other than the sound of Keenan decimating his dinner, the room was quiet. When I wandered back to the table, salsa in hand, I pretended like everything was good, that his words hadn't rattled me. I was good at pretending.

The moment I settled into the wooden chair, my body recoiled.

Both Brecken and Keenan's attention tracked my direction.

"Need your pillow, Mom?" Keenan was already moving into the living room to grab one of the small pillows I used for more than decorative purposes on occasion.

"What is it?" Brecken set down his glass, looking like he was about to get out of his chair too.

Lifting my hand, I shook my head. "Nothing." When he grunted, I added, "My tailbone. I fell and bruised it the other day and it's still tender."

Keenan had already returned with the small pillow and was waiting for me to lift up so he could put it into place for me.

"My hero." I winked at him after he'd slid the pillow beneath me, which made him puff out his chest and strut back to his chair.

Brecken was still appraising me like I was writhing in pain or something.

"Really. I'm fine."

But my assurances seemed to do the opposite of convincing him.

"How's the unpacking coming along?" I focused on my dinner instead of him since he was looking at me in a way that had me feeling like he'd found my darkest room and just flicked on a flashlight.

He answered after a moment. "Slowly."

Setting my napkin in my lap, I thought about the boxes I'd seen on the porch. If that was the extent of them, it wasn't that much. But I could understand how it could feel overwhelming. Going through a person's things, one item at a time, unable to recall some or most of them.

"What about furniture? You'll need that, right?" I asked.

Brecken had lived in the base dorms, where most of the furniture had been provided. The house he'd purchased wasn't huge, but it would feel that way without some things to fill it.

"I've got a couch and a card table." Brecken picked up a taco, watching how Keenan was eating his. "So I'm set in that department."

"You might need more than a couch and a card table."

"Like what?" He took a big bite of his first taco, waiting for me to explain.

"Like a bed for starters. A kitchen table and chairs. Maybe a television."

Brecken's forehead creased while Keenan seemed perfectly content looking between the two of us as we talked, like we were live entertainment.

"Why do I need a bed when I have a couch?" he said once he'd finished chewing. "And I don't need a table specifically for the kitchen when I've got one I can move to whatever room I want. And the last thing I want is a television droning on all day and night."

Based on the fact that I couldn't turn on the television without hearing about Lance Corporal Connolly in some capacity, I could understand where he was coming from on that topic.

"You're going to use a couch as a bed?" That revelation was enough to get Keenan to hit the pause button on his taco massacre.

"Believe me, a couch feels like a plush pillow-top mattress when you've slept on the floor for as long as I have."

Keenan blinked. "They made you sleep on the floor?" he cried, like it was the worst form of torture one could receive. If only that were the truth.

"That couch is sounding pretty nice, right?" Brecken clinked his glass against Keenan's, getting back to his dinner.

"Well, if you need help getting settled in, let me know. I'm here almost all the time. I'd be happy to help." As I nibbled a small bite of taco, I found myself actually tasting it. The spices, the oils, the textures. I couldn't remember the last time I'd really tasted a taco.

The way Brecken was downing his, it was like he was experiencing the same thing.

"And me too," Keenan added, wiping his hands on his shorts. Since the napkin tucked beside his plate was so far away. "I could help you unpack. And Dad too."

Brecken's and my eyes met, but mine were the first to drift away.

"Thanks for the offer. I might take you and your mom up on it."

After that, Keenan wouldn't stop talking now that he'd finished his dinner. He had an endless stream of questions, all of which Brecken answered in a way that was fitting for a child.

An hour passed and we were all still staggered around the table before Brecken pushed his plate away. "I'm stuffed."

When I noticed his plate, I could see why. "That's because you ate a million tacos."

He patted his stomach, smiling. "I only counted eight."

Keenan stared at Brecken's plate and gave an impressed nod.

"None of my old clothes fit me anymore, and I don't want to go shopping for a whole new wardrobe." He slid the bottom of his shirt up just high enough to expose his buckle. He'd had to drill a new hole in the belt a good few inches from where the last notch was. He was fuller than the last time I'd seen him, but he was still thin. Emaciated when compared to the size he'd been.

"They didn't feed you either?" Keenan nearly shrieked.

"Oh no, they fed me," Brecken answered. "Fava beans."

Keenan leaned forward in his chair. "With what?"

"More fava beans."

"Breakfast, lunch, and dinner?"

"They preferred the one-meal-a-day way of doing things, but yeah, fava beans for every meal. Occasionally with a side of vitamins."

Keenan's nose crinkled. "Mom makes me take vitamins too. She says it keeps my bones and muscles strong."

"Keeps you from going blind too," Brecken replied, his expression drawing up like he should have caught himself before saying that.

I played interception before Keenan could glom on to that topic. "Why don't you bring down some of your Legos so Mr. Connolly can see what you've built?"

"Brecken," he said. "He can call me Brecken. If that's okay with you."

He and Keenan were both watching me, waiting. I wasn't sure what Keenan should call him, but I supposed Brecken wasn't totally inappropriate.

"Okay, why don't you bring your Legos down so *Brecken* can see what you've built?"

Keenan was already out of his seat, his feet thundering up the stairs, before I'd managed to slide out of my chair.

"How are things?" I asked now that Keenan was gone. For however long it took him to gather up his favorite towers.

"Specifically or all-encompassing?" Brecken handed me his plate, his fingers grazing mine.

"However you want to answer."

He shifted in his seat. "Things are weird." His words were slow, deliberate. "I was only gone for six years, but it feels like six lifetimes sometimes. I can't remember what a taco is, but I can remember some random equation Mr. Murdoch taught us in algebra. It's like I'm having to pick up pieces of my past, one at a time." As I set the plates in the sink, I didn't expect him to say anything else, but he did. "I feel lost. My old life feels like a dream, and this one feels like I'm living someone else's life. The only time I feel hints of my old self is when I'm …" His head turned toward the window as he closed his mouth. He wasn't going to finish his sentence. Then his head rotated back to where I was hovering at the sink, his eyes clearing. "When I'm with you." His words echoed off the kitchen walls. "I remember who I was, who I *am,* when I'm with you."

My heart crawled into my throat when I let myself look at him, my hands curling over the edge of the sink. That had been another life. I'd been another person. Who he remembered, that girl he'd loved, that person wasn't in the woman he was staring at now. That girl had died with that boy. The woman was a mirage.

Keenan burst into the room right then, making me jump. Before he could notice, I turned on the sink to pretend like I was doing the dishes while Keenan spread out an armful of Lego constructions on the table. Brecken didn't say anything else to me after that—he focused on Keenan, who could have gone on for hours about each and every structure like they were an engineering feat rivaling the first pyramids.

I let him stay up an extra half hour before wrangling him up to his room for bedtime. He fell asleep almost instantly, the Lego soldier figurine clasped in his hand. When I went back to the kitchen a few minutes later, I found it clean and empty.

"Brecken?" I called quietly, peeking into the living room.

"Out here." His voice floated into the house from the porch. The door was open, but the porch light was off. When I stepped outside, Brecken reached back inside, reaching for the porch light. "Sorry. Sometimes the lights still get to me."

"It's fine. Leave it off." I covered the switch before he could fire it back on. "Sometimes they get to me too." I closed the door, leaving it open a crack so I could hear if Keenan called for me.

As I passed Brecken, all I could see of him were the whites of his eyes. Going from the light straight into the dark like this was blinding. Strange how the reverse was true as well.

"Do you want a beer? Crew has some in the fridge." At least, he had as of last night.

His head shook as he sank into one of the porch chairs. "No, thanks."

"Something else?" I asked, trying to remember what I'd last seen in Crew's cupboard in his office.

His fingers curled around the arm of the chair. "I'm afraid if I let myself start drinking, I'm never going to stop."

I moved toward the other chair. "I know the feeling."

"You don't drink?"

"No."

His head tipped. "Why?"

"Because I've seen it turn men into monsters." The words were out before I'd felt them forming. Even if I could take them back, I wouldn't have. I'd held so much in for so long, letting that one particle out felt like a victory.

"You have your old man to thank for that." Brecken stared into the night, his chest moving evenly. "But booze can't make a monster; it can only free one."

My eyes closed. Everything went darker.

Time went by and we let it, sharing the silence together. It was different though, having him close. The dark, the silence, it was gentler with Brecken near. It was almost comforting.

"Listen, I know I flunked more than one math class in my day, but a five-year-old kid plus nine months of pregnancy about equals six years, right?"

I'd known the peace couldn't last, but I hadn't expected for it to be broken like that. When I shifted, a ripple of pain burst up my spine from my bruised tailbone. "Brecken …"

"I'm not asking for an explanation." His chair whined when he leaned forward, his head turning toward me. "Just a confirmation."

"A confirmation of what?"

"That I'm doing my math right."

His stare was too much to hold. It wasn't accusation in his eyes though—it was forgiveness. That was harder to accept from him.

"You are," I whispered.

"Figures." He shoved out of his chair, his hands sliding into his pockets as he scanned the quiet street. "The one answer I wished I'd gotten wrong, I got right."

My head lifted. "There is an explanation."

"You don't owe me one." His head barely shook. "And it doesn't change the outcome."

"What outcome?"

Brecken did half a turn, motioning at the house behind me before indicating at me. "You belong to someone else now."

I couldn't deny it.

Yet I couldn't confirm it either.

"It's okay," he continued, his throat moving. "I'm happy to have you in my life. In whatever capacity I can. Even if it's saving my ass every once in a while when I flambé my scrambled eggs."

I stood from my seat and moved beside him. Regardless of everything else, he was alive. "I'm happy to have you in my life in whatever way too. Even if it's saving my ass from something else."

His shoulder touched mine. "I'll save your ass from whatever you need saving from."

"Hero complex?" My eyebrow lifted at him.

"Far less noble," he replied, his eyes dropping behind me. His mouth stretched into a grin. "You've got a nice ass. Totally worth saving."

Elbowing him, I feigned appall, but he saw through the act.

"I better get going. I don't want to overstay my welcome." He moved down the steps, holding the handrail as he took them backward. "Let me know what you decide to tell Crew. If you decide to tell him anything."

My arms folded as I moved to the edge of the porch, watching him lower himself one step at a time. "Things between Crew and I are—"

"Complicated. Yeah. I was listening. I know that." Brecken stopped when he stepped onto the pathway. "I don't want to make things more complicated for you, so just let me know how I can do that. Unless you want me to complicate things for you, then by all means, let me know how I can do that as well." He was joking, the glint in his eyes told that, but he wasn't entirely. His face told me that.

When I went to reply, all that came out was a sigh.

"Listen, you're with him, you have a kid. I know you're his wife." He was staring at me, still holding onto the handrail. Not able to let go. "If he wants to hear me say that to his face to make him feel better, I will."

"You know what question Crew will follow up with."

He nodded once. "If I'll respect the fact that you're his wife."

My silence was a confirmation.

"Well, that's simple," he said, his voice sounding like the one I remembered. It didn't waver. It didn't rasp. Brecken's eyes didn't leave mine as he backed away. "I'd tell him that I have every intention of showing him the same amount of respect he showed me when he moved in on my girl weeks after my fake execution."

# Seven

This window had been a portal to a different life. At first, after Keenan's birth, I'd spent what felt like months trapped at home with a colicky newborn, rocking him in the chair I'd pull up to this window. Watching our neighbors live their lives, one window to the next, admiring the snow when it fell, dreaming of a different life that I imagined was just on the other side of that pane of glass.

Now, I watched something else. I watched him. I no longer pulled up the old chair to stare out of the window for hours, but I took a few stolen minutes when no one else was watching. That other life felt farther away than just one pane of glass now though. It wasn't a different life I saw anymore at all actually. It was someone else's life.

Crew was in his office, finishing up a few things, while Keenan was in his bedroom, picking a few toys for his backpack to take over to his grandparents' monthly Sunday brunch. Alone, I took my stolen moments at the window.

It had been over a week since the night Brecken had come over for dinner. Other than from the window, I hadn't seen him. He'd kept his distance, and we'd kept ours. Keenan hadn't mentioned anything to Crew about our dinner guest, and I couldn't help but wonder why. It wasn't because he'd forgotten about it, but there must have been a reason. I hadn't asked him not to mention it because I couldn't pull our son into a lie, especially one as dangerous as this.

Crew pretended our new neighbor didn't exist, insisting the curtain to the window facing east be kept closed both day and night. However, each day, the tension tethered to him seemed to loosen. The longer Brecken kept his distance, the more Crew seemed to accept that him moving in next door wasn't some play to steal me away.

Brecken usually stayed inside during the day, but he was outside on the porch most mornings and nights, wrestling with some kind of weighted object. The day after he'd moved in, a bench, a few different barbells, and racks of weights had been delivered and assembled out on his porch. The boxes hadn't budged or looked as though they'd been unpacked, but the weights had definitely taken their residence in the place.

He spent hours out there every day, grunting as he moved weights, dripping sweat as he wrestled them, almost as though they were fighting back. He was getting stronger. More weight was being added to the barbell, heavier dumbbells were being lifted above his head—he was putting himself back together. Sometimes I watched him and wished it was so easy to put one's soul back together.

"We're going to be late, Keenan!" Crew's office door burst open, his voice booming through the house. "Put some hustle in it!"

I had just enough time to close the curtain and whisk away from the window before Crew marched into the living room.

"You got the pie, right? The one from the freezer section, not the bakery?" Crew asked as he adjusted the cuffs of his dress shirt.

He wavered in place as he did, but when he looked up, I pretended I hadn't noticed. Crew's parents weren't the easiest people to be around, and he usually needed a drink or two before we made our monthly visits. I couldn't blame him for it. If I'd been the drinking type, I would have downed those shots with him.

"I've got the pie, the freezer one, and the homemade rolls your mom asked me to bring. Everything's packed up and ready." Pulling a sweater jacket from the coat closet, I cinched it on before shouldering the bag with the pie and rolls.

"You didn't add too much salt this time, did you?" Crew glanced at his watch, checking up the stairs with an impatient look. "Dad has to watch his salt—"

"I halved the salt this time."

When Keenan started bouncing down the stairs, I exhaled, pulling the front door open. These brunches were as stressful an ordeal for me as they were for Crew.

"Got everything?" I combed Keenan's hair with my fingers a few times before following Crew out the door.

He was already marching down the stairs, acting like we were five minutes late, when we'd probably be five minutes early.

I knew, in his parents' book, that was five minutes late.

"Do we have to stay very long?" Keenan whined to me, smart enough to keep it quiet enough so that Crew didn't hear.

"As long as we need to, and not a minute more." I took Keenan's hand as we moved down the stairs, trying to ignore the figure standing on the porch next door. The one who'd stopped lifting those dumbbells to watch us.

I wanted to wave. We were neighbors; no one could accuse me of anything other than being friendly. But if Crew saw, he could accuse me of more. Maybe he'd even be right.

Instead, I lowered my sunglasses over my eyes and did my best to ignore the man whose eyes were trained on me as I moved down the sidewalk. Thankfully, Crew was distracted enough by what was waiting in front of him than who was watching behind him.

His parents still lived in the same house he'd grown up in at the end of the block. The blocks were long in this part of the city, more like three blocks in the newer subdivisions. The walk only took a few minutes, but it felt like we were traveling back in time a couple of generations.

Lester and Margaret Graves' household—the home where casseroles, plastic-covered furniture, and old-fashioned values thrived.

Crew didn't say anything the whole way there. He just kept a steady charge in front of us, looking like he was going to war instead of a meal with his parents. He waited at the door for us to catch up, adjusting his collar and cufflinks once more.

"Be good," he said, pressing the bell. I guessed his suggestion wasn't just for Keenan.

The heavy, measured steps of his father could be heard from inside. Crew was a decent-sized guy—until he stood next to his father. Lester towered a few inches above him and was a good margin wider. Even though he was in his fifties, he still had the body and bearing of a man half his age. He was an intimidating figure who clearly liked people viewing him that way. Keenan and I did our best to keep our distance, but Crew was of the opposite mind. He stayed by his dad's side like a trained companion.

When the door pulled open, Lester seemed surprised to see us. Then realization must have set in. "It's the fourth Sunday of the month. The one day we're lucky enough to be graced with the presence of our only son and his family."

Even Lester's voice was intimidating, though he was wearing a smile as he opened the door for us.

"Margaret?" Lester boomed through the house. "Is brunch almost ready?"

"Five more minutes. I'm just carving the chicken," Margaret replied from the kitchen.

Lester exhaled under his breath, waving his arm inside. "I can't close the door unless you come in. You want to pay my air-conditioning bill?"

Keenan was silent, my steady shadow whenever we crossed the threshold of that front door. He'd been getting chided for crying since our first visit as the three of us. He'd been two weeks old at the time.

"I'll see if Margaret needs some help." I gave Crew's arm a reassuring squeeze before moving through the house. "Keenan can help set the table."

"A boy doesn't need to know how to set no table." Lester laughed, Crew joining in.

"Then I'll have him sharpen the knives or something instead," I said under my breath as I steered Keenan and myself into the kitchen.

As expected, Margaret had everything under control. The silver was gleaming, the crystal sparkling, the kitchen nearly spotless even though she hadn't finished preparing an impressive meal.

"What can I help with?" I greeted, indicating the chair in the corner for Keenan to wait. It was getting easier to leave him to his own devices now that he was older, but trying to protect heaps of fine china from a grabby two-year-old had been a fiasco.

"I've got everything under control," she replied, her focus unmoving as she carved the chicken. "Thank you for the offer though."

She never looked up once. Not until she'd finished layering each piece of chicken onto a serving plate. When I moved up beside her to carry it to the table, she gave me an amused smile before carrying it herself.

When she glanced up, she almost looked surprised to see the boy sitting in the corner, playing with a couple of his action figures. "Hello, Keenan."

The plastic figurines stopped smashing together, Keenan's blue eyes flickering toward the table. "Hello," he replied in the same hesitant voice I favored in this house.

"Why don't you have a seat and your mother can get you situated?" She adjusted the plate on the table another degree before leaning back and appraising the spread with a critical eye. Whatever tests she ran it through must have passed. "I'll grab Lester and Crew."

By the time I'd scooted all things of an extremely breakable nature back from Keenan's seat, the others were in the kitchen and settling into their chairs. Lester sat at the head. No one sat at the other head. Ever. It was an unspoken rule. Though I guessed he'd have something to say about it if someone tried.

Brunch was a silent affair most of the time, a pattern of events I'd memorized years ago. Lester started by serving himself from the main course before passing it around the table, moving on to the next dish. Crew and I praised Margaret for her culinary skills while Lester usually had something to address, whether it was the roast being too rare or like, last month, my rolls having too much salt.

More eating in silence except for the scrape of forks on china plates. Keenan bouncing in his seat when he got restless. Crew pulling at his tie as he checked his watch. It was a sequence of events that we followed without orchestrating it beforehand.

"Someone's got an awful lot of spinach left on their plate," Margaret observed, peering across the table at Keenan's plate.

I sighed to myself. I'd been trying to sneak tiny bites from his plate when no one was looking, but clearly I hadn't sneaked enough. Keenan ate more vegetables than most kids, but he was still a five-year-old.

Crew came back to the here and now from whatever escape he'd found. "Keenan"—he pointed his fork at Keenan's plate—"finish your spinach."

Keenan's mouth turned down with extra flair. "I don't like spinach," he said in just a whiny enough voice that I was already bracing myself before Lester cleared his throat.

"You see? How many times do I need to tell you, Crew?" Lester pushed back his empty plate, shaking his head. "You're letting that boy run wild, letting him do what he wants, say what he wants. He needs discipline."

The mother hackles in me rose with a serious vengeance. I found my body angling in front of Keenan, like I was shielding him from Lester.

"All of these hippie parents raising their kids with all of this positive discipline bullshit. They're raising a generation of spineless pussies." Lester snorted as he leaned back in his chair. "You mark my word. By the time your boy's a man, Canada will be able to invade our country and take over with the sissies we're breeding these days. I'll welcome them to it too."

Heat surged through me. Keenan was getting old enough to be affected by what he heard Lester say, and I didn't want my son growing up under the impression people could say those kinds of things. I didn't want my son to grow up as Crew had, under the iron fist of a man raising soldiers instead of sons.

I was just pushing out of my chair to guide Keenan out of the kitchen, consequences be damned, when Crew set down his silverware, his head lifting toward Lester. "I didn't like spinach when I was his age either. It's not a big deal."

Lester's gray brow cocked, a look I was familiar with settling into his face. It was the same one his son gave me when I challenged him on something. "Sure. What kid does? But you *ate* your spinach. And you sure as hell didn't whine about it at the dinner table." Lester's forearms settled on the table on either side of his plate, his gaze unyielding.

He wasn't even looking at me and I found myself wanting to shift in my chair. Lester's size made him intimidating, but it was his demeanor that made him menacing. I'd been scared of him before marrying his son—in the six years since, I'd become even more so.

Crew's eyes were the first to break, his posture following. Clearing his throat, he motioned at Keenan's plate. "Eat your spinach, Keenan."

"But—"

"Eat it!" Crew threw his napkin on the table.

Keenan wasn't as used to Crew's bursts of anger as I was. He did a better job of masking it around Keenan, and I made it a priority to try to shield Keenan from it. You could see from the look on Keenan's face how hurt he was by Crew's outburst. He was trying to conceal it, but his eyes betrayed him. The first tear took a moment to fall, but once it did, the rest followed right after.

"See? Proving my point." Lester lifted his arm in Keenan's direction.

I angled myself more in front of Keenan, feeling my own burst of anger crawl out from deep within me.

"You did used to cry like that though, Crew. Whenever you got the lightest little tap or smallest scrape." Lester chuckled in that dark way of his, grabbing a chicken leg from the serving plate. "You and your son actually do have something in common—who would have guessed it?"

Crew didn't need me to defend him and I knew he probably didn't want me to, but I couldn't help it. "Crew got attacked by a man he was arresting last month. Finished what was left of his shift before realizing he needed to head to the ER for a cut he got in the midst of it. Twenty stitches."

Lester's attention was on me now, his eyes emitting something that resembled amusement. His gaze cast to the man across the table from me, who was giving me a look of his own. One that was the opposite of thankfulness.

"You have your wife sticking up for you now?" Lester grunted, tearing into the chicken leg. "Need that kind of confirmation that you're a man or something?"

Crew didn't say anything. In word or expression. He just rose from his seat and left the kitchen. In the midst of that, I managed to scoop most of Keenan's spinach onto my plate without anyone noticing. Well, Keenan noticed, but the smile that tugged at his mouth as he wiped his eyes told me I wasn't in danger of him telling on me.

"Keenan has to use the restroom. We'll be right back," I said.

"A boy doesn't need his mama to escort him to the bathroom, contrary to the popular opinion of the contemporary times," Lester announced through a mouthful of chicken.

I pinched the bridge of Keenan's nose as I gave him a private wink. "I think he's getting a bloody nose. I don't want his nice shirt to get stained."

Keenan played along, getting up with me and moving out of the kitchen.

"Probably brought on from all that crying," Lester muttered before we were out of earshot.

Crew was nowhere to be found when we passed through the living room on our way to the bathroom. I supposed he could have been halfway back to our house, though I doubted that. Crew was nothing if not predictable. He showed up on the last Sunday of every month, even the time he'd been sick with the flu. He stayed through dessert and coffee, every time, no matter what his father said to him; or on a few occasions, when his father didn't say anything to him, as in one single word. Not even hello or good-bye.

We almost ran into Crew as we were turning into the bathroom.

"What are you doing?" The edges of Crew's face were still damp. He'd been throwing cold water on his face. It was his preferred coping mechanism when he got over-whelmed and a bottle wasn't accessible.

My fingers went back to Keenan's nose. "I think he's about to get a nosebleed. I didn't want it to get on anything."

Crew slid by us. "Well, hurry back. Mom will be serving dessert soon."

"In a jiff," I replied as I guided Keenan inside the bathroom before closing the door.

Once I'd turned the lock over, we both let out a breath. Keenan leaned into the wall like he was as exhausted as I was.

"How are you holding up?"

Keenan made a face. "Is it time to go yet?"

"Almost." I was counting down the minutes myself. No more than sixty, maybe forty if we were lucky.

He sighed one of those long, full-body ones. "Why is Grandpa so mean?"

Leaning into the wall across from Keenan, I drudged up a smile. "Because he's sad, Keenan. Usually the meanest people are the saddest ones."

His eyebrows came together. "But you're sad."

My chest seized, not expecting a talk about Lester to involve myself. "I am?"

Keenan nodded. "But you're not mean."

"I'm glad to hear you say that." I pulled at the tie of my sweater.

"So Grandpa's mad because he's sad ... but why are you sad?"

"I'm not sad."

"Sometimes you are."

"Everyone's sad sometimes."

Keenan gave that a moment's thought. Then his eyes cut through me, like the five-year-old could see straight into me the way his dad could. "But why are *you* sad?"

"I'm sad, sometimes, because when you get older, you have to make hard choices. You have to make decisions when you feel like there's no good solution." My head turned toward the bathroom window. Another pane of glass to stare through, another barrier confirming my imprisonment. "That's what makes me sad."

Keenan pushed off the wall and came toward me. His hand took mine as I'd taken his so many times. "But I make you happy."

That it was purely a statement, no trace of a question, warmed what had frozen inside me after the reminder of the choices I'd had to make. The ones I wasn't sure I'd made correctly anymore.

"You make me *very* happy."

"And Dad? He makes you happy?"

My free hand lifted to Keenan's face. "Yes. Your dad makes me happy too." Moving toward the door, I kept his hand in mine. "Ready?"

"I guess," he muttered.

"The sooner we eat dessert, the sooner we can get out of here. I'll take you to the park later, okay? We can stay as long as you want."

His eyes went round. "As long as I want?"

"As long as we come home before bedtime." I ruffled his hair before stepping out into the hallway.

We both sucked in a breath before turning into the living room. Crew was the only one in it, slowly pacing behind the couch and looking like he was waiting for his sentence to be read.

"Are they still finishing?" I asked.

Crew was about to answer when a crash came from the kitchen. From the sounds of it, something had broken. It was a sound I was familiar with from my own household. Crew went back to his pacing while I started for the kitchen.

"Stay here, please," I told Keenan when he started to follow me. If there was broken glass, I didn't want him around it.

As I was about to enter the kitchen, Lester was leaving it. He barely took a second glance at me as he stretched his arms and continued into the living room. "The damn chicken was dried out again. Every single time."

When I made it into the kitchen, I found Margaret on the floor, looking like she was curled over.

"Margaret?" I rushed toward her. When her arm blew behind her back, her hand raised, I slowed, but I didn't stop. "What happened?"

Crouching beside her, I found that she was curled over the plate she'd served the chicken on. It must have been what I'd heard break. She was picking up each piece carefully, placing them into her lap.

When I moved to help, she threw her hand out to stop mine. "I've got it."

"Let me help."

"I don't need your help. You need to take your help and direct it toward your family. If I neglected mine the way you neglect yours …" She left the rest unsaid, though it was perfectly explained with the look she gave me. "I warned Crew when he married you. Having no mother figure around growing up. What can a man expect when he marries a girl who didn't have an example of what a mother should be?"

I stopped trying to help her with the mess scattered on the floor. She clearly didn't want it. Leaning in so she was forced to look at me, I noticed the red mark stretching across her cheek. Her eyes weren't red from crying or shiny from fighting back tears. They looked just as hard and calloused as ever. I doubted she'd always been this way. I guessed there'd once been a gentleness to her in some capacity, a vulnerability, a reason to smile. She hadn't been born this way; she'd been created this way.

For one moment, I saw myself reflected back in her dark eyes. I saw myself in the hard, empty woman kneeling beside me, picking up the damaged pieces of a platter. She'd become this because of circumstance. Because she'd chosen to stay with a man who abused her in more ways than one. She became hard because that was the only option in this kind of a life.

Rising above her, I finally gave her my reply. "Lucky for me, I've had your example to watch. And I've learned everything I need to know about being a wife and a mother from watching you."

After that, I couldn't get out of the kitchen fast enough. Seeing her like that, getting a glimpse of what my life could look like in thirty years, it was too much harsh reality for one Sunday.

Crew and Lester were in the living room, settled into chairs set diagonally from one another, while Keenan had gotten back to playing with his action figures, this time hiding behind the couch. He was a smart kid; out of sight, out of mind was the policy to follow in this household.

"How's that POW friend of yours?" Lester cracked his knuckles, his big legs stretched out in front of him.

I wanted to march up to him and hit him right across the face like he'd hit her. I wanted him to see how it felt to be taken by surprise like that—how much it messed with a person's sense of security. How being hit by a human being who was supposed to love them made a person feel worthless … and hopeless … and *less*.

Less of the person they'd been. Less of the person they were meant to be. Less of a person at all.

"He *was* my friend. Isn't anymore." Crew looked toward the kitchen, probably hoping Margaret would be emerging with dessert so we could get out of here.

"Of course not." Lester clucked his tongue. "He made something of himself. That's a man this country needs. Six years in a damn Iraqi torture camp and they couldn't break him." He clapped, his stare unyielding on Crew. "Now that's a son who makes his father proud. Damn fucking proud."

I glanced behind the couch. Keenan was oblivious.

"Connolly barely knew his dad. Bailed on him as a kid." Crew shifted on his chair, taking another check of the kitchen.

"And look at how he turned out. The whole nation knows his name and won't ever forget it either. Just think what a boy who grew up with an actual father could do if he put his mind to it and applied some discipline in his life." Lester's mouth lifted as Crew shifted again. "So what's that hero of a neighbor been up to? He's your new neighbor, right? Maybe some of that greatness will rub off."

Crew's hand slid down his thigh, his jaw working beneath the skin. "He keeps to himself. He's messed up. Probably going to lose it one day."

Lester tsked, waving off Crew's worry. "You should invite him over. Get to be friends again. Take notes."

"I'd rather not have a mentally unstable man sitting at the dinner table with my family when he has a sudden flashback."

"If that boy's head was breakable, those fucking terrorists would have cracked it years ago. That boy's head's made of steel. Balls of the same stuff."

Crew's knuckles were white. "Whatever you say."

"Didn't you and Hero have a pretty hot and long-running relationship, Camryn?"

When I didn't answer, Lester's gaze shifted toward me. When Crew saw me standing in the living room, it looked like he'd only just realized I was there. He was waiting for my answer too, but not with the same look of anticipation.

"For a while. A long time ago."

Lester cracked another knuckle. "Planning on marrying him, weren't you?"

Swallowing, I wandered up behind Crew's chair and laid my hand on his shoulder. His hand found mine. "But then I married Crew."

Lester laughed a sharp note. "Well, honey, if nothing else, you have firsthand experience of what it's like to go from a hero to a zero."

Crew's shoulders stiffened. Lester never had a kind word to say about his son, but he didn't usually have so many cruel ones to serve.

My protective streak rose to the surface. "Crew's not a zero."

That only made Lester laugh again. "Well, he fucking sure ain't no hero, is he?" He leaned forward in his chair, waiting for my response.

Crew's hand tightened around mine, wringing out whatever fight I had in me to argue this topic any longer. I slid my hand free and stepped away.

Margaret carried in the dessert and coffee a few minutes later. The pie I'd brought from the *freezer* section instead of the bakery was precisely sliced and served on the same china plates we ate off every month. Coffee was served black, without even the option of adding milk or sugar. This was a house one expected to drink black coffee in.

Margaret had just cleared our dishes and we were making our good-byes, heading toward the door, when Lester decided he wasn't quite done with us yet.

"Any plans to expand that nest of yours?" he asked, looking at my stomach before his son.

Crew lifted a shoulder, reaching for the door handle. "We're trying."

"It's been five years." Lester gave a crooked grin. "*Try harder.*"

This conversation was making me more uncomfortable than the ones before. I reached for the door handle too.

"I knocked your mom up plenty," Lester continued, waving at the kitchen dismissively, "but the only one she was able to carry to full term was you." No hiding how he felt about that.

Keenan turned in front of me, his eyes bright. "Are you going to have another baby, Mom?"

Giving an internal sigh, I found a smile. Lester and Margaret had asked us plenty of times about future family plans, but Keenan had either been too little or too preoccupied to notice. "I don't know."

"I want a brother or sister. All of my friends have them."

The door couldn't have opened at a better time. "Say good-bye to your grandparents, Keenan."

"Good-bye." He took my hand as I led him out the door.

"And what—"

"Thank you," he said instantly, waving.

Crew and his father exchanged their usual formal good-bye while Keenan and I headed down the walkway. We both sucked in a breath, taking in the fresh air as though we'd been deprived of it for days.

"Good job," I said quietly, nudging him as we made it to the sidewalk.

"You too." The seriousness in his tone made me laugh. "Good job to you too, Dad," Keenan said when Crew caught up to us.

He was holding his wrist, shaking out his hand discreetly.

"You okay?" I asked.

His pace picked up. "I'm fantastic."

Keenan and I had to clip along to keep up with him, but the movement felt good after being locked in that cage for two full hours.

"Hey, what's the matter?" I asked when we were halfway home.

Crew ignored me. He never left these things with a smile, but he wasn't usually so obviously upset. His dad had been particularly vicious today though.

"If you can't stand to be there, why do we keep going every month?" I lowered my voice, watching Keenan jog in front of us.

"Because they're my family, Camryn. And to me, that means something." Crew broke to a halt, pulling me with him. "You wouldn't know the first thing about family, so just keep your opinions on the matter to yourself."

The domino effect of hate. From Lester to Crew. From Crew to me. I didn't allow it to keep going from me though, to keep spreading until everyone around me had fallen. I was a victim of it, but not a perpetrator. Although, I supposed there was a side effect of bottling all that hate inside. The only thing hate had left to latch onto was me.

I directed plenty of hate at myself.

Crew was towering in front of me, waiting for something, his fingers tightening around my arm. I knew that whatever he was waiting for, I couldn't give him. No one could.

From the corner of my eye, I noticed a bright flash of color across the street.

"Crew!" Gina called, waving as she stopped jogging. "Camryn!" She didn't shout it with the same level of enthusiasm, but that could have been because she was out of breath from all of the running she never seemed to stop doing. Checking the road, she jogged across the street toward us, wearing a sports bra that had me wondering yet again if it was meant to hold in a woman's assets or better display them.

Crew stiffened when he saw her, his hand leaving my arm to drop at my side. "Gina," he said, his voice rising just enough to indicate he was asking what she wanted.

She bounced to a stop in front of us, her skin shining with sweat, her chest still bouncing from the way she was breathing. Her eyes roamed the two of us. "Sunday brunch?"

Crew's head bobbed.

Up ahead, Keenan had noticed we'd fallen behind and was jogging back toward us.

"How's Brecken been?" She tightened her ponytail, glancing down the sidewalk toward our house. "Things have been quiet, way quieter than I thought they would be with him coming back, and the city doesn't seem to be overrun with the pap the way I thought it would be."

My forehead creased. "The pap?"

"The paparazzi." She nudged me with her hand like I was being funny.

The only thing funny around here was the way she was checking out my husband in his Sunday best. Nothing like having a half-naked woman shuffle through a few fantasies about your husband with you standing a foot away.

I'd gotten used to it though. Gina had had a thing for Crew since middle school, and she'd been about as subtle about it then as she was now. If subtle constituted practically rubbing one's breasts against a married man's arm.

"He keeps to himself. We don't really see him." Crew sniffed, looking off in the distance. He was clearly pissed about all of the Brecken talk today.

"Really?" Gina tipped her head, looking confused. "What about that night he was over a week ago?"

That was when I realized what was happening. Why Gina had pranced-slash-bounced over. To say hello to him. And screw you to me.

Gina had also had the same feelings for another certain someone since middle school—me. Although they weren't feelings of affection. More the opposite kind. Apparently Crew had liked me even back then, and since she liked him … go do the middle school jealous bitch math.

Crew crossed his arms. "He wasn't over."

"But I'm sure that was him. He's not exactly hard to mistake." Gina's attention diverted to me. She was waiting for a confirmation. Expecting one.

My lips stayed sealed.

"He was there for a while, it looked like. Around dinnertime. Still hanging around a couple of hours later. I thought you were there on the porch with them, but maybe it was just Camryn and him." Gina nibbled at the ends of her hair like she hadn't meant to say so much. Even though she had meant to say exactly that and more.

"Camryn?" Crew turned to face me. "What's she talking about?"

Keenan had made it back and knew something was wrong. His head was moving between Crew and me.

"We had him over for dinner," I said. "To be nice."

Crew's expression didn't change, but his face reddened. It started in his ears, spreading across his face, into his neck.

"He was going to starve, Dad," Keenan piped up, stepping between the two of us. "He burned eggs."

"He's used to starving. He would have survived." Crew's voice trembled. "Clearly he can survive just about anything."

Gina's hand covered her chest. "Oh god. I didn't know." Her other hand went to her chest. "You weren't there. You didn't know. I should have realized that from the look you were giving me, Camryn, sorry." She exchanged a look with me that looked friendly, but was the opposite just beneath the surface. "I'm sure it was nothing. Just a couple of old friends catching up."

The more she said, the more Crew's eyes darkened. The monster inside was waking up.

"He invited us over for dinner sometime too, Dad." Keenan took my hand, still staggered between us. He knew something was wrong, and in his five-year-old way, he was trying to protect his mom.

I never wanted that from him though, touching as it was. I never wanted my son to grow up feeling like he needed to protect me, that it was his job.

His job was to be a kid.

"The three of us," I added, ignoring Gina as she excused herself to finish her jog.

I knew she didn't know what she was doing, at least not the full scope, but she was a far cry from innocent. She gave Crew's arm a little squeeze as she passed, her eyes offering something I wasn't sure her husband would approve of.

"What do you think, Dad? Can we have dinner at Brecken's one day?" Keenan asked as Crew moved us along down the sidewalk.

"I'm not stepping foot in Brecken Connolly's house." Crew's neck rolled, his eyes narrowing when our houses came into view.

Keenan took off again now that our house was a few yards down. He could never wait to tear off his dress clothes after Sunday brunch.

"Why don't you like him?" I asked Crew, lifting my head and shoulders to give the illusion of strength if nothing else. "He doesn't hate you. Even though he has a reason to."

"Why? Because I married his girlfriend, who fell into bed with me weeks after he died?" A rush of air came from his mouth. "Please, I did him a favor."

"You did yourself a favor." With that, I knew I'd crossed whatever line there was. I knew there would be consequences for it.

"I don't want you seeing him again," he announced in a voice that boded no argument as he marched up the porch steps.

"He lives right next door."

Crew stopped. "I don't want you seeing him again." His voice was dark, low. "He comes out onto his porch and you're watering the flowers, you go inside. He passes a window you're looking out of, you look away. He comes to the door because a piece of our mail wound up in his, you pretend you're not home. He starts having a heart attack and needs CPR, you let him die."

Keenan had disappeared inside to get changed, so he wasn't around to hear what Crew was saying, but that wouldn't always be the case. Eventually, he'd overhear something, if he hadn't already. The pull of a belt or the blast of an accusation. I had a sudden urge to grab Keenan and get the hell away from here. Forever. For good. Like I should have done right after he was born.

I was willing to sacrifice my own life, but not my son's.

I started up the stairs toward Crew, tired of being scared. Tired of breathing fear. "Brecken already died. He can't die again."

For a moment, Crew looked at me like he didn't recognize me. That didn't last. Leaning in, his hand found my waist. I tried not to squirm as his fingers dug into me, clawing at my hipbone like he was trying to exhume whatever was left of my spirit to be crushed.

"I'm really hoping you give me a chance to challenge that." His mouth stayed outside of my ear, his hand squeezing my flesh, for another minute before he let go and retreated inside the house.

I stood there, chest pounding, head throbbing, staring at the threshold. I knew what would happen when I crossed it. I knew what waited beyond it. When I heard the clink of bottles echo from Crew's office, I flinched. It was a conditioned response. A learned behavior. The clink of glasses preceded the insurgence of my living nightmare.

"Keenan!" I called, lurking outside the door.

His feet pounded down the stairs. "Yeah, Mom?"

"Park time?"

His face lit up as he finished bounding down the stairs. "Park time!"

"Let's go." I waved him out the door, my eyes flitting toward the half-open office door. I could have told him we were leaving, where we were going, and when we'd be back. But it wouldn't change what I'd find waiting for me when I made it back and crossed the threshold.

As Keenan and I moved down the stairs, I noticed someone watching us. It wasn't the man one would expect to be concerned.

Brecken was watching us from the shadows of his porch, his hands gripping the handrail, his brows pulled together. From his expression, he looked like he was trying to figure something out, but with the way he was gripping the handrail, he already had.

He didn't say anything. He didn't follow. He just kept watching, like he was trying to tell me something. That he knew my secret. Or that he knew I had one. Either way, I knew Brecken wouldn't stop until he'd figured it out. He would, sooner than later, and once he did, he'd realize we had one more thing in common.

Torture.

# eight

Keenan was asleep. The real asleep, not the fake kind he sometimes pretended to be so I'd have to carry him from the couch to his bed. It was the first time he hadn't begged me for just another few minutes at the park before coming home. It was also the first time we'd stayed at the park until ten o'clock at night.

Afternoon had bled into dinnertime had fused into nighttime. We'd had such a carefree, simple day, I'd been tempted to never leave the park bench Keenan had fallen asleep with me on. We could just stay there forever. Happy, safe, playing freeze tag.

The thing about living the life I had was that fantasies never lasted long. There was always something close by to strangle the life right out of one. This one especially.

When the house came into view, my steps slowed. I wasn't in a hurry. At the same time, I was in a hurry to have it over with.

Keenan hadn't stirred once on the whole half-mile trek from the park to home, and I was grateful he'd found such peaceful, heavy sleep. That had been part of my plan in taking him to the park. Let him run and jump and scream himself into a sleep coma.

My arms were burning from carrying him, but it was the kind of burn I liked. It was the feel of my body being strong, fighting exhaustion. It was the knowledge that I was strong enough to carry my son through the night.

I didn't realize I was watching the house next to mine, but when I did, I focused on it as I started up the walkway. Brecken's house was dark—he was gone or asleep.

The steps didn't creak as I climbed them. Maybe because I'd become more voyeur than human.

The door was unlocked, open a sliver. An invitation. A welcome home.

My heartbeat was echoing in my ears, my lungs straining when I stepped inside. He was waiting for me somewhere in the dark. I couldn't see him, but I could feel him. He was close. I could practically taste the whiskey in the air.

"Where have you been?" Crew's voice was nearly unrecognizable, slurred from alcohol, low with anger. "*Wife?*"

I kept moving toward the stairs, not daring to stop. He was propped in his chair in the living room, sitting in a dark room. The glass he was drinking from caught fragments of light streaming in from the window behind him. He looked menacing. It was a demeanor he'd mastered years ago, perfecting only recently.

"The park," I answered, kicking off my shoes before climbing the first stair, scrambling for the last remnants of energy in my possession.

"For eight hours?" The ice cubes in his glass clinked when he finished drinking the last of it. "If I didn't know better, I'd say you were trying to avoid me."

"Let me get him into bed, Crew." I didn't wait for permission—I kept climbing the stairs. "Then we can talk."

He swirled the ice cubes in his glass, the whites of his eyes shining. "You know how I love our talks."

A tremor spilled down my spine, but I kept climbing, practically breaking into a jog when I reached the second floor. There was no getting out of this prison. It had windows and doors and had the look of a place a person could come and go from, but it was a lie. I was bound to this jail, a prisoner who would one day die in her cell. I'd accepted my fate, but my son's wouldn't be the same.

Never.

Moving as fast as my depleted body could, I lowered Keenan into his bed, then I slid off his shoes before tucking the covers up around him. I placed the sound-canceling headphones around his head, securing them around his ears. Some parents bought them for their children to muffle airplane noise—I bought them for my child to stifle the noises that erupted from this house at night.

"Sweet dreams," I whispered, too worried he'd stir if I kissed his forehead.

Backing out of his room, I closed his door without making a sound. My eyes closed, letting out the breath I'd been holding since crossing the threshold. Keenan was tucked away. I was ready.

A few steps later, I realized Crew wasn't where I'd left him. He'd moved onto the second floor and was propped at the top of the stairs. It was dark up here too, but Crew was a creature of the darkness. He could see in it, he did his best work in it, he thrived in it. I might not have been able to see him well, but from the way his lips were stretching to reveal a gleaming set of teeth, I thought he could see me so well, he didn't miss the way my heartbeat was firing in my pulse points.

"Have I told you recently how beautiful you are?" His voice spread around me, entombing me in its web.

"No. You haven't." My hands were starting to tremble, so I tied them behind my back. The more scared I became, the more fear he could sense in me, the more it fed his addiction.

His addiction to power. Exerting it. Forcing it. Displaying it.

"Maybe that's because you haven't shown me how beautiful you are lately." His hand rubbed his chin, his eyes roaming me. "Take off your dress."

"Crew," I whispered.

"Remove it. Or have it removed for you." His hands had lowered to his belt, working it open.

The option of him removing it involved far more noise, and being up here, so close to Keenan's room, noise wasn't something I wanted to make any extra of.

Pulling off my sweater, I let it fall onto the carpet behind me. When I reached behind my back to lower the dress's zipper, Crew's fingers stopped tugging his belt free of his slacks.

"Did you fuck him?"

Pulling the straps down my arms, I let the dress fall at my feet. "No."

Crew's eyes wandered down my body. "Did you want to?"

My legs were shaking, but I moved toward him. Every step close to him put us farther from Keenan. "No."

"You lied to me." His hands came back to life, pulling his belt from his slacks, one loop at a time.

I didn't argue that I'd never lied to him, that I just hadn't told him about it. That would only inspire more violence. "I know." Stopping a few feet in front of him, I made my eyes meet his. Now that I was closer to him, I could see in the dark too. "I'm ready to accept my punishment."

His forehead creased, the end of the belt falling to the floor. "You're not usually so agreeable."

"I know I made a mistake. I know I upset you." My voice wasn't shaking, but everything inside me was.

Crew looked almost disappointed. "The rest." Alcohol perfumed the air around me from his breath. He'd drunk a lot. More than usual. "Take it off."

As he started to roll the belt around his fist, my feet carried me back a step. He didn't miss it. His mouth twisted up on one side. Focusing on my breath, trying to let it give me strength, I took off my bra then slid out of my underwear.

Taking me in, Crew rubbed his groin, grunting as he stroked what was straining against his zipper. "Turn around." When I did, a ragged moan came from him. "So fucking beautiful."

I felt him appraise me the way an artist would his masterpiece. When his fingers brushed along my back, I flinched.

"On the floor."

My legs were shaking now. I couldn't control them. It had been a while since the last time, months, but I still remembered the sting of the belt. I could still remember the taste of blood from biting my tongue so I wouldn't cry out and wake Keenan.

I'd barely dropped to my knees and elbows before the first lash cracked across my spine. My head fell to the floor, a muffled cry coming from my mouth before I could swallow it back.

"Do you still love him?" Crew let the end of the belt brush along my back as though he were trying to soothe the pain.

My head shook as I struggled to regain the function of my lungs. "No."

Another crack. This one I'd been bracing for though, so no sound came from my lips. Inside, everything was screaming. All of my body was shaking now, tears streaming down my cheeks from the kind of pain that demanded their payment.

"Admit you do. Be honest. Stop lying to me, and I'll stop." This time it was his fingers that brushed along my back, his breathing accelerated from the effort and excitement.

When I refused to answer, the sting of his belt whipped across my lower back. My legs gave out for a moment as my body broke out in a cold sweat. I'd never passed out from the pain before, but I guessed he was angry enough that this might be the time I experienced it.

"I know you think he's a better man than me. I see it every time you look at me. Every time you look at him."

Another crack sent white hot pain shooting through me, blinding my vision. A few more immediately followed. Crew's grunts of exertion tangled with the snap of the belt against my skin, until the two became one. Him, the belt, they became one being.

"Admit it. Say it out loud." He stopped, having to rest against the wall behind him as he struggled to catch his breath.

The belt hung from his hand, and that's what I found myself focusing on as I looked behind me. An inanimate object. Something a person used to keep their pants cinched in place. A tool of torture.

From the look on his face, Crew was moving into the next phase—regret. Where he'd take me into his arms, tend to whatever wounds he'd inflicted, the entire time whispering tender words and reminding me of his unending love for me. Sometimes he'd carry me to bed after that, put himself inside me, and promise he'd never hurt me again. He'd rock himself asleep after spending his seed inside me with the promise of filling me with another child.

Those nights, I'd wait until he was breathing evenly before I crawled out from beneath his suffocating body, and I'd escape into the bathroom to take the birth control pill he didn't know I was taking. Then I'd step into the shower and not leave until I'd washed every drop of his seed away from between my legs.

Strength was an odd thing. The way it filled us one moment, leaving us at the next. I'd been the strongest person in the world before. I'd been the weakest one too. Strength wasn't a guarantee. It was a fickle whim that came and went as it pleased.

It visited me again right at that moment.

Getting my hands and feet beneath me, I started to rise. My legs shook, the rest of me felt about to crumble, but I didn't stop until I was standing tall in front of him. When he noticed me, he pushed off the wall he'd been resting against. His face was dotted with sweat, his pupils so large I couldn't tell where the iris started and ended.

"Say it." His jaw worked as he stepped toward me.

I backed away a step, but he matched it. He matched every one until I couldn't go any farther without going down the stairs.

My eyes lifted to his. I held them there for what felt like a whole minute. I didn't say anything. I just let him know that I saw him for who he was, what he was. Not the man who'd promised to love me for eternity—the one who endeavored to torment me until I expired.

"Say it." Crew's eyes flashed, his chest bumping against mine.

I didn't blink as I met his request. "I don't need to tell you he's the better man. With every hit, every word, you prove he is."

I watched Crew's face crumble.

For half a second.

Right before anger flamed through his eyes.

Leaning in, his mouth hovered beside my ear. "I love you."

My skin prickled from the tone in his voice—right before I felt his hands shove me. Hard.

I didn't realize I was falling until my body came crashing down on the stairs, feeling as though it were being cracked open, one stair at a time. Limbs rolled over limbs, tangling together as I crashed down the staircase, an endless journey from the top to the bottom.

The sound of my body banging down the stairs had stopped, but I still felt the sensation of falling. My ears ringing. My body throbbing. My brain feeling like it was pounding inside my skull.

I couldn't feel my body. I didn't feel the pain anymore. That only lasted a moment before, one by one, sensations trickled back into my consciousness. The feel of the cool wood floor on my back. The throb coming from my wrists and ankles. The warm trickle spreading down my face.

I wasn't dead. But I wasn't alive either.

"Oh, fuck. What have I done?"

Crew's voice echoed from the top of the stairs, so similar to a small boy's that I pried my eyes open to make sure Keenan hadn't woken. It was only Crew though, the monster back in his cage. The man stared down at me, blinking like he was trying to convince himself he was dreaming.

More of my body was coming back, one piece at a time, every part throbbing. Crew started down the stairs, swaying on a few of them, catching himself before he fell down them too.

"What have I done?" he whispered to himself, seeming afraid to look at my body as he stepped over it on his journey toward the door.

I didn't call out for him. I didn't beg him to stay or warn him to never come back. I just let him go, praying that wherever he went, he stayed. The door flew open, bouncing against the wall as Crew escaped through it. He was running away from something. He was being chased by something too.

Outside on the lawn, I heard noise. Voices.

"Crew?" It was Brecken. "What's going on? I heard something."

Crew sounded like he was saying something, but it was the same thing, over and over, too quiet for me to hear.

"Crew, stop!" The sound of Brecken's uneven footsteps pounded on the sidewalk, followed by the whine of a car door being opened.

I was finally able to make out what Crew was saying. "I need help. I need help."

"What the fuck?" Brecken's voice went louder, the sound of more shuffling. "Is that blood on your shirt? Is that *her* blood?"

Crew repeated those three words before I heard the sound of his car starting.

"Where is she? Where's Camryn?" Brecken was shouting above the noise of the engine, sounding like he was pounding on the windows. "Get out of the car. Get out of the fucking car."

More pounding, followed by the squeal of tires on asphalt as Crew's car sped away. Brecken bellowed Crew's name a few more times. The uneven cadence of him running outside for a few moments. Trying to scoot away from the stairs so I could find something to cover myself with or hide behind, I didn't miss the sound of my name being shouted. The shuffled footsteps getting louder before they started to pound up the stairs, sounding like they were making the whole house shake.

"Camryn!" He burst through the door before I had a chance to move anywhere, his eyes scanning the room for a moment before they found me. They went wide when he saw me, his throat moving.

Before he shouted anything else, I lifted my finger to my mouth and pointed up the stairs. That Keenan's bedroom door was still closed was the only miracle I needed tonight. He hadn't seen. He hadn't heard.

That was what mattered.

"What the fuck? What the fuck happened?" Brecken's voice was quieter as he rushed as quickly as he could toward me. He stopped short, his eyes flickering to the phone in the kitchen. "I'm calling 9-1-1."

"No. Brecken, don't." Getting my hand beneath me, I managed to sit up a little.

He didn't seem to realize I was naked until right then. "Camryn, what the hell?" His voice broke, his eyes taking me in as he moved toward a chair to pull the throw off of it. He stopped in front of me, kneeling slowly. He looked away as he draped the blanket over my body, his jaw about to break from the looks of it. "Did he do this to you?"

His hand tucked the corner of the throw up over my shoulder, resting there when he was done. My eyes closed. I was unprepared to answer him. Felt unequipped to explain any of this. I'd endured my torment in silence for so long, it felt almost impossible to talk about it.

There wasn't a part of me that didn't feel like it was burning or had already been burned, and my head felt like it was about to explode from the throb building inside. Sitting up a little higher, a shot of pain burst up my leg, twisting my face.

"I'm getting you help."

As he started to rise, I took his hand. "I don't need that kind of help."

"You need stitches." He indicated my forehead, the source of the warm trickle winding down my face. "You might have broken something." His hand opened to make room for mine before closing around it.

"I don't, and I haven't," I said.

"You don't know that."

"Yes, I do." He grabbed the corner of the blanket when I sat up some more, to keep it from falling down my body. "I know what needs stitches. And I know when something's broken."

"How do you know that?" His tongue worked into his cheek. "How do you fucking know that, Camryn?"

The sound of a door whining open stopped my heart, right before a sleepy voice came from upstairs. "Mom?"

"He can't see me like this," I whispered, checking up the stairs. My hand squeezed Brecken's as I tried to slide away from the bottom of the stairs. The thought of my little boy seeing his mother like this made me desperate. To promise anything, to say whatever needed to be said to save him. To save him from the life he'd been born into. "Brecken, please? I don't want everything I've gone through to be for nothing. He can't see me like this. *Please.*"

He was looking up the stairs now too, warring with his own emotions. "You'll tell me what happened? What's been happening?" His eyes returned to mine. A storm was raging in them, but unlike Crew, he was able to control his anger. He controlled his emotions instead of letting them control him. "You'll tell me everything?"

I'd give anything to protect my son. I'd given so much.

"Yes," I promised, letting go of his hand so I could continue to move out of sight just in case Keenan started down the stairs.

"Mom?"

Brecken was already moving up the stairs, one foot faster than the other. "I'll be back down as fast as I can."

The breath I'd been holding came rushing out. "Thank you."

Once I'd pulled myself a little farther out of sight, I paused to catch my breath.

"Hey, little man. Your mom's taking care of something real quick and asked if I'd come up and check on you." Amazingly, Brecken's voice gave nothing away. He sounded like we'd been doing nothing more than chatting over lemonade on the front porch. "Want me to tuck you back in?"

"Is Mom okay? I thought I heard noises."

There was a moment of quiet. "She's okay. I'm here now, so you don't have to worry about anything happening to her. Or you." Another pause, the sound of Brecken clearing his throat. "Let's get you to bed."

Peeking around the wall, I saw Brecken kneeling in front of Keenan.

"Tell Mom I love her. And tell her thank you for taking me to the park." Keenan rubbed his eyes, yawning. "Better just tell her thank you for everything. Then I'm covered."

Brecken chuckled a soft note then wound his arms around Keenan before lifting him. "I will," he said, carrying Keenan back down to his room.

I waited until they'd disappeared inside the bedroom before I tried to stand. It was going to hurt like hell, but I needed to get into the bathroom and start getting myself cleaned and bandaged. It wasn't just Keenan I didn't want to see me like this—it was Brecken too.

When I put weight on my feet, flames burst up my legs, spreading into the rest of my body when I started to walk. The right side of my body had taken the brunt of the fall and would probably have a nasty collection of bruises for a few weeks. I had plenty of clothes to conceal them, but the forecasted heat wave could have come at a better time.

My bad wrist was throbbing, but I didn't think I'd sprained it again. The worst pain was coming from my back, which felt like it had been torn open to the muscle by the belt. Keeping the blanket around me, I padded into the downstairs bathroom. The first thing I did was crank on the shower to get it warm. The water would wash away the blood, and the heat would soothe my aching muscles.

Before the steam had a chance to coat the mirror, I examined the worst of my injuries. The cut on my forehead was just below my hairline. It was bleeding like crazy and might need the aid of a little superglue, but I'd survive without stitches.

Twisting so I could see part of my back, I sagged with relief when I took in the damage. Only a couple of lashes were open, a few drops of blood leaking from them. The rest were just angry red marks that may or may not add to the permanent scars scratched across my back.

A few minutes later, I heard the thump of footsteps coming down the stairs. Stepping into the shower, I ducked under the water, letting it wash away the blood and pain.

"Camryn?" Brecken knocked lightly on the door before coming inside. "He's asleep. He's fine. Doesn't know what happened or anything like that."

My eyes closed as I let the water rain down on my face.

"How long has this been going on?"

I moved my face out from beneath the shower. I'd promised him. "Aren't you going to ask if he did it first?"

"No. Because I already know." His voice filled the room.

I watched the water swirl around the drain, the red fading to pink to clear. Blood could be washed away, if not much else in life could.

"You need to tell the police. You need to turn him in."

"No."

"Yes," he said slowly, through a gritted jaw.

"No, Brecken."

"Why not?"

My arms crossed, and I kneeled in the shower. Standing was taking too much of my energy. "He works for the police. They all play poker together. They have a summer baseball league. They go out for beers every week." Fear settled into my stomach from just thinking about taking this to the police. "He could be standing over my dead body, the gun still smoking, and they'd find some way to make it seem like self-defense. They take care of their own."

Through the fogged glass, I could just make out Brecken's form pacing, his arms looped around the back of his head. "Then we'll take it another step higher. To the state. Or federal. I could make some calls. I'm sure someone will have some idea of what we can do. He's beating you, Camryn. There are laws against that. There are punishments in place for the bastards who do it."

Unable to stand the shower beating down on my back any longer, I twisted so it was streaming down my front, and I leaned into the shower wall. "Everything I've done has been to keep Keenan from finding out about all of this. Everything," I repeated to myself. "How's making national headlines going to shelter him from it?"

Brecken was quiet, just the sound of his muffled footsteps moving across the tile. "I understand you wanting to protect Keenan. I do. And I respect you so damn much for it …" He paused, his feet stilling too. "But there's a difference between sacrificing yourself for your child and straight-up sacrificing yourself."

I held out my bad wrist, letting the warm water soothe the dull ache that never went away.

"And what do you think will happen when Crew beats you to death one day? Who's he going to go looking to next to take it out on when you're gone?"

The tears fell after that. I could endure physical pain, to every degree, but the thought of someone I loved enduring the same was more than I could take. Brecken wasn't saying anything I hadn't considered before, but the thought of what would happen to Keenan if I were gone didn't lead down any happy avenues. I preferred not to think about it, electing instead to believe that I was invincible and could take whatever Crew gave me.

It was a lie.

But in my world, lies were easier to accept than truths.

Brecken must have guessed he'd struck a sensitive spot, because he didn't keep pushing the topic. He gave me a few minutes to myself, maybe needing those few minutes for himself too.

"How long's this been going on?"

My tongue went into my cheek. I'd never talked about my abuse with anyone. One of the urgent care doctors I'd visited had asked how I'd gotten my injuries. When I answered that I'd fallen off my bike, she'd looked at me with just enough doubt and sympathy for me to guess she knew, but this was different. Open conversation. Blunt questions. Stark answers.

"Why do you want to know?"

"Because I have to." He exhaled slowly through his nose. "Because you promised you'd tell me everything."

"You don't want to know everything." My arms roped around my legs.

"I want to know everything there is to know about you. The good. And the bad. I want to know the shit you were going through at the same time I was going through my own shit over the past six years. I want to know what I missed out on."

I watched him through the shower door. Even though his form was blurry from my tears and the steam, he felt like the most solid thing in the world. Like I could tie myself to him and no storm could pull me away. "Why?"

"So I don't hold back the next time Crew is standing in front of me." His voice was different, less human. "When did it start?"

My mind went to the first time Crew had ever laid his hands on me. It had just been a slap, but I remembered being so surprised by it that I started to wonder if I'd imagined it. That was followed by feelings of self-doubt that had me questioning if Crew was right and I had deserved it. Those firsts abuses had been the worst because they'd stolen the biggest parts of my soul. All that was left now were a few measly remains.

"After Keenan was born," I said. "A few months after."

I could hear Brecken's breathing even with the shower beating around me. "How often?"

"What do you mean?"

"I mean, how often does he fucking beat you?" His voice broke at the end.

"It depends."

"Depends on what?"

My chest was lifting harder from the way I was breathing. "How much he's been drinking. How stressed he is."

He was quiet, a sigh rolling from him. "Which with me coming back …"

"You didn't do this."

"No, I didn't. But I'm going to be the one who makes him pay for it."

My head shook. "I already told you, no police."

One dark note came from him. It wasn't a laugh. It wasn't a grunt. It was something all its own. Something that gave me a window into the darkness he endured for half a decade.

"My brand of justice doesn't involve the police or the legal system. I have a more eye-for-an-eye policy when it comes to punishment." He moved closer to the shower. "There's an obvious solution to this. One I'm not afraid to address. Or execute."

My nails dug into my palms. "No, there isn't. Not when it's a police officer you're talking about. They won't rest until they figure out who killed one of their own. And they'll make sure you spend the rest of your life in prison, wishing you'd died with him." My forehead pressed into my knees. "I can't stand the thought of you going back into another prison after what you've been through."

He moved closer and kneeled outside the glass door. "I spent years in an Iraqi prison because my squad drew the short straw. I'll spend the rest of my life in another prison for something actually worth going to jail for."

I lifted my head to watch his hand press into the glass. I spread my hand out over his. "Like what?"

The glass was too foggy to see through, but I swore I could see his eyes looking into mine right then. His stare went right through that pane of glass. "Like you."

My fingers curled like they were tying through his. His did the same.

"Why didn't you leave him?"

The hot water was starting to run out. I wasn't sure that once it was gone, I could get up and out of the shower on my own. Already I could feel my body going stiff from the fall, petrifying. "For Keenan. I stayed for him."

"It's important for a boy to be around his dad. *If* he's a good one. If he doesn't hit his mom. If he doesn't leave her bloodied and broken at the bottom of the stairs before running off." Brecken's head twisted away.

"I didn't stay for that reason." Taking a breath, I braced my hands on the shower floor and pushed myself up. It felt like every nerve in my body decided to fire at the same time.

Brecken rose when I did. "What other reason did you have to stay?"

I needed a few seconds before I could reply. The pain was so intense, my vision was vacillating from black to white. "Crew's threatened to seek full custody of Keenan if I leave. He promised me he'd get it too. With his connections."

"Even with his connections, what dad gets full custody unless the mom is an irresponsible, negligent junkie?"

Twisting off the shower, I stood there letting the water finish dripping off of me, unable to open the shower door. "That's what he'll prove. He's got an entire file of proof, evidence, that will incriminate me if it comes to seeking custody."

"What kind of evidence?" Brecken snorted, pulling a towel off the rack. "The kind that testifies that you're an amazing mom? Let him try. He'll look like an asshole for even trying to make you look irresponsible."

I took the towel when he handed it over, but I let it drop at my side instead of wrapping it around my body. "My fingerprints on things that would prove otherwise. Photos of me. A whole line-up of character witnesses that would prove me unfitting as a mother."

I couldn't hear Brecken's breaths anymore. It was like he'd stopped breathing. "Drugs?"

My fingers curled into my palms. "And more."

The only sound was the shower dripping.

"Is it true?" His voice was quiet. "Any of it?"

"No. But that doesn't matter, because he'll make it true. I know it." I wound the towel around my body as best as I could. "He's a police detective. He knows about evidence. He knows how to make it convincing. No judge is going to side with me, a stay-at-home mom with no job, no real friends, when all of that evidence is stacked against me, when Crew's the upstanding person in the community he is."

"Crew's a piece of shit," Brecken snapped. "Not upstanding."

"We're not the ones who need to be convinced of that." My fingers closed around the shower handle. "Can you close your eyes? Please?"

"I already saw what he did to you, if that's what you're worried about. I should look you over, just in case you need to get something looked at."

I tucked the towel around me tighter. "You haven't seen everything."

"I saw enough to make sure I go real slow when I sever his dick from the rest of him," he grunted.

"Just, please, close your eyes."

An exhale. "Fine. They're closed."

Peeking out, I made sure they were before opening the door the rest of the way. "And maybe turn around too."

"I won't look," he promised, turning around anyway.

"Thank you." I yanked my bathrobe from the hook on the back of the door and threw it on. It was one of those long, bulky ones, which was perfect since it would conceal most of the damage. My hand rested on the side of Brecken's arm. It surprised him, making him flinch. A moment later though, his hand lifted to cover mine. "I stayed for Keenan. Because the thought of him being raised by Crew is enough to make me endure ten times this every night of my life if that's what it comes down to."

"It won't come down to that. This won't ever happen again." Brecken lifted one brow, his eye opening a slit, waiting for me to give him the okay.

"You can look now."

Whatever he saw made his throat move as he swallowed. Turning around, he lifted his hand and combed my wet hair back from my face. His motions were slow, gentle, like he knew how to handle a wounded animal following an attack.

"That's the last time I'm ever taking my eyes off of you. Please don't ever ask me that again." He scanned my face, the skin between his eyes creasing when he got to my forehead. "That's going to need a bandage. A big one." He looked away, his throat bobbing. "Where do you keep them?"

"Above the sink." I indicated the medicine cabinet before I started out of the bathroom. I needed to lie down. Before I fell down.

"Do you want something for the pain? The military docs gave me a ton of stuff when I gave back. Pills I could probably sell for a whole lot of money on the streets." The whine of the cabinet opening sounded, followed by some riffling. "I hear some of it's supposed to be pretty fantastic."

"Thanks for the offer, but I'll stick to my ibuprofen." When I reached the bottom of the stairs, I found myself staring at the spot where I'd fallen. There wasn't much to show for it: a few smears of blood, a scuff mark from Brecken's boot when he'd come rushing in. No indication that a human had just crashed into a million little pieces right in that very spot.

"Yeah, I didn't take any of that stuff either." Brecken stopped in the living room when he saw me standing there staring at the spot where he'd found me. His hand holding the bandages fell at his side.

"What's your reason?" I asked. "Why didn't you take them?"

Brecken moved up beside me so we were shoulder to shoulder in front of those stairs. Then he took my hand. The same hand as my bad wrist. "Because you and me, what we've been through, the pain makes us sharp, keeps us on our guard. Without it, we're vulnerable." Leading me away from the stairs, he turned toward the couch. "If we start dulling our pain—looking for ways to mask it—we become no better than those who caused it to begin with."

My other hand curled around the top of my bathrobe. "What makes us better is we don't let our pain become a disease, allowing it to infect others."

He stopped moving, his eyes narrowing on the front door. "Oh, I have every intention of allowing my pain to infect a certain other. It's taking everything inside of me to stay here with you and not go after him so I can take all of that pain I carry and share it with him. Every last piece of it." The sinews running down his neck stiffened, showing through his skin.

"Revenge isn't the answer."

He helped me lower to the couch, his jaw clenching when he noticed my face draw up from the movement. "I'm not looking for an answer. I'm looking for retribution."

Once I was seated, he collected the throw pillows, fanning them on one end. "Blankets?"

"In the closet." I ground my teeth together and twisted on the couch so I could lie back. My head pulsed from the motion, the rest of my body feeling like it was being whittled away one layer at a time.

"Is Crew carrying a gun?" He grabbed a stack of blankets from the top shelf, pausing at the front door to lock it. Then he hooked his foot under the wall table and slid it in front of it. "Just so I know what I'm dealing with if he comes through the door tonight?"

"He won't be back tonight. He'll go somewhere. He'll drink some more, feel bad, maybe call to apologize tomorrow and promise it will never happen again, but he won't be back tonight." My head fell heavy into the pillows as I adjusted my robe so it was covering as much of my body as it could.

"Whenever he decides to show up, I'll be right here. Waiting for him."

"I'm not worried about Crew right now. I have to figure out what to tell Keenan in the morning."

When Brecken started unfolding the blankets beside me, he couldn't seem to look at my face for more than a moment at a time. He was an adult, had been through something truly horrendous, and could barely stand to look at me. What would my five-year-old son do when he saw his mom like this?

"It's always worse the next day. I can hide most of this, but I won't be able to hide how I move." I tucked the first blanket around my head and body, knowing I couldn't hide forever behind a blanket. Or even for long.

His eyes narrowed in concentration as he layered another blanket over me. "We'll say you're sick. You can rest. I'll take care of Keenan. Keep him occupied." After spreading the last blanket over me, he grabbed one of the chairs across the room and pulled it toward the couch. "I might need a few pointers on what might keep him entertained though."

"He gets to spend a day with you?" My eyebrow lifted. "He will be plenty entertained."

His face ironed out. "Pizza delivery? That's still a thing, right?"

The seriousness of his question made my mouth twitch. "It's still a thing. You haven't been gone that long."

"Thank god." He stretched back into the chair, scooting closer. "My cooking skills still have room for improvement."

"Improvement?"

"I tried making Easy Mac yesterday."

"It's called that for a reason."

"I forgot to add the water. The silver lining is that I fried my microwave, so I can't make that same mistake again."

A small laugh rattled in my chest. "Delivery it is then."

He smiled, tucking the blanket around me tighter. He handed me a couple of ibuprofens and a glass of water, taking the cup from me when I was done.

"What have you been eating all week if you haven't been able to cook and you had to ask if delivery is still around?" My gaze roamed him. He seemed like he was getting bigger every day. He was starting to fill out his old clothes again, cuts and grooves working back into his arms.

He didn't resemble the man I'd seen at the homecoming party a month ago.

"Protein shakes. Protein bars. Pretty much anything I don't have to apply heat to and potentially light on fire."

Another laugh rattled out of me, making it sound like my lungs were straining.

Brecken held his smile, but his forehead folded. "Just sleep." He smoothed my hair back from my forehead where my cut was. "I'll be here if you need anything. I'll be here if Keenan needs anything. Just let yourself rest."

My eyes closed, sleep sweeping me under instantly.

"You're safe."

# nine

For the first time since Brecken left six years ago, I woke up feeling rested. I woke up having slept the whole night through.

I doubted it was a coincidence that it was the first night I'd spent with him beside me. We might not have been sharing the same bed or tangled up in each other, but I'd felt his presence.

"It's not even six yet. Why don't you get a little more rest?" The chair made a noise when he sat up, his face mirroring his strong voice. His eyes didn't look tired, but I knew he hadn't slept. Brecken didn't know how to break a promise. Him making it back after we all thought he'd died years ago testified to that.

"Keenan gets up around seven." My throat was dry, my head felt like it was about to break open, and the rest of me felt like it already had.

"I'll take care of him when he does. Sleep." His hand smoothed the blankets down.

When I rolled onto my back, I had to choke back the cry that rose. I'd been expecting the pain to be worse this morning, but I still hadn't been fully prepared for it. Instead of taking a tumble down fourteen stairs, I felt like I'd been thrown down a cliff face and landed on a bed of jagged boulders.

"Can I have some water?"

"One step ahead of you." He reached for something on the floor. "I remember waking up so many times and feeling like I would have told them anything they wanted if I could just have one sip of water. There's something about pain that makes a person thirsty." He unscrewed the water bottle's lid and held it out for me, guiding his hand behind my head to help lift it.

Half the bottle was gone before he pulled it back.

"And a couple more of these." He held two pain relievers in front of me and set them on my tongue when I opened my mouth. He lifted the bottle to my lips again after I swallowed the pills. "I would have told them everything else for a couple of those." He painted on a smile and let me finish what was left of the water. "More?" He lifted another bottle off the floor.

When I shook my head and tried to sit up, flashes of pain licked up my spine. My back felt raw from the damage Crew's belt had done, and Brecken didn't miss it.

"Did you break a rib?" He was already sitting up, scooting my robe down my back to check. His hands froze.

A ragged breath spilled from his mouth.

"Camryn ..." Another uneven breath, his fingers barely skimming over the marks on my back.

"Nothing's broken."

His fingers traced an old scar running across my spine. "I might be," he said in a voice that was balancing the knife's edge of tormented and defeated. "Last night. His belt. That wasn't the first time." His eyes lost focus as I felt his hand ball into a fist against my back. "He's been torturing you."

A sob rocked my body. Hearing him use that word, experiencing it spoken out loud ... I'd been able to pretend it was something else, something less cryptic, but if anyone understood the concept of torture, it was Brecken. Abuse and torture might have been related, but they weren't identical. I'd experienced both in my relationship with Crew, but only one felt capable of breaking me. Only one felt like it had.

Brecken was taking strained, uneven breaths, his body trembling just enough I could tell. Reaching for something else on the floor, he lifted a bag of ice. He pressed it gently to my back, wincing with me. His other hand stayed in his lap, balled into such a tight fist, his knuckles looked like they were about to burst through the skin.

"You do realize that the next time I see him, I'm going to kill him, right?"

"Brecken ..."

"He's dying or I am," he said, moving the bag of ice down my back. "And I don't die easily."

"Yeah, I think you've proved that to the world by now." I pulled the blanket up my body, feeling naked even though it was only my back that was bare. "But what good would killing Crew do when you wound up spending the rest of your life in another prison?"

"If he's dead, he can't hurt you." The skin between his brows creased. "And the rest of my life in prison is a good trade for that guarantee."

I should have put up a few more protests, but my mouth felt like it had lost its ability to defend Crew one more time.

Brecken's eyes shifted to the door. His body was still here, but everything else was somewhere else. "Back in Iraq? There were a couple of really bad ones, so evil it seemed like they'd been born like that, you know? Birthed in hell or something." The corners of his eyes creased. "I'd lie awake plotting the things I'd do to them if I ever had a chance, ways I'd kill them." His eyes came back to meet mine. The emotion in them made my breath stop. "My worst fantasy looks like a picnic compared to what I'm going to do to Crew."

He moved the bag of ice to another patch of my back. He was making the pain go away, one piece at a time.

"Brecken, please ... violence isn't the answer."

"Tell that to your husband." A black flame flashed through his eyes. "There's only one way to beat a monster, Blue Bird."

"What way is that?" I whispered.

"Playing the game by their rules. *Winning* the game by their rules."

"You're a marine. That's what you know."

"I'm a man. Staring at a woman I've loved, trying not to break down in front of her broken body." His voice broke, matching the look on his face. "Trying to be strong when I've never in my life felt weaker. Trying to look like I can handle seeing her like this when I can't fucking handle seeing her like this."

His gaze shifted to my back, his eyes squeezing closed right after. This was the one time I'd ever seen Brecken appear weak. The only time I'd seen him broken. He'd been through every brand of hell created by man, and the thing to break him was me. I wasn't sure if that should make me feel special or unworthy. I supposed I felt a little of both.

He shifted the ice to another spot, cracking his neck as he rolled it. "Just to warn you, there's going to be some media floating around the next week or so. I agreed to give a few interviews."

I exhaled, thankful for the shift in conversation. "I thought you'd decided not to give any interviews."

"I didn't think I was going to give any. But they're offering money. Quite a bit of it. Crew's got power in the form of the police force covering his corrupt ass. I'll take mine in the form of cold hard cash."

"Money can't buy everything," I whispered.

His shoulder raised as he moved the ice across my ribs. "No, but I'm not above trying to let it buy me whatever I can to keep you safe."

Again, a clash of emotions. Guilt for knowing he'd never have taken the interviews if it hadn't been for my situation. Gratitude because of it. I welcomed them both. I fought them both too.

My phone beeped from inside my purse resting on the table by the door. Brecken and I both fixed in on it.

After balancing the ice bag on my shoulder, he rose from the chair and started for my purse. His limp was more pronounced this morning, probably from being stiff after spending all night propped up in a chair. When he returned, he settled my purse gently in my lap, distracting himself with the bag of ice while I dug out my phone. I hadn't missed any calls, only the one text that had just come in. It was from Crew. Simple. Concise. No drawn-out apology. No elaborate defense. Just a statement.

"He's checked into a rehab program," I said, rereading his message before lifting the phone at Brecken. "A twenty-eight-day one."

This time when his eyes closed, he let out a deep breath. When they opened a moment later, the Brecken I remembered was looking at me. "That gives me twenty-eight days to figure out a way to save you."

The relief in his voice was matched by what I felt inside, though my relief came from a different place. He was thankful for the time so he could figure out a way to save me. I was thankful for the time so I could figure out a way to save him. From me. From this life. From tying his rope to me and drowning with me.

There was no "out" for me. No heroic rescue.

I was a mother who'd do anything for her child. Including staying in a gruesome situation. Others might have argued that I was setting a bad example for my son by staying in an abusive relationship, but I didn't give a shit about setting examples—I cared about keeping him safe. That wouldn't happen if I tried to leave Crew and he proved me an unfit mother and earned sole custody. If I tried running away with Keenan, every cop in the country would keep an eye out for us.

I had twenty-eight days to get Brecken to realize that it was too late to save me, but it wasn't too late for him.

The familiar creak of a bedroom door opening caught both of our attention.

"The table," I whispered, motioning at the wall table still buttressed against the front door.

Brecken dropped the bag of ice on the floor and rushed toward it. He heaved it back into place in the same amount of time it took me to adjust my robe and blankets to make myself look asleep.

"Don't say anything to him about Crew. I'll figure out something to tell him, okay?" I tucked one of the blankets up around my head to cover the bandage Brecken must have finished putting on after I'd fallen asleep. I didn't want Keenan to see it and ask questions before I'd figured out the right answers to give him.

Brecken made eye contact with me, nodding. He might have wanted to announce to the whole world what he really thought about Crew Graves, but at least on this, with Keenan, he was with me. No little boy needed to find out that the man who'd raised him had been beating his mama for years.

I closed my eyes when I heard Keenan's footsteps start down the stairs. Brecken's started up to meet him.

"Hey, little man," Brecken whispered, his voice giving away nothing. "Your mom's not feeling good this morning. She called me a little bit ago and asked if I'd come over to watch you so she could rest. That okay with you?"

There wasn't a fraction of a pause before Keenan gave his answer. "You get to be my babysitter?"

"I've never had any formal babysitting experience, so I can't promise to know exactly what I'm doing, but if you give me a few pointers, we should be able to make it work."

I had to tuck the blanket over my mouth to hide my smile. My body felt like it had been run over by an SUV, but hearing my son's voice, hearing him happy, was enough to cancel out all the rest. If only temporarily.

"We do breakfast first in the morning. Sometimes eggs and toast. Sometimes Cheerios and sliced bananas."

"Cheerios and sliced bananas it is." The thud of their footsteps coming down the stairs echoed through the whole house, bringing life into it.

"Still can't cook?" Keenan asked.

"Without lighting something on fire?"

Keenan's laugh came to a halt when they made it to the first floor. "Is Mom really sick?"

"Pretty sick. But she'll be okay," Brecken added, like he knew what he was doing when it came to kids. "She just needs some rest and she'll feel better."

"Should I get her a popsicle and cold washcloth for her forehead? That's what she does when I'm sick."

"How about we let her keep sleeping, and when she wakes up, we'll bring her in a popsicle and cold washcloth. Sound like a plan?"

Keenan made a sound of agreement before his slippered feet padded across the living room. He barely made a sound, and he didn't touch me other than the spot where his lips touched my cheek. He was just as quiet rushing back toward where Brecken must have still been stationed at the bottom of the stairs.

"Mom always needs her kiss from me in the morning."

The sound of what I guessed was a high-five followed. "Good man."

"Where's Dad?" Keenan asked, like he'd suddenly remembered Crew. "I didn't think he had to work today."

My lungs stopped working the longer Brecken's silence ran. I wasn't sure what he was going to tell Keenan, but all I hoped was that it wasn't the truth. Not all truths were meant to be told—especially to the innocent.

"He had to leave for a while. Came up really suddenly. Your mom knows more about it than I do, so she can tell you when she wakes up." Brecken paused for a moment, then I heard footsteps. "Come on. Breakfast of champions time."

Keenan's muffled footsteps hurried after him into the kitchen. "So what do we get to do today?"

"I don't know. I was thinking we could start off with some skydiving, followed by some rock-climbing, cliff-jumping, then target practice. Then we should probably take a break for lunch. You know, to refuel for the rest of the day."

Keenan was laughing again, the sounds of cupboards opening and closing joining with it.

"What? Did you have something else in mind?" Brecken asked, pouring cereal into a bowl.

"Running through the sprinkler? Playing Legos? Digging in my sandbox?"

"So no to the skydiving?"

"I don't think Mom would like me jumping out of planes," Keenan said, crunching on a bite of cereal. "She likes to keep me safe."

Brecken was quiet, so just the sound of Keenan eating came from the kitchen.

"She does. She'd do anything to keep you safe." Brecken's voice drifted into the living room, settling around me. "And I'd do anything to keep you both safe too."

# ten

The living room had never looked like this before. Demolished. Blankets draped around kitchen chairs that resembled the most giant, misshapen fort ever. Games scattered on tables and the floor, play money and pawns everywhere. Half-eaten bowls of popcorn, empty pizza boxes, and soda cans mixed in with the rest. It looked like the kind of mess Crew would lose it over. He liked order and coming home to a tidy house—he thrived off of predictability.

But we had twenty-eight days to ourselves, to make a mess without the need to have it cleaned up before Crew came in from work. To eat junk food without having to keep it hidden in the back of the cupboards. To laugh and be silly without being met with a raised brow. It was just a messy living room, but it was freeing. Like someone had opened the cage door and let me escape. It was a temporary reprieve, but one I wouldn't let be tarnished by the knowledge of its expiration date.

"I think he's out. It finally hit him." Brecken was propped in front of the couch I was still stretched out on, his back leaning into it.

Where he was, how he'd positioned himself, it felt as though he were guarding me. Silly, but I also hadn't missed the way his eyes shifted every couple of minutes during our movie marathon—toward the front door. We were both holding our breaths for when Crew would come marching through that door again, but for different reasons. He was anticipating it, while I was dreading it.

"What finally hit him?" I whispered, peeking at Keenan. He'd fallen asleep with a half-eaten bag of fruit snacks clutched in his fist, his other hand gripping his favorite superhero action figure.

Brecken motioned at him. "The sugar crash or the exhaustion coma."

"Probably both." I shifted onto my back, since my side was numb.

I'd only left the couch a couple of times today, and both instances were to use the restroom. Both times, I'd needed Brecken's help to get there. I'd made sure Keenan was good and distracted so he wouldn't see me hobbling around, being practically carried to bathroom, and when he saw my bandage, I'd explained I'd fallen and hit my head the night before. Which wasn't a lie. I just left out the part about Crew pushing me down the stairs first.

The wet washcloth, which was mostly dry now, was still on my forehead, and I'd gratefully accepted my popsicles when Keenan had brought them to me whenever he heard me stir. We'd survived the day, and Keenan didn't know the real reason for me barely being able to move or the reason Crew was gone. He'd accepted the stories about me being sick and Crew having to leave for an extended work training. It was easy to convince a five-year-old his mother was sick, not beaten to an immobile pulp. It wouldn't be so easy with a fifteen-year-old.

"Must have been the manual labor. Slave driver," I tacked on as Brecken clicked off the television.

"Oh, please. He loved getting to swing a hammer and work a wrench."

I blinked at him. "He's five."

"Your point?" His brow carved into his forehead as he leaned over to pick Keenan up off the floor.

In between running through sprinklers and playing with just about every toy in Keenan's possession, they'd taken breaks to fix the broken board in the fence out back, take care of the leaky faucet in the laundry room, and change the back porch light that had burned out. It was strange to see Brecken wearing Crew's tool belt as he saw to the things that needed maintenance around our house. Hold Crew's hammer, climb his ladder, move around his garage.

It all seemed to fit Brecken better than any of it had Crew.

"I'll carry him up to bed. Then I'll be back for you." Brecken started for the stairs, Keenan carefully tucked into his arms.

"I'll just sleep down here again."

"You'll feel better in a bed," he replied, disappearing up the stairs.

He was gone a couple of minutes, which gave me a chance to try to sit up on my own. Tomorrow I'd feel better, but I hated feeling so incapacitated. I'd never been so immobilized after one of Crew's attacks, and the voice in the back of my head kept whispering at me about domestic abuse getting worse until the victim wound up dead.

But that wasn't going to happen to this woman. Not me. I was strong. Crew was getting help. I just hoped it would be enough to get me through the next thirteen years before Keenan was an adult and out of the house. I'd be one step behind him.

"He's all tucked in." Brecken's soft footsteps came down the stairs. "Next."

I attempted to lift myself up off the couch. I made it. A whole half inch.

"You don't have to carry me up." I sighed as his arms slid around me.

"I know I don't have to." He glanced at me once he'd lifted me up. "I just know I want to."

"Is that the hero you try so hard to keep hidden speaking?" My body felt like it was melting into his arms as he wove around the fort and mess. He wasn't limping.

"I spent six years picturing this." His arms tightened around me. "It might have been a different sort of picture, but I'll settle for this. I'll settle for whatever I can have of you, even if it's just carrying you from a couch to your bed. I'll be that guy."

My head relaxed into the bend of his arm as he moved up the stairs. "You'll be what guy?"

His light eyes found mine, seeming to illuminate the darkness surrounding us. "The one waiting in the wings."

My lungs struggled. My heart fought the same battle. "I'm married, Brecken. You know the situation. You know there's nothing I can do to change that for a long time. I married Crew."

"So? That might change your feelings for me, but it doesn't change my feelings for you. I told you forever ago that I wasn't going anywhere. That there was no one else for me. No one else I wanted to love. Nothing can change that. If you think a piece of paper and a couple of vows can end my feelings for you, then you really don't know who I am."

He hadn't stopped staring at me, and it was making me feel things I wasn't allowed to feel. His body, his words, his stare, they weren't mine to covet. They weren't mine to want to claim anymore. He was free to follow the tenor of his feelings, but I was not.

"Sorry. I'm staring. Again." Clearing his throat, he tore his eyes away before we rounded into the bedroom. The guest bedroom. I'd been so distracted when his arms came around me, I hadn't noticed the direction he'd taken me— away from the bed I'd known for years, the one I'd shared with him, toward one that held no ownership or designation.

He flipped on the light switch as we entered the dark room, inspecting it in the same way I knew he'd been trained to clear a room. He was still waiting, like I was, for Crew to appear out of nowhere.

"I've been thinking …" He set me down at the foot of my bed, then he moved around the room, turning on the lamps. "Crew's got all of this evidence against you, right? Proof that could make you seem like an unfit mother."

He glanced at me when I didn't answer.

"Yes," I said. "He does."

"Then we need some of our own evidence." He said the words slowly, his eyes moving around the room, away from me. "Camryn …"

I knew what he was about to say the moment before he said it. "What? No." My feet carried me backward until I rammed into the footboard.

"I'd take the pictures on my phone. No one would see them, I swear on my life, unless you gave me your permission first. He wants to lie about you being a bad mom? We'll prove he's a bad man. We'll prove he's a monster." Brecken swallowed and stepped toward me. "But we need to be able to show what that monster's capable of."

My arms wrapped around myself. "I don't want you to take pictures of me. I don't want you to see me like that."

"I see you exactly the same way now as I saw you back then." His voice rose, his finger thrusting at me. "As a strong, beautiful woman who seems to know exactly what to do to take the ground right out beneath my goddamn feet and the air straight out of my godforsaken lungs. The same girl I grew up admiring from a distance, and the same woman who was foolish or charitable enough to let me love her when I was a dumbass kid with nothing to my name. When I look at you, I will always see you. The real you. Not the one he's trying to make you."

My breath was making my chest ache. Too fast. Too hard. His words echoed in my head, spreading. I felt like that same woman when I was with him, but if he saw me exposed and vulnerable, he'd realized I wasn't that same person. She'd been broken in too many places to hold her old form. She'd been forced to take on a new shape, a form designed at the hands of her abuser.

"No. I can't." My head whipped back and forth as Brecken pulled a cell phone from his pocket.

"I know you can," he said, moving toward me. "You won't be able to just tell people he abused you and hope they'll take your word for it. That's not how the legal system works. You're going to need to show them he abused you."

As he moved closer, my arms tightened around my body, starting to coil up like I was more a cornered animal than a confronted human. When he was a few steps away, he stopped. His eyes wandered up and down me, taking me in as I stood there trembling, cowering, silent tears streaming down my cheeks.

He let out a long exhale as he reached for the bottom of his shirt. He didn't say a word, but his eyes went to mine, only losing their connection for the moment it took him to tug his shirt over his head. He stood there for a moment, his shirt falling to the floor, staring at me. Waiting. The light in his eyes shuddered, like a gust of wind had blown by it, as his breath picked up speed.

Then he raised his arms at his sides and slowly turned around. Without his eyes claiming mine, my eyes dropped. When they landed on his back, the breath I'd been taking hitched in my throat.

My hand flew to my mouth. Then my other joined it. There were no words for the sight before me. No words of apology or anger or consolation. It was still Brecken's back I was looking at, but it had become the canvas of a tormented beast.

My fists were no longer curling into my bathrobe out of fear for myself but anger for him. Blinding rage made me wish I could face just one of his captors and attempt to inflict a tenth as much damage as they had to him. God knew I would have passed out in exhaustion from the effort.

Every size and shape of scar spanned the stretch of his back, some jagged and angry looking, others precise and calculated. Brands had been burned into his flesh, most in symbols of a language I didn't know or ever want to understand. A few universal symbols needed no translation to understand. They'd marked him. Branded him. Attempted to strip him of all his humanity. They'd torn his back to pieces then carefully stitched it back together so it could be shredded again. Scars were layered over scars, the mark of one flowing into the pucker of another.

My stomach folded when my mind started down a dark path, imagining the smell of his flesh as it burned, picturing the things they'd done to him to leave him with those kinds of scars, hearing his cries as they ripped him open. Again. And again.

And again.

My knees gave out, but my hands grabbed onto the footboard before I could fall to the floor. Bracing myself, I buttressed my body against the bed to remain standing. He wasn't saying a word, he hadn't glanced back once, but I still felt his silent need for me to be strong.

This wasn't just torture he'd endured. This was something else. This was experimentation on the human soul, an effort to push it to its threshold before exterminating it. This was murder. A murder of one's humanity.

He stood there, arms at his sides, head turned, shoulders raised, letting me stare at him. Letting me see him exposed and vulnerable. He didn't once waver or start to turn away. He trusted me with his darkness.

I knew I could trust him with mine.

"I never wanted you to see this." His voice was hollow, far away sounding. "I never wanted you to see *me* like this." He took a breath, his head turning slightly back. "Does it change how you think of me? *What* you think of me?"

I didn't wipe the tears away—they were the only part of me that didn't feel numb. "No."

"Does seeing this make me less of a person?"

I wanted to look away from his back, but I couldn't. "No."

"It won't make you less of a person either. It won't change the way I see you." Brecken started to turn, his eyes finding me before the rest of him made it around. "Our scars prove we're strong. They testify to what we can endure. It's not weakness carved into them—it's strength."

His chest wasn't marked up quite as badly as his back, but it still looked more pieced together than part of a whole. He'd left me as a whole man, been broken into pieces, then sewn back together.

"I'm sorry." The words tumbled out, inadequate and messy.

Brecken was still clutching his phone, waiting for me. "Let's stop feeling sorry for ourselves and start making those who did this to us sorry. Let's make them sorry for not just taking away six years, but a whole entire life we'd counted on. Let's make *him* sorry for putting a hand on you. God knows I'm going to make him sorry for the first time he put his hand on you, to this last time."

My heart felt like it was beating between my ears as my hands moved to the belt of my bathrobe. My fingers wouldn't work right as I tried to untie it, so Brecken moved toward me. His hands had no problem undoing the knot.

Twisting around, I felt like I could have passed out from what I was feeling. Fear, shame, embarrassment, vulnerability.

"It's okay, Blue Bird." His hand dropped to my wrist, his thumb caressing the inside of it. His voice was calming to my soul, his breath satin grazing my skin. "You're still you. This is something that's happened to you. This isn't what defines you."

One arm at a time, I slid out of the robe, still clinging to it so it covered me. I didn't want to let go. I felt like I couldn't.

"You're safe," he promised.

All at once, the bathrobe fell to the floor, collecting at my feet. The first thing I noticed was how quiet it was. He wasn't breathing. But neither was I. When I heard him finally take a breath, it was a choking kind, like he'd been drowning and just taken his first breath at the surface.

"Are you okay?" My head turned over my shoulder to find him staring at me in much the same way I'd just appraised him. Horror in his eyes, anger in his jaw, sadness tying it all together.

"No." His head shook as he lifted his phone.

He didn't add anything else, and I didn't know what else to say. Of course he wasn't okay. I wasn't okay with what I'd seen either. But we were still standing, fighting, and that counted for something.

"Turn around," he asked a minute later, his voice unrecognizable.

Lifting my arms so I could cover my chest, I stepped around to face him. I was naked, and he was bare from his waist up. We were in a small bedroom alone, late at night, and had once upon a time been lovers, though we still harbored feelings for each other to some degree. There was nothing heated or sexual about this moment though. He was only focused on getting the right pictures, his brow drawn into a hard line as he studied each bruise and mark, while I focused on being the kind of brave person he was convinced I was. Pretending to be strong was infinitely better than accepting I was weak. He took a few more pictures, trying not to show any emotion as he went from one spot to the next.

"I think I've got everything." He rose from where he'd been crouched beside my leg, taking pictures of the bruising and swelling from the fall. Grabbing the robe, he stood and held it out for me to slide back into.

He was trying so hard not to show his emotions. He was trying not to show how close he was to driving his fist through the wall and letting out all of that pent-out anger with a bellow that would know no end.

I'd seen his scars. And now he'd seen mine. I wasn't ready to cover them back up again.

My arms found their way around him as I pressed myself against him. His arms slipped around me instantly, dragging me closer. So close, I could feel his heart's steady rhythm against my chest. We stayed like that for so long, I started to feel sleepy, like I could fall asleep standing in his arms. His chest felt so strong against mine, even though it had shrunk from the last time I'd felt it bare against mine. His arms felt unbreakable, even though they'd been broken several times. He felt invincible, and maybe he was, but I was made of lesser things.

"I know I need to let go, but I'm not sure I know how." My hands were stuck in place around him, my arms welded to his flesh.

His head angled down at me. "You don't have to."

"Maybe not right now, but eventually, soon, we'll both have to let go."

His mouth dropped to my ear. "We could run away. All three of us. Out of the country. He could never find us."

The idea of running away with Keenan and Brecken was like the sum total of every dream and fantasy I'd dared to conceive of. A life of peace. A life of love. A life where my son could grow up without a dark shadow drawing him in. But it was just that. A dream. A fantasy.

"That's not the way I want to show my son to deal with a problem," I whispered, finally finding the strength to let go. "Running away. Letting fear rule your life. Keenan deserves a better life than that."

"A better life than escaping his piece-of-shit father who can do this to his mother?" Brecken waved his arms at me as I stepped away from him.

"I can protect him from Crew. I can keep him from finding out."

"Look at yourself, Camryn." He motioned at me again, his face giving away exactly what he was seeing. "How much longer do you really think you can hide this from him?"

Yanking the robe from his hand, I threw it on and moved around the bed, trying not to show any signs of pain. "I'm tired, Brecken. Enough for one night. We can argue about this again tomorrow, but no more today."

"Looking forward to picking up where we left off tomorrow then." He followed me around the bed, rolling the blankets down for me.

"What are you going to do?" I crawled into the bed and let him pull the covers over me.

"I'm going to stay right here, keep watch."

"You didn't get any sleep last night. You need to rest." I yawned, wondering what time it was. I'd lost track hours ago. I lost track of lots of things when Brecken was around.

"There was a time they kept me awake for ten days straight. Tied up to a metal chair, stuck in a cold room." He pulled the armchair out of the corner, scooting it to the edge of my bed. "This is the lap of luxury by comparison."

As he moved around the room, turning off the lights, I scooted over in bed to make room. When he headed back to the chair, I pressed my hand into the empty spot beside me. "Get some rest. Please. He's not coming back tonight. We've got this night and twenty-six more. I feel safe with you, whether you're awake or asleep. "

He stared at the empty space, his forehead creasing. "I'm not sure it's a good idea."

"I'm not sure it's a good idea either," I said, looking at him. "But it feels right."

He stood there for another moment before crawling on-to the bed and sliding his legs beneath the covers when I opened them. The air in the room changed suddenly. It went from calm to restless, the way the air felt before a storm rolled in. I felt hyper focused on him—every breath, every move he made that shifted the mattress. My body felt tuned to his, waiting for him to play the first note.

His heavy arm draped around my waist right before the rest of him scooted up behind me, molding to the bends of my body. His head settled beside mine, his chest spanning my back, his legs tucked behind mine. His breath was warm against the back of my neck, familiar in a way that had my body responding the way it had before when he'd crawled into bed beside me and touched me.

"Brecken?" I whispered, my voice sounding off.

He made a sleepy sound of recognition, his arm wind-ing tighter around me.

"I'm not sure this is a good idea."

His leg slid between mine, tangling around one. Then his head turned just enough that his lips touched, not just his breath, the back of my neck. My skin prickled, my chest moving so hard I felt certain my heart was about to break free.

"I'm not sure it's a good idea either. But it feels right."

# eleven

"Brecken," I whispered as quietly as I could, checking the time on the clock again. It wasn't even six thirty, but I wanted to have plenty of time to get out of the bed Brecken was in so my son wouldn't find me tangled up with him. Clothed or not, he was sure to have questions.

He was sleeping hard apparently, because he didn't even budge when I whispered his name again. When I went to try to pull his arm off of me, however, he snapped awake.

He squinted at the clock before dropping his head back on the pillow. "It's not even six thirty. Sleep."

Winding his arm around me, he pulled me back against him, settling the bend of my body into the bend of his. That was when I felt something strange. Or maybe not strange, but *inappropriate*.

"Brecken," I hissed, prying at his forearm like I could actually budge him.

"What?" he said drowsily.

"You're having morning … issues." I tried to ignore the feel of him hard against my backside, but it would have been easier to ignore the sun blasting two inches in front of my face.

He was silent for a moment, then a grunt of realization came from him. "That's not a morning issue." He adjusted himself so his lap wasn't pressed against me. "That's a *Camryn* issue. There's a difference."

"Yeah, but it's the morning."

"And I've woken up the past six years of mornings without this"—he cleared his throat to fill in the rest—"issue."

My cheeks felt hot from talking about what we were. My body felt hot from feeling what it just had. Both of us coming off the night we had, the scars we'd born to one another … it seemed like the very definition of the wrong time to be having these kinds of feelings.

But right or wrong, there they were.

"Sorry," he said, shifting around in bed to grab a pillow. He stuffed it between us. "There. Taken care of."

"Sorry it happened?"

"Sorry it made you uncomfortable." He adjusted the pillow a little lower before reattaching his arm around me. "Not sorry I feel that way about you."

My head tipped back to find him already looking at me, like he was waiting. "You *feel* that way about me," I repeated, raising an eyebrow. "As in you want to have sex? You're not sorry for that?"

"I'm not sorry I still want to love you. In every way I can." His voice was clear now, the sleep gone from his eyes too. "I haven't been with a woman in more than half a decade. The last woman I was with is the one beside me in bed right now. I can control my hands, I can control my mouth, I can control most of my body, but I can't control that, and I can't control my thoughts."

"Well, there's a pillow to solve the problem of one issue you can't control." I found myself smiling back at him, despite the awkwardness and the tragedy of our whole situation. He was smiling back. "There's got to be something to solve the 'not being able to control your thoughts' issue."

"There is," he stated, leaning his head farther over mine. Then he drilled his finger into his temple. "It's called a lobotomy. I'd rather not. Thanks anyways."

I turned my head to muffle my laugh. My body still ached this morning, but it felt like a paper cut by comparison. There, noticeable, stinging, but not like the open, pulsing wound of yesterday. "Hungry?"

This time when I moved to leave, he let me go. He was fighting his initial instinct, I could feel that from the twitch in his arm, but he wouldn't hold me by force. In play or otherwise, I guessed he'd never hold me against my will after what I'd revealed to him last night.

"I have six years of eating actual human food to make up for. I'm always hungry."

When he started to crawl out of bed, I motioned at him to stay. "I'll make something. Not a lot of places do delivery of eggs and bacon."

He gave me his best scowl, which crumbled a moment later. "Just five more minutes. Then I'll be down." His head crashed back into the pillow as he rolled onto his back. The blankets and sheet were twisted and tangled, like we'd been doing something other than sleeping last night. "We've got a big day."

I paused outside the door, checking to make sure Keenan's bedroom door was still shut. "We do?"

"I've got my first interview later this afternoon."

"Where?"

"Here. In town. The journalists thought it would add some 'personal flavor' to the interview to have it filmed walking down the sidewalks I grew up on." He gave me a look that suggested he thought otherwise. "Tomorrow I'm meeting with some magazine writer who is flying in to talk to me about the other members of my crew that were captured with me. The day after, some editor from a publishing house who's interested in writing my story. The day after that, I don't remember the few others I set up."

Leaning into the doorway, I searched for the right way to phrase what I was thinking. "Are you sure you're ready? To talk about all of that? To have people ask hard questions, to have them publish your answers for the world to hear?"

I hadn't been through anything like he had and couldn't conceive of talking with a stranger about my abuse, let alone having it out there for anyone I'd ever met in life to know about. Brecken was brave, I knew that, but I wondered if this was the blind kind. The variety that would come back to haunt him.

Brecken sat up on his elbows in bed. "I'm ready." He held my stare, unblinking, challenging me to challenge him.

"Five minutes." I lifted my hand, five fingers spread. "Bacon or sausage?"

"Like you even need to ask." His voice was back to normal as he fell back into bed.

"Bacon it is. Extra crispy," I added just before he got it out.

"Hey, Camryn? His voice stopped me. "I booked a cabin by Upper Klamath Lake for you and Keenan."

My feet carried me backward until I was looking back inside the room. "What?"

"Until the interviews are over, I booked a cabin for you guys to stay in."

My mouth turned down. "Why?"

"I'll be busy almost all day. I won't be around in case he comes back." He sat up in bed again, swinging his legs out over the side of the bed. He still didn't have his shirt on, and I couldn't seem to forget the way his warm chest had felt pressed against mine last night when I'd stepped into his arms. "I want you guys away from here. Somewhere he won't be able to find you."

"He's not coming back."

"You could have his statement written in blood, death being the penalty for breaking it, and I still wouldn't wager your and Keenan's safety on it." He scrubbed his face when I sighed. "Just, please. Do this? For me? There's no way I'm going to be able to do those interviews if all I'm thinking about is him walking back through that door when I'm not here to protect you."

"You don't need to protect me. It's not your job to keep me safe."

"Then whose job is it? Your husband's?" He huffed, shaking his head.

The other kind of heat washed into my blood. "Mine. It's my job."

"You haven't been protecting yourself, Camryn. You've been protecting him. Your son." Brecken motioned down the hall, rising to his feet. "And no one, including me, can fault you for it, but you need someone to look after you while you're looking after your son. That's me. That's my job because I'm making it mine and it was mine to begin with. I don't care that you married him or that you have his last name. You're mine. To love. To honor. And to fucking protect."

He stayed where he was, and somehow I found the strength to stay where I was, even when every cell in my body was being pulled toward every cell in his. My feet stayed in place while the rest of my body gravitated toward him.

"Please, Camryn. Please do this. It's only a couple hours away. Keenan will love it. Fishing, swimming, hiking, whatever. It's only for a few days."

My shoulders slumped, admitting defeat. "Do these cabins have running water?"

His body visibly relaxed. "Running water. A private bathroom. Even comes equipped with a roof." Picking up his shirt, which was still on the floor, he pulled it on. To-gether, in the privacy of this room, we could share our deep-est scars with one another, but when confronting the world, a shield was needed.

He took my hand, closing the door behind us. When we came to the stairs, he angled himself ever so slightly in front of me. So if I fell, he'd be there to stop me.

"**M**om! Come swimming! Puh-leeeeease!" Keenan bel-lowed from the knee-high water he was doggie-paddling around in.

"Mom forgot her swimsuit. You look like you're doing enough swimming for the both of us." I waved at him from my folding chair propped in the sand where I'd spent the last six hours just … *relaxing*. I think that was what it was.

Doing nothing, lounging, not checking the time every few minutes. It had been so long since I hadn't lived my days checking over my shoulder, tiptoeing through life, that this had taken me a while to adjust to. Relaxing. It was nice.

"They had some in the gift shop. Go buy one of those." Keenan swam closer to the shore.

"I don't think they had any in my size." I smiled and checked behind me, where the two cabins Brecken had rented were. The used truck he'd recently purchased wasn't there yet. He'd said he probably wouldn't be back until after dinner, but it was already seven.

"Mom," Keenan whined, dragging one syllable into five.

I glanced down at what I was wearing. Jeans, a long-sleeve blouse, and a camisole under that. Oh, and a sunhat to attempt to disguise the bruise forming around the gash bandaged at my hairline. I won the most dressed award at the beach today. It had been a warm day and I'd been sweating like crazy in my layers, but there wasn't an alternative. If I pranced around in a bathing suit with the way my body looked, I'd scare everyone, including my son.

"Come on, Mom. We haven't been to the beach in …" Keenan paused to think, his eyes going skyward as he did. "Ever. Swim with me. Swim with me!" He was splashing water all around now, jumping up and down to create more of a splash.

I'd taught him to swim at the public pool in Medford, but he was right; I couldn't recall a time we'd been to the beach. Crew didn't like sand getting everywhere, and he said open water was a deathtrap for young children. It wasn't scary though. Not at all. Keenan was having the time of his life, and I hadn't and wouldn't take my eyes off of him.

"You want Mom to come swimming?" I rose out of the chair and moved until the water was lapping at my toes.

Keenan stopped splashing, looking at me like he was trying to figure out if I was being serious. "Yes!"

"Okay." I lifted my arms out at my sides. "I guess I'll just have to go swimming then."

As I stepped into the water, Keenan's eyes went round when he noticed my jeans getting wet. The next look he gave me suggested he was worried I'd lost my mind.

"But you're coming with me!" Grabbing him, I lunged deeper into the water until I was up past my waist, then I bobbed up and down until the water was splashing around our faces.

Keenan was shrieking in delight, waving his arms to disrupt more water. I hadn't realized I was laughing with him until he stopped. His head tipped, and he gave me a thoughtful look as my bobs slowed.

His arms tied around my neck. "I like your laugh, Mom. It's nice."

He smiled right before leaning in to kiss my cheek. Then he wiggled out of my arms and swam toward the shore. He paused when he was halfway back to see if I was following him, but I was still in the same place.

My laugh. It was such a strange thing for a five-year-old to comment on—liking his mom's laugh. I knew why he'd mentioned it though. It was because he'd heard it so infrequently. Even when it was just him and me, I carried around a sadness that didn't leave a lot of space for laughter. It wasn't something I'd been aware of until just now, how much my secret abuse had trickled into the rest of my life.

Keenan didn't know why I didn't smile and laugh often, but I wasn't sure that was a comfort when I'd just had to witness my son stare at me with wonder as I shared a laugh with him.

I'd managed to hide the truth from him so far, but not the repercussions of that truth. I thought I'd been protecting him, but now I just felt like I was depriving him. Of myself. Of joy. Of laughter.

Instead of second-guessing the past or worrying about the future, I made a decision right there, my toes buried in the sandy loam of Upper Klamath Lake, the water lapping at my chest as I watched my son drag a shark floatie into the water—I was going to live in the now. The day. The moment. The past wasn't going to haunt me, and the future wasn't going to daunt me. This was what mattered. Now. This breath.

"Mom!" Keenan shouted, rolling off his floatie. "Brecken's back!" He broke out of the water, dropping his shark, and sprinted toward the old truck that had just lumbered up between the two cabins.

"He's had a long day! Give him a minute to unwind before you attack him."

Keenan was too far away to hear me, and I realized I was recycling a statement from my survival warning bank. Crew had had long days. Crew had needed time to unwind before dealing with a five-year-old wanting to play.

Crew wasn't Brecken.

Although I supposed the significant distinction was that *Brecken* wasn't Crew.

As I made my way out of the water, dripping wet and smiling, I didn't miss the way Brecken dealt with Keenan flying toward him. Open arms. An expression that was welcoming instead of annoyed. Throwing him up on his shoulders instead of waving him off. Striding down toward the beach to join us instead of disappearing behind a closed door to be alone.

I couldn't stop watching the two of them as Brecken lumbered down the beach, still wearing his khakis and dress shirt from the interview. The slacks were wrinkled now and the shirtsleeves were rolled up to the elbow, but he looked good. Having Keenan on his shoulders made his limp more pronounced, especially when he made it to the sand. By the time they'd made it to the stretch of towels and toys, I'd emerged from the water.

Brecken took one look at me, his grin stretching. "Nice suit."

Keenan laughed with him, looking like he was on top of the world when sitting on Brecken's shoulders.

"I knew you'd like it." I wrung out my hair, moving a few steps closer. "Want a hug?"

When I held my arms out and moved closer, Brecken backed up. "No, thanks. I'm good. I'm already nice and wet from the shoulders up." He glanced up at where Keenan was, dripping down on him.

"I think you need a hug. A nice warm, dripping-wet one."

Keenan started clapping while Brecken gave me a warning look. "I've got your son on my shoulders. I can't run away from you."

I gave an overdone smile then lunged. "Exactly," I exclaimed, winding my arms around him and wiggling the rest of my wet self against him.

Brecken let out a drawn-out groan, but he stood there and took it, hanging on to Keenan while I hung on to him.

"Mature. So mature." He sighed all dramatic-like. "Wonderful example you're setting for your son here."

I tipped my head up, eyebrow raised. "This coming from the man who mixed Frosted Flakes and Cocoa Puffs this morning?"

His eyebrows lifted. "I'm setting the example of how to behave like a proper five-year-old. You're the parent. You get to set the parental example."

I was quiet for a minute after that, having nothing else to say—having everything else to say. Instead, I stood there looking up at the two of them. Brecken's face above mine, Keenan's above us both. The sun was breaking behind them, pulling out the golden shades in their hair. Keenan's nose was speckled with a few freckles from spending a day in the sun, water drops running from his lashes whenever he blinked. If happiness was having exactly what you wanted, if only for one fleeting moment, then I'd found it. I had it. No matter what came, I'd always carry this with me.

"Can we still go fishing, Brecken?" Keenan glanced at one of the rental fishing boats tied up at the main dock.

"It's late," I started.

Brecken lifted his wrist from behind my back to check his watch. "Night-fishing is the best kind of fishing in my opinion."

"Night-fishing?" I repeated.

"No sun baking down on you, and they bite better at night." He shrugged like it was obvious.

"And how many times have you been fishing? Outdoor sportsman?" I stepped back and propped a hand on my hip, trying not to smile when I saw the dark, wet outline of where I'd just draped myself around him.

"Lots of times," he said, feigning outrage that I'd question him. But he lifted his fingers a moment later, where Keenan couldn't see. "Two times," he mouthed.

I covered my mouth to muffle my laugh. "So should I plan on cooking fish for dinner tonight? Or should I have a backup to be safe?"

Brecken shot me another appalled look. "I will not dignify that question with a response," he announced, looking up at Keenan and shaking his head. As he started toward the rental shed, he spun around, mouthing, "Have a backup."

This time, I didn't muffle the laugh.

"Doesn't Mom have a nice laugh?" Keenan said as they lumbered down the beach.

Brecken's answer came instantly. "She's got the best laugh in the whole world."

# twelve

It was after nine by the time the fishing boat came back, the full moon illuminating the dark lake just enough for me to see them. "Backup" dinner had been cold for an hour, and I didn't care. It was after Keenan's bedtime, and I didn't care. He was getting to be a kid, getting to go fishing like he'd always wanted. That was what mattered.

Crew had fished plenty of times growing up, but could never seem to be inconvenienced to take Keenan out for a few hours, despite the begging. Brecken had fished twice in his life, and it had probably been at some carnival where they baited and caught the fish pretty much for you. I doubted they'd caught anything, but I knew that wouldn't bother Keenan.

Today, he got to fish. It was a good day.

Shoving out of the rocker on the porch, I wandered down to meet them. Brecken was carrying a couple of fishing poles and a tackle box in one hand, and in his other hand was Keenan. When I started down the dock toward him, I realized why he was carrying him.

"When this kid goes out, he goes out," Brecken said softly, letting me take the poles and box.

"I don't know anyone else like that," I said, nudging him.

Keenan was almost snoring he was breathing so loudly, still zipped up in his life jacket.

"Well? Did you catch anything?"

"Does seaweed count?"

I smiled at the dock. "You should have brought some back. We could have made sushi."

Brecken snorted. "We got a few bites, but that was about it. And I managed to hook my thumbs a couple of times. Pretty successful first attempt, I think."

"Thanks for taking him out. He's been dying to go fishing."

Brecken nodded as we headed for the cabins. "He's a good kid."

I gave Keenan's hand hanging down Brecken's arm a little squeeze. "Well, he takes after his mom."

Brecken grunted. "Lucky kid."

As we walked up the steps of my cabin, I glanced at the dark one beside us. Brecken had rented two to keep things simple for Keenan. He'd been worried what Keenan might think if the three of us shared the same cabin. I appreciated the extra thought—and expense—he'd put into it, but I doubted it would have even crossed Keenan's mind. He was five and wouldn't have the first clue why it would be inappropriate for his mom to share a cabin with a former boyfriend while her husband was away. Innocent intentions or not. Which made me wonder if the second cabin had more to do with Brecken's benefit than Keenan's.

Had he accepted what I'd been trying to tell him? Had he embraced the impossibility of us? Circumstances being what they were?

The thought made me relieved as much as it made me depressed.

"What time do you have to leave tomorrow morning?" I asked.

He was about to answer when a boom sounded, echoing across the lake. Brecken stiffened for half a second, then he was a swirl of motion. I found myself pinned against the wall of the cabin, Keenan cradled against my chest, while Brecken stationed his body around us. Almost like he was shielding us from something.

It took me a moment to realize what had happened. It took me another to say it out loud.

"Fireworks," I said softly, wiggling off of the wall. Then I pointed across the lake where I could just make out the last few green sparks drifting out of the sky. "It was just fireworks."

Brecken didn't move at first—I wasn't sure he was breathing—but after I lifted my hand to his face, the lines in his forehead started to erase. His shoulders relaxed some as an uneven exhale spilled from his lips. Once he realized what had happened, his eyes dropped to Keenan, still in his arms, asleep. Another exhale, this one more sigh than breath.

"I'm sorry," he said, his brows pulling together as he glanced back at where the boom had come from.

I leaned in a little closer so he'd know I wasn't afraid. My other hand formed around his face so I could turn it around to face me. Then I waited for him to look at me. "It's okay." My thumbs slid down his cheeks. "It's oh-kay."

He didn't look convinced, instead allowing his eyes to swim with guilt. When the next firework cracked across the lake, he didn't throw himself around the two of us again, but

I didn't miss the quiver that ran down his back—like he was restraining himself.

"Where do you want me to put him?" Brecken cleared his throat and moved toward the screen door. He was avoiding looking at me.

"We made out the futon in the living room earlier. He wanted to camp out on his own instead of snuggle with his mom."

He didn't smile as he moved inside, the screen door screeching closed behind us. He moved across the room quickly, setting Keenan on the futon in the same rushed fashion. He was acting like he was dangerous, a threat, capable of breaking us if he wasn't careful.

"I experience the same type of thing, you know? Well, it's different … what sets me off, the triggers …" As I spoke, his jaw stiffened and he stared at Keenan. "But it results in the same thing."

"What result is that?"

"Doubting myself. Questioning if I'm going to hurt the people I care about. Wondering if I even deserve to be cared about in the first place." I tucked my jacket around me tighter. "I know what you're feeling."

"No. You don't." Brecken's head turned before his body. Then he started for the door. "Because if you did, you'd know I don't want to talk about it."

I slumped in place where I was, eyeing the table I'd set for dinner. He probably wasn't hungry. He probably didn't want to talk.

Too damn bad.

Grabbing the plate I'd made for him, I threw it in the microwave to warm it up before I took it outside. He was probably in his cabin, but I'd bang the door down if I had to.

I knew the retreat-from-the-world technique, and it never helped. It only made things worse.

Instead, I found him standing outside our cabin, staring at the dark lake.

"I brought you out dinner. Backup dinner." When I held out the plate for him, he took it, but he didn't really see it. I slipped off my sandals and took a seat at the top of the stairs. "How was the interview today?"

"Fine."

Rolling my feet from heel to toe, I searched for what to say next. "What types of questions did they ask you?"

"All kinds."

My back slouched as I blinked at him. "I'm trying to have a conversation here. Kind of hard when all I'm getting in return is one- and two-word responses."

Finally, his eyes drifted down to me. Whatever he saw crouched on the stairs below him cleared the brooding expression. "Sorry. I didn't realize you were trying to have a conversation. I thought you were more going for interrogation."

My hands lifted. "We can talk about whatever you want. You take the lead."

Before taking a seat beside me, he snagged a towel hanging over the rail. "Here. That wood looks hard." He set his plate down to fold the towel, then he scooted it behind my back, waiting for me to sit up. When I did, he slid it under me.

"That wood *was* hard." I smiled, shifting to get comfortable on the folds of the towel.

Brecken set the plate on his lap and picked up the fork, but he didn't move to take a bite. "They asked me questions about what actually happened once I was captured." The skin between his brows folded together. "What they did to me, if I remembered their names, what the conditions were like. That kind of stuff."

I nodded, but I stayed quiet.

"Then they asked me what I remember thinking about when I realized I was being rescued."

"Relief that you were still alive?"

"You." He set down his fork, his head turning toward me. "That was all I thought about when I was rescued, that was all I thought about during the six years I was there. You." He slid a wisp of hair behind my ear. "You were what kept me alive in that hell. And you're what will keep me alive in this one."

"You're free. Alive. How is this hell?"

"It might not be a wall of metal bars and a half a world of distance, but there's still something keeping me separated from you." He set the plate down beside him and glared at the world like it had betrayed him. "It's hell to go from loving someone, thinking of them every minute of every day and thinking you'd never see them again, only to make it home and see them and realize they aren't yours to love anymore." His back stiffened as he continued. "But instead of baring my soul to those people today, you want to know what I told them? You want to know how I answered their question as to what was the first thought that went through my head when I'd been rescued?"

I didn't answer him.

"A cheeseburger," he barked, rolling his neck. "A fucking cheeseburger."

"I'm sorry, Brecken." My head lowered as I stared at my hands in my lap. "I'm so sorry."

"I am too." He paused, his head twisting my way. "But sorry doesn't change a goddamn thing."

My nails dug into my palms. I wasn't sure what the look in his eyes was. It might not have been an accusation, but I felt like the accused. I felt guilty and wrong, and mostly, pissed off at the whole entire world.

"You know what?" I said, my voice already trembling. "I *do* know what it's like. I do know what it's like to love someone, to think of them every second of every day, thinking I'd never see them again, only to see them and have to accept they aren't mine to love anymore." I glanced inside the cabin to make sure I hadn't woken Keenan with my tirade. Then my eyes flashed to Brecken again, fire burning in them. "I *do* know what that feels like, so stop acting like you're the only one hurting here. Because you know why we can't go back to that, you know what's at stake. Him. That little boy's life inside there." My arm flew toward the cabin, my finger pointing inside. "You've made sacrifices. Well, so have I."

Brecken rolled his neck, his gaze drifting away. "Is that why you waited a whole hot minute after I 'died' to hook up with Crew Graves?"

My breath caught. He hadn't just said what I thought he had.

"Speechless?" he added as my silence continued.

He really had just said that.

I scooted away, unable to stand being close to him. "You have no idea what happened. No idea why I did what I did."

His expression stayed unaffected. Like he didn't give a shit how upset he was making me. "Well, it sure wasn't because you were hung up on me and mourning my death."

I couldn't stay seated. I couldn't stay beside him. I couldn't stay in the same universe. Jogging down the steps, I didn't stop until I'd put some space between us. The sand was cool against my feet, the night air coating me like a blanket.

My eyes narrowed on him, my whole body shaking. "How fucking dare you."

He refused to look at me. He looked over my shoulder. Above my head. Below my feet. Everywhere but at me. That made me angrier than his words.

"I loved you. I *loved* you." I glared at him, wishing so badly I could hate him right now. Knowing how much easier this would be if I did. "How dare you question that."

That was when his face betrayed him, a crack forming in that crafted facade of indifference. He lowered his face so I couldn't see it, his hands clasped in front of him. "Why did you marry him? Why him? Why right after?" He exhaled, his voice quiet. "Why?"

The band on my left hand cut into my skin when I crossed my arms, reminding me of its presence. "Because I had to."

Brecken's head lifted just enough his eyes could reach mine. I was looking at a man I'd known my whole life, but I was staring into unfamiliar eyes. "Because you were afraid of being alone."

I fell back a step as though he'd just shoved me. Like fists, words carried just as much force.

I recovered, taking that step back. "You son of a bitch."

He flinched when the words hit him. Barely. Just enough for me to see it.

"I loved you like crazy. I thought about you every day you were gone. I've thought about you every day since I thought you were killed. I loved you like I've never loved anyone. Like I never thought I could love anyone. I *still* love you."

His head lifted, his eyes not so strange anymore.

I didn't know what I was saying anymore, just that I had to say it. "How dare you try to make what I did seem so cheap and desperate. It killed me to move on. It killed me. I died with you that day. So don't pretend you're the only one who knows pain and loss. I might not have been trapped behind those bars with you, but I've been in my own kind of jail. And I might not know torture the way you do, but the kind I know is pretty damn cruel too. Don't pretend you're the only one who lost something." My words were an avalanche spilling out of me, my body a swirl of motion. I'd carried this inside me for so long, and I felt like I could breathe now that I'd said it. "This person today is not the same one you left behind. There's nothing left of that girl to love, so there's no need to feel like you're missing out. Save yourself the torment, and save me the guilt."

Brecken hadn't stopped staring at me. He was so still, his only movement coming from his chest as he breathed, his eyes as he blinked. He sat there staring at me like I remembered he used to from before. The way he'd admire me from a distance before moving in. The way he'd appraise me with that glimmer of possession in his eyes. The confidence in his brow that read that no matter how far away I got, he knew I'd always find my way back.

My stomach tightened as the fire surging through me receded. What took its place was a different kind of fire. The kind that burned stronger—an endless supply of tinder keeping it alive.

He rose from the stairs, moving toward me. His steps weren't hesitant or slow. "That girl I left behind is right here, standing in front of me," he said, his eyes unyielding. "There's everything of her still to love."

Suddenly, I wanted to get away from him for a different reason. My heels sank into the sand as I stepped back. "I'm married."

His steps didn't slow. "So?" He said it in a way that suggested it didn't matter—that it was trivial compared to the bond we shared. "You could have married the best guy in the world and never looked my way again, and I'd still be here." He motioned at the sand separating us while he strode closer. "Loving you. Waiting for you. Biding my time."

My feet stopped moving. I couldn't take another step away from him. "Biding your time? Brecken, Keenan's five years old. He won't be an adult for thirteen more years. That's two times longer than you spent in prison."

He didn't stop until he was directly in front of me. "Does it look like I flinched?" He waited. Not blinking. "Shit, I know I'm not supposed to. I know you're married. But I love you. Still. Always. There's nothing you can say or do to change that."

I dropped my arms at my sides, tired of crossing them, tired of closing myself off to him. "It's been six years. Everything's changed. I have. You have." My eyes lifted. "Why? Why are you trying to win me back?"

He exhaled, his lips parting. "I'm *going* to win you back."

When his hand slid around the bend of my waist, winding behind my back, I jerked. His touch was different tonight, hungry, determined. My head clouded, blocking out reason or letting it surface to the top, one or the other.

"I married him," I whispered even as my hand found his chest.

"But you belong to me."

My eyes closed as he bowed me against him. I wasn't sure how two bodies that had been as broken as ours could be so strong when joined. "How do you know?"

"I can see it in your eyes. Every time you look at me." His other hand lifted to my chin, tipping it until our eyes connected. His brow rose slowly, like I was proving his point right that very moment.

"That's a rather confident statement." My voice shook, but my body felt steady. Unwavering.

"It's the truth."

My chest was moving so hard, it brushed his with every breath. What was I doing? Where had I found myself? The man holding me had died only to be resurrected six years later. It was too late, but it wasn't over.

No matter what, Brecken Connolly and I would never be over.

"Twenty-six days," I said slowly. "That's all I have to give you. That's all I have to give. Four weeks. Once he's back, you know the way it has to be."

His face broke, but his hold didn't budge. "It's not enough."

My fingers curled into his shirt, looking for some way to hold on to him. "I know."

His other arm suddenly looped around me and he lifted me off the ground, his grip going around my backside when my legs tied around him. "But a fucking eternity wouldn't be enough either, so it'll just have to do."

He carried me through the sand and up the stairs of the cabin, then he propped me against the wall so he could open the screen door. Something slipped out of my mouth when he flexed his hips into mine.

"Told you it wasn't a morning issue," he whispered in my ear, but I could hear the smile in his voice. "Just a Camryn one."

He made the same motion with his hips, applying a little more friction this time, causing a louder sound to echo from my lungs.

Opening the screen door as silently as he could, he carried me inside, both of us glancing at the futon. Keenan was out—nothing was waking him. Brecken closed the door and locked it before slowly moving around the room to switch off the lights. His hold never loosened.

"You can set me down, you know?" I whispered.

His brows came together like I was crazy. "I know," he said, his arms tying tighter. Once all of the lights were off, the cabin closed up for the night, he padded down the hall.

"You know where you're going?"

His head nodded beside mine. "I've always known."

My hands went behind his neck. His skin was warm and familiar. "And where's that?"

He exhaled against my skin as he closed the bedroom door. "Toward you."

He set me down once he'd untied my legs from around his waist, and he took a few steps back. He stared at me for a moment then reached for the lamp on the dresser.

"What are you doing?" I asked.

"Turning on the lights."

I watched him flip on another. "Why?"

"Because I want to see you. Because I want to watch your face as I move inside you. Because I want to see your skin flush when I make you come." He flipped on one more light, then all of his attention turned to me. "Because I want to see everything."

My heart took off as I imagined being intimate with him with every light in the room on. My body wasn't the same one he'd left. It had since carried a child, it had carried a burden, it bore the scars of a shattered soul and a broken body. "I don't want you to see me. Not like that. In the dark, you can imagine the way I was before."

When I reached for the closest lamp to switch it off, he stopped me. "I don't want to imagine." His hand curled around mine, guiding it away from the lamp. "I want the real thing. I want the real you."

"You've seen my body. You know what I look like beneath all of this." I motioned at the fresh clothes hanging off of me, covering me from my wrists to my ankles to my neck.

"When I look at you, I see beauty and strength, and the one person in the world who gives me a reason to live and a reason to die." He drew me to him, his face creased in lines of concentration. "That's what I see when I look at you."

When his fingers skimmed beneath the hem of my shirt, starting to slide it up, I went stiff. Noticing, he let go of my shirt and reached for his instead. He had it up and over his head in one seamless motion.

He threw his shirt across the room and stepped back, holding his arms out at his sides. "What do you see when you look at me?"

He swallowed, waiting, then began to turn. I studied his back as he revolved, but what I'd noticed last night wasn't what I saw tonight.

My eyes were waiting for his when he finished his revolution. "I see the man I love."

His chest froze, his expression doing the same. Then his whole body relaxed, like a lifetime of burdens had just been lifted. "Then fuck the scars," he whispered, half of his mouth turning up. "They don't define us. We define them."

Whether it was courage or stupidity, something had me reaching for my shirt. I didn't think I breathed as I pulled it up my body, removing it over my head with my jacket. My instinct was to cross my arms over myself, to curl into a lesser self, but I fought it. I let Brecken's eyes steady me as I dropped the clothing onto the floor.

He wet his lips, taking a large stride toward me, but he stopped in his tracks when I reached behind my back to undo my bra. Quickly peeling each strap down my arms, I let it fall to the floor with the rest and forced my arms to rest at my sides as he stared at me.

"Blinking." I fought a smile from the way he was looking at me. "It's good for the eyes. Keeps them from drying out, that kind of thing."

"It's not my eyes I'm worried about." He managed to blink a few times as his fist came to his chest. "It's my damn heart." He pounded on his ribcage a few times, like one knocked on a door. "If this thing gives out before we finish, I'm going to be seriously pissed."

Still fighting a smile, my thumbs hooked under the waistband of my leggings. "Then we'd better hurry."

"Okay." Brecken was fighting with his belt then his jeans. They clearly couldn't come off fast enough. "At least this time."

"Stamina confidence?"

"It's been six years, Blue Bird." He balled up his jeans and tossed them over his shoulder. "That's a lot of celibacy to make up for."

Having him tease along with me, seeing him smile and behave like the boy I'd fallen in love with lowered whatever inhibitions were still weighing me down. Lights on, more scars and bruises between us that an entire division of rugby players, so many obstacles waiting outside that door that we might never make it past the first step ... my love for the human being standing before me overcame all of that. His love for me overcame it.

I'd heard it said that love conquered all, but I'd never believed it until that moment.

After peeling off my leggings, I took a deep breath when my fingers looped around the sides of my underwear.

Brecken started to tug on his boxers. "Me first?"

My teeth sank into my lip, and I shook my head. Then I slid my underwear over my hips, down my thighs, until I let them fall when they reached my knees.

"Holy fucking hell." A breath rushed out of Brecken's mouth as he fell back a few steps as though he'd been shoved.

"Isn't that an oxymoron? *Holy* hell?" I settled my hand into the bend of my waist, painting on what I hoped was confidence.

His fist went back to his chest, thumping on it. Almost like he was giving himself CPR minus the mouth-to-mouth.

"You're not going to have a heart attack on me, are you?" I slid closer when he kept thumping at his chest.

"Not planning on it, but if I do, just keep going. Don't stop. I'll be smiling in heaven. Or hell. Or wherever a tortured soul like mine winds up."

I wasn't hiding my smile anymore. "Your turn." My eyes dropped to his boxers.

He had them off his body and in a ball sailing across the room in one and a half seconds flat.

Now it was my turn to feel chest pains. I restrained myself from grabbing at my chest and pounding at it, but damn, that man had always had a body capable of making a girl lose her mind. Six years later, nothing had changed. I didn't see the scars and breaks when I looked at him, nor the burns and brands. I didn't see his limp as he moved closer or miss the muscle that had deteriorated. I saw him. Brecken Connolly. The person I'd planned on spending a lifetime with but would have to settle for spending the next twenty-eight days with. Or twenty-six now.

The reminder had me rushing toward him, not about to waste one moment of a second. I'd slow down time until a minute became a year, a day a decade. By the end of this, we'd have our lifetime.

When the end came, I'd have no regrets.

"You're not saying anything." Brecken moved toward me. Naked. Scarred. Beautiful.

My gaze returned to his. "Holy fucking hell."

A deep chuckle resonated in his chest. "Packs a punch, right?"

"This is the part where you close your mouth and make love to me."

He stalked closer until a few steps separated us. "I have to open my mouth to kiss you." His eyes dropped to my lips. "At least to kiss you the way I want to."

"I guess you can open your mouth for that."

He stepped into me, pressing his body into mine, backing me against the wall. A sharp breath rushed out of me when I felt how hard he was against me. Not just what resided between his legs—presently pressed into the softness of my stomach—but the expanse of his chest, the planes of his abdomen, the muscles running down his legs. He was hard, strong, and felt capable of saving me from whatever the world decided to heave at me. If I could just stay tucked into the shelter of his body, I'd be safe. I'd be happy. I'd know peace.

His head angled against mine, the heat of his breath touching my mouth before his lips did. My arms wound around his back, my hands carving around the slope of his shoulders and looking for a place to hang on. Needing a solid grip to hold onto when he carried me wherever it was he was planning on leading me to. With the way he was kissing me, it could have been anywhere.

His mouth was gentle at first, letting me take the lead. When my tongue touched his, a baritone sound vibrated in his chest. Hearing him make that sound, feeling it rattle against my body, knowing it was the result of what I was doing, made me feel things I hadn't felt in years. Power. Persuasion. Control. They hit my bloodstream like a shot of the best kind of positive endorphins, swimming inside me until I felt invincible.

The way he was allowing me to lead, submitting to my weaker physical strength, following the tenor of my need, had me feeling other things I hadn't felt in years. Trust. Reverence. Love.

As I lifted up to wind my legs behind his back, I arched my back, letting him feel the physical manifestation of what he was making me feel emotionally. His groan reverberated into my mouth, our kiss never breaking stride.

"I have to open my mouth to make the sounds you're going to force out of me," he whispered before gently sucking my bottom lip into his mouth.

My legs tightened around him. "You've made your point."

He leaned back just enough for me to see the glimmer in his eye. "I have to open my mouth to …" He dropped his mouth to my ear, whispering the rest of it.

A tremble wound down my spine, the rest of my body feeling like every nerve was firing.

"Are you—"

"I'm ready," I said, lifting my hips.

"You're sure? We don't have to. I can wait. Until you're ready. Being like this with you is enough, I swear." His breath was so uneven, each word sounded like its own sentence.

"It's not enough." I tipped my hips until I could feel him pushing against me. Our chests started rising and falling faster. "With you and me, nothing will ever be enough."

As I lowered myself onto him, his arm flew out behind him, bracing into the wall. He pushed against me until my back was hard against the wall, his chest hard against mine. His hips flexed slowly, sinking deeper into my body.

My head rolled back, my mouth falling open. His one hand was braced against the wall, the other lowered to the bend of my hip, his fingers sinking into it as the rest of his body pushed into mine. A sound came from me that I didn't recognize. I had to cover my mouth to contain it. When my head lowered enough to see Brecken, his face was turned up in a partial smirk.

"The bed?" I breathed, letting myself adjust to him inside me again. Letting myself grasp the reality that I was making love to Brecken Connolly again.

"I lived inside four walls for six years. There wasn't a bed." He kissed the bend of my neck, his lips tracing down the column of my neck. "I made the most of my situation by imagining you in those four walls with me, up against any one of those four walls with me inside you." His body smashed into mine a little harder, managing to sink the slightest bit deeper. "Just doing a little fantasy fulfillment."

I smiled even as he started to move inside me. "This seems like a nice wall."

Brecken was breathing hard, his forehead beading with sweat. "It's a nice wall wherever I have you pinned against it."

His mouth returned to mine, claiming ownership in the same way he was the rest of my body. I felt him every-where, inside, outside—he was a part of me.

"Brecken?" I breathed against his lips, squirming as I tried to slow my body down.

"Me too, Blue Bird." His forehead fell into the wall be-side me, his back going rigid. "Me too."

A pulse shot through my body right before my orgasm surged to life. His fingers dug deeper into me when he felt me come undone, his own release following. He rasped my name once, then again when his body stopped moving inside mine.

"That was …" He shook his head against the wall.

My fingers dragged down his back, my whole body feeling as though it were floating. "Quick?"

A raspy chuckle emanated from him. "Insane."

"Insanely quick?"

His head tipped against the wall to look at me. "Insane-ly good. Insanely amazing. Insanely unreal. Insanely the best thing to ever happen to a guy in the history of ever."

My body rocked against his when I laughed. "Now I understand." I paused, loving the feel of the sweat dotting his back. Loving the way it felt gliding along the pads of my fingers, the raised ridges of his scars with it. "But I might need a repeat. Maybe this time though, insanely slow?"

Brecken's arms wound around my back before turning me away from the wall. He started toward the bed, his steps strong and sure. If he was limping as he carried me across the room, I didn't feel it.

"Do you mind if insanely slow translates to all night?"

My head shook against his neck, a gasp escaping from my mouth when I felt him harden inside me. As he laid me down on the bed, his hands cupped around my left hand. His eyes stayed on mine as he slid the platinum band from my ring finger. He held it for a moment, then he opened his fingers and let it fall to the floor.

"I've always been yours." My fingers braided through his as he lowered his body over mine. "Nothing changes that."

"He was too blind to see what he had. I never was. I always knew what I had when I took you into my arms." His arms knotted behind me, drawing me into him, as his hips rocked into mine. "The whole fucking world."

# thirteen

My body still ached the next morning, but it was different. The aches from pain had dimmed, being replaced with aches from pleasure. Brecken had managed to take away the pain, one gentle touch at a time, one loving word at a time.

I was waking to the same life, but I was a different person traversing through it. The time on the alarm clock beside the bed read a little before six in the morning. I recalled seeing four something before my eyes had finally given in to sleep. I'd never felt so rested though, even on only a couple hours of sleep. That might have been because I hadn't slept with the proverbial one-eye open, anticipating when the next attack would come.

When I rolled over, I found the other side of the bed empty. On the pillow though was a pink wild rose he must have plucked from one of the bushes outside, and a note. On it was a little stick figure with exaggerated eyes. *Sorry. Staring again.* It was signed *Pretend, Stick-Figure Me.*

Most mornings I woke up with some version of dread or resolve on my face. This one, I woke with a smile. Collecting the flower and note from the pillow, I pried myself out of bed to get showered and dressed. I wasn't sure where Brecken had gone, but I assumed his cabin since we'd both decided it was important to keep our relationship, as far as it went beyond friendship, hidden from Keenan. It would only confuse him, and I wanted to keep confusion to a minimum in his life.

After showering and dressing, I went back to straighten up the bedroom and made sure none of Brecken's clothes were left lying around. I didn't miss that he must have picked up my ring sometime early this morning and put it on the dresser for me to find.

I slid it on with a heaviness. He knew the way things were between us, and he'd also accepted the way things had to be once Crew was back from rehab. It was a strange reality to accept that the man I loved would gladly rip out the throat of the man I was married to … if it wasn't for me asking him not to.

Checking my phone where I'd left it charging in the living room, I saw I'd missed a text from Crew. He'd sent me one each morning since he'd checked into the program, each within a few minutes of each other. Each one started with a countdown to how many days were left, followed by some quip about missing us and being sorry. Like the two mornings prior, I erased this one.

Keenan hadn't moved from the position he'd been in last night, his chest still moving in slow, even motions. Nothing like a day at the lake to deplete a kid's energy stores.

He was going to wake up starving though, so I figured I should get started on breakfast before he woke up. Actually, I was hungry too. I couldn't remember the last time I'd actually eaten because I'd been hungry, instead of just eating to keep from wasting away.

We'd picked up a few things at the grocery store before heading here yesterday, so I tore open the box of pancake mix and pulled the carton of eggs from the fridge. I was just cracking the last couple of eggs into the frying pan when I noticed a figure running along the lakeshore. It was barely detectable, but his stride was a bit uneven. Smooth on the right, choppier on the left. Not that it was slowing him down any. Brecken looked like he was training for the hundred-meter sprint instead of out for a morning jog.

His footsteps echoed on the stairs a few minutes later, his heavy breaths sounding similar to the ones I'd experienced against my skin last night. I made myself focus on breakfast so it didn't burn, instead of the reminders of the night before.

The screen door whispered open, followed by Brecken slowly stepping inside when he noticed Keenan still sleeping. When he saw me, his eyes softened, right before they roamed me in a similar fashion to the way mine were roaming him.

"Hungry?" I said quietly, waving my spatula at the plate of steaming pancakes.

His brow lifted before he wiped his face off on his shirt. "Famished."

The way he said it had me clearing my throat. Hormones, be gone. Libido, save it for later.

"Exertion?" I eyed his sweaty running attire.

He grinned. "Plenty."

"Tired?"

His forehead creased as he gave me a look. "Negative."

"More?"

"Positively." He nodded once as he moved closer.

"Tonight?"

He grabbed an apple from the table and lifted it to his mouth. His teeth sank into it, his eyes aimed at me as he chewed. "*All* night."

"Sounds ..." I started, scrambling the eggs.

"Amazing?"

"Strenuous."

His brows bounced as he took another bite of the apple. "If you're doing it right."

"Which you make it a point to."

He gave a half bow, followed with a wink. "Are we done with the one-word sentences conversation?"

"Maybe." I smiled into the pan when he grumbled.

A moment later, the sounds of someone starting to wake up came from the futon. Keenan had a ritual when he woke. Couple of yawns, arm stretched above the head, another yawn, long and drawn-out, followed by bouncing up in bed, all ready to take on the day.

"Hey, sleepyhead."

"Hey, Mom." Keenan rolled out of bed and padded into the kitchen. "I'm starving."

I glanced at Brecken as I carried the plate of pancakes to the table. "Seems to be the theme this morning." Giving his messy-haired head a kiss, I layered a couple of pancakes onto a plate for him.

"Hi, Brecken. Why are you all sweaty?" Keenan stopped reaching for the syrup when he took a good look at Brecken, who was moving toward the stove.

"I went out for a run this morning."

"Can I go on a run with you tomorrow morning?"

"Yeah, sure. If it's okay with your mom," Brecken added, grabbing the spatula and giving the eggs a look, like he was trying to broker a truce.

Thankfully, I'd turned down the heat before taking the pancakes to the table.

"Is it okay, Mom?"

"It's okay with me," I answered, cutting his pancakes into small pieces as he poured a stream of syrup over them.

"Why do you work out so much, Brecken?" Keenan asked.

"Because I need to be strong," he said, carefully stirring the scrambled eggs. He seemed surprised when flames didn't start shooting from the pan.

"Why? You're not in the marines anymore. Why do you need to be so strong?" Keenan stuffed a forkful of pancake into his mouth.

"Because I want to keep the people I care about safe." He spoke facing the stove, but I could feel his words aimed toward us.

"I guess that's a good reason." Keenan shrugged, inhaling a few more bites of pancakes while Brecken finished scrambling the eggs.

After inspecting the eggs and turning off the burner before we went from scrambled to scorched, I nudged Brecken. "Nicely done."

"I'm a quick learner."

"Or I'm a good teacher."

"Fine." He smirked at me, carrying the pan of eggs to the table. "Then I'm an *eager* learner."

"True story." I found a smile as I dished up two more plates of pancakes.

"So what are we doing today? More fishing?" Keenan's eyes lit up, his head whipping toward the window in the direction of the lake.

"Sorry, little man. I've got more work to do today, and I'll probably be back too late to take you out night-fishing again." Brecken scooped some eggs onto Keenan's plate, then mine, before taking a seat.

Keenan slumped in his seat for a moment before shooting back up. "Mom?" He turned toward me, blinking those big blue eyes. "Would you take me fishing?"

Picking up my fork, I paused. "I don't know anything about fishing."

"Brecken didn't know anything about fishing, but he took me out." When Brecken shot him an injured look, Keenan shrugged.

"My secret's out. I don't know anything about fishing." Brecken dished a portion of eggs on his plate. "But we still had fun trying, right?"

Keenan's head bobbed. "Come on. Please, Mom? I'll do anything. I'll do the dishes. Fold the laundry. Just please, try? For me?"

The bite of egg I'd been about to take was still frozen in the air in front of my mouth. Brecken had joined in with the clasped-hand begging, puppy-dog-eyed guilt-tripping. They looked like twenty-year age difference clones, from the drooping lower lip to the ramrod posture.

I lowered my fork, glancing out at the dock where the fishing boats were bobbing in the water. "Let's go fishing."

"This is the best day ever, Mom. The bestest," Keenan announced from his seat in the fishing boat a few hours later, a pole resting in his hands.

"You said that about yesterday too." I checked the tip of my pole for any movement at all, like the guy who'd rented the boat to me had instructed. Nothing. I was starting to wonder if the lake was fresh out of fish.

"Yesterday was the best day ever. But now today is."

I tipped his hat down lower over his head to cover more of his face. It was hot out again, and the midday sun was beating down on us. My long-sleeve shirt was plastered to my back from the sweat, made worse by the restrictive orange life jacket I was stuffed into.

Keenan hadn't complained once, but he had to be roasting. Thankfully, Brecken had suggested I pack a small cooler with some water and snacks in case we were out here for a while.

"We're fishing," Keenan announced a minute later, grinning at me. "We did it, Mom."

Despite the heat and the sweat and my unfavorable opinions on the topic of fishing, I was struck with something. A feeling of accomplishment, a sense of confidence. I'd known nothing about fishing other than how to spell it and that there was a pole involved, yet here I was, out on a boat in the middle of a big lake, *fishing* with my son. Crew wouldn't have believed it. No one who knew me as the person I was now would have believed it.

For so long, I'd bought into the theory that I was weak and incapable and inadequate, but I realized what a lie that was. I had everything I needed to face any challenge. It was all inside me. Maybe it was hiding, but it was there, waiting for me to find it.

My back relaxed and I exhaled, admiring the scenery around us. "You know, this really is the best day ever."

Keenan was in the middle of a smile when the end of his pole wobbled. "I got one! Mom! I caught one!" He leapt up from his seat, making the boat rock some.

"Reel it up! I'll get the net!" I was shouting with him for some reason, my heartbeat pumping in my throat.

Keenan's hands were a haze of motion as he worked his reel while I wrestled to get the net untangled from the tackle box. If anyone was watching us, they were probably getting a good show.

"I can see it! There! I can see it!" He stopped reeling long enough to point at the flash of silver rising from the dark water.

"It's a big one, Keenan! I don't think it'll fit in our net."

Keenan's mouth made a round shape as he stared at the net before getting back to his reeling. When the fish was close enough to the surface, I dropped the net into the water, scooping the fish into it.

"Does it fit? Does it fit?" Keenan was bouncing in excitement, leaning over me to try to get a look.

"Barely."

Once I had the net in the boat, I turned it over to let the fish slide out of it. It flopped around on the bottom of the boat, the hook hanging from its mouth, splashing droplets of water onto us.

"It's ginormous!" Keenan hooted, leaning down to touch it before thinking twice about that.

"Biggest fish I've ever seen."

I leaned over the fish to shield it from the relentless sun. Truthfully, it was a little puny and all banged up. One

fin looked mangled, and there were a bunch of marks running all along its belly. Even one of its eyes was cloudy. It
was a fish that had seen a hard life, even though it had clearly been a short life gauging the size of it.

"Should we keep it, Mom? We can cook it up for dinner tonight. Brecken won't be able to believe it." Keenan
was leaning over me, still shaking in his excitement.

"I don't know. What do you think?"

I kneeled back, finding myself feeling almost sorry for
this poor little fish that had been looking for a means to stay
alive, been tricked into taking the wrong bait, and was now
going to pay with its life. It was a fish. Not an emotionally
intelligent animal, if you could even classify it as an animal.
Fish. Slimy. Scaly. God, it wasn't like it was some adorable
polar bear cub I'd just lured into my boat for the sake of entertainment or a meal.

Keenan continued to stare at the fish with me, his body
starting to quiet. Eventually, his little hand made it the rest
of the way so his fingers could brush across the fish's metallic scales.

"Let's put her back," he said, moving toward the tackle
box like he knew what he was looking for.

"You sure?" I turned my head to watch him dig around
in the tackle box, surprised. From how excited he'd been
about fishing, I'd guessed he'd want to have his first one
stuffed and mounted.

Keenan held out a pair of needle nose pliers for me.
"Let her go."

As I worked the tiny hook from her mouth, I told my
son the reason for my tears was the bright sun reflecting off
the metal boat. I couldn't tell him the real reason. So instead, I pulled him under my arm as we both lowered the

fish back into the water, letting her go so she could swim to see another day.

# fourteen

He wasn't back yet. He'd thought he'd be back by nine, ten at the latest, but it was almost eleven. He wasn't back.

I guessed that what had happened to him back then would always haunt what happened now. I told myself he was fine, just running later than planned. I reminded myself this wasn't a war zone; it was Southern Oregon. It didn't matter. Nothing was capable of calming my worries.

Keenan had been adamant about staying up until Brecken got home, but even he'd crashed in the middle of a game of checkers half an hour ago. Another long day of fishing, swimming, and hiking had worn him out. It had worn me out too, but the more minutes that went by without hearing from Brecken, the more awake I became.

He'd said he'd try to pick up a cell phone sometime today so I could get ahold of him if I needed to, but that didn't do me any good tonight. To distract myself, I picked up all of the games Keenan and I had scattered around the living room, collected the pieces of popcorn we'd tossed at one another. After he'd fallen asleep, I'd changed into a soft cotton nightgown, unable to keep myself covered in billows of fabric any longer. The bruises and evidence of my beating were still evident, but being able to display them for once, instead of making concealment the priority, felt freeing.

When Keenan was awake, that was different, but this … this was for me. A manifesto in my new creed. I might have wanted to hide what had happened to me from my son, but I didn't want to hide it from myself. I wanted to be reminded of what I'd been through, so I remembered I could get through anything.

Once the mess was cleaned up, I tucked the blanket over Keenan again, knowing he'd probably kick it off again in a minute, then headed for the screen door. The days were hot here, but the nights were perfect. Clear skies, cool fresh air, light breeze.

As soon as I stepped onto the porch, that breeze caught the hem of my gown, playing with it, and tugged at the ends of my hair. The lake was reflecting moonlight in stripes of silver and ivory.

I took a picture with my mind, adding another one to the pile. These moments, these experiences, were the ones I'd go back to when the cloud of reality closed in around me again. People said all you needed was a glimmer of light to lead you out of the dark. I was going to put that theory to the test. Soon. Twenty-five and a half more days.

When my gaze went from the lake to the dark cabin next door, it took me a minute to realize what was parked in the space next to my cabin. Brecken's truck.

With him inside.

My feet jogged down the steps, carrying me toward him.

"Brecken?" I said quietly, not sure if he'd fallen asleep or had just gotten back. When I came around the front of his truck and examined the look on his face, I guessed he'd been sitting there for a while.

He didn't see me at first. He didn't see me at all. He was somewhere else. His body here, his mind in a different world.

"Brecken," I repeated, reaching for the driver's side door handle.

When the door screeched open, he broke out of whatever daze he'd been in.

"How long have you been here? Are you okay?"

When I swung the door open, I found his hands curled around the steering wheel, his body stiff and primed. A sheen of sweat covered his skin, and his eyes had a wildness to them.

My hand curled around his wrist, guiding his hand away from the steering wheel. The truck was in park, the engine turned off. I reached for his other hand, leading it away from the wheel, feeling the muscles down his forearm tight and tensed.

"It's okay," I whispered, letting go of his hand so I could turn his head toward me. "It's okay," I repeated once his eyes drifted near mine.

All at once, he sprung out of his truck, his body crushing against mine. The wildness in his eyes was now a make I recognized. His hands formed around my back, his fingers sinking into me as he spun me around.

My heart took off, my body already spiraling out of control from the look of need in his eyes alone. He moved me against the side of his truck, pressing himself into me from behind. His head dropped beside mine as all he did was breathe me in for a minute, like I was his ticket back home. One hand slid up the bend of my body, slipping inside the top of my nightgown when he reached my chest. The other hand reached for the back of my nightgown, fisting it up over my backside.

When he pressed his hips into me, his erection straining against me so I could feel his need, a whimper crawled up my throat. He paused, pulling himself back just so there was enough space for him to turn my head toward his. I saw the question in his eyes. I heard the unspoken one on his lips. I felt it in every part of him pressed against every part of me.

He deserved so much and I had so little to give him, but this, my body when he needed it, my love in unconditional form, I could give him. At least for the amount of time we had left.

My lips touched his as I reached behind me to work at the buckle on his belt. "Yes," I whispered, touching his lips once more. "Yes."

That was all he needed to hear. All he needed to know. His hands left me just long enough to undo what was left of his belt and zipper, then his body smashed back into mine at the same time he moved inside me. I felt him quiver against my back, his warm breath breaking across my shoulder. He gathered my hair into his hand, closing his fist around it as he thrust himself inside me. The sounds he was making as he took me spurred my release from the depths. His truck was hard and cool against my front, his body hard and hot against my back, his hands pulling on me, his mouth sucking at me, driving me closer, one thrust at a time …

I'd thought this was what he needed when I looked into his eyes a minute ago. What I realized, as I felt my orgasm join his, was that I needed it too. I might have even needed it more. To trust another human being enough to let it all go.

To give myself over to another soul, in body and mind, and trust that wherever they led me, I'd be okay.

I'd experienced rough sex before, the kind that accompanied no foreplay or warning. I'd come to fear it. This though, *this* was different. Not forceful in the way of exerting and abusing one's power, but in the way of two people's passion fusing together and combusting. This was trust at its pinnacle, not control at its most corrupt.

He shuddered against me, exhaling as his body relaxed into mine. His hold loosened around my hair, letting it slide out of his fist, while his other moved until his arm was tied around my waist.

"Are you okay?" he rasped, leaning his forehead into the truck and turning it toward me. His forehead was creased, the storm retreating from his eyes. "I didn't hurt you, did I?"

My hand lifted to his face, tracing the lines drawn into his skin. "You didn't hurt me."

His eyes dropped, taking in the sight of my body crushed between him and the truck. He swallowed. "Did I scare you?"

I waited for his eyes to return to mine. "You could never scare me. Never." When he exhaled, his body leaning away from mine, I grabbed his hand.

Turning around, I pulled him back to me. When my chest was spilling against his, I drew him closer. "Turn me on like crazy, yes, but scare me, never."

He rearranged my nightgown, smoothing it down my stomach. Then he leaned in and kissed my forehead. "Thank you."

"Thank *you*."

This time, he tipped my chin toward him, kissing my lips slowly. He kissed me the opposite way he'd just fucked me. My head was reeling from it all.

"The interview …" I said, as he started to refasten his jeans and belt.

His jaw moved, his eyes staying away from mine. "It was long."

"Anything else?"

"It's over." He took my hand and led me around his truck toward the cabin.

"Brecken—"

He spun around. "It's done, Camryn. Finished. They asked their questions, I answered them, they wrote me a check, that was that. I spent all day talking. I don't want to spend the rest of the night rehashing it."

I slid my hand out of his. "You didn't use to hide stuff from me. You didn't use to not want to talk about things. You used to tell me everything."

"Yeah, and then I was captured by some bad people who did bad things to good people. I had to listen to my crew being tortured while I sat helpless in a cell." His voice rose with each word, his movements choppy and agitated. "I had to watch—" His jaw clamped closed as he glared at the lake. "You don't tell me everything anymore either, Camryn. So don't start accusing me of hiding things when you're keeping your own secrets."

My mouth fell open. I hadn't expected him to turn this around on me and wasn't prepared for how to respond. "What are you—"

"Don't. Don't play it off." His eyes cut back to mine. "You want to keep some things to yourself, that's fine. I respect that." He started backing up toward my cabin. "Just please return the favor."

Disappearing up the stairs, he moved through the screen door. I stood there for a minute, thinking. Debating. He had secrets. I had secrets. I knew we were entitled to them, but what concerned me was what secrets like Brecken's and mine could do to such a fragile relationship as ours. Secrets came with a price, a steep one most of the time. I'd already paid so much to keep mine. I wasn't sure if I was in too deep to change course now or if I could afford to lose anything else to keep them.

We only had a limited amount of time together. Would it make a difference? Either way?

As I followed him inside the cabin, I entered with more questions and what felt like no answers.

The lights were still all off in the main space, Keenan still sound asleep, the blanket still tucked around him miraculously. However, I noticed it was tucked differently. Up over his arms, almost under his chin. Someone else had pushed pause on the brooding long enough to tuck a blanket around a sleeping boy.

The sound of the shower sputtering on had me heading toward the bathroom. I'd saved him dinner from earlier—Keenan and I'd made hot dogs and potato salad since we were officially catch-and-release fishermen now—but I guessed he wasn't hungry. He probably just wanted to shower, crawl into bed, and fall asleep, but I wasn't sure that was what he needed right now.

The bathroom door whined open when I slid inside, steam already billowing over the top of the small shower. Brecken's head sat above the showerhead.

"Camryn, please."

I didn't say anything as I slid aside the plastic curtain and stepped in to join him. His brows came together when he saw me, and he tried to keep the shower from beating down on me in my nightgown by blocking it with his back.

"What are you doing?" He held the curtain open, gently trying to guide me out.

I didn't budge, and he didn't force me. He could have, but he didn't. He wanted to, but he knew better.

I felt myself fall more in love with him, right then and there. It didn't seem possible to love a human being that wasn't my own child more than I already did, but somehow … against the odds … I could.

"You don't have to talk." I placed my hand on his chest, looking up at him. "But I'm not going anywhere." Then I stepped into him, wound my arms around his back, and settled my head on his chest.

At first, he tensed up, like my touch was painful, but then he relaxed. Letting out a breath, his arms scooped around me as he stepped closer, his chin tucking over my head to bind me to him.

"You don't have to talk either." He angled our bodies so the warm shower was raining down on me as well. "I'm not going anywhere."

He was naked, and my thin nightgown was saturated and transparent. He was hard and pressed against me as the signs of our love-making ran down my legs. There was nothing sexual about this moment. Everything about it was intimate though. Being close to him like this, realizing I could choose to tell him what I wanted or didn't want and that he wasn't going anywhere, was where love proved itself.

"I was the only one they kept alive. The only one who survived." Brecken's fingers curled around me, hanging on. "My crew, they all died in that place. Their bodies? God knows where they are or what became of them." He stopped to take a couple of breaths. "I was their leader. It should have been me."

My head shook against him, but he kept going. "At first, they kept us all together in the same cell, so we had to look at each and see what they'd done to us. I didn't think there could be anything worse than having to watch the limp body of one of my marines being drug into that cell and dropped, but I was wrong. It was worse when they separated us. Different cells. We never got to see each other—we just had to hear. The screams, the whimpers … I had to listen to them suffer. That was the worst part of it all."

My arms tightened around him. God, I wanted to cry. I wanted to release the sob I felt about to brim over, but I didn't let myself. I knew if I started crying, he'd stop talking in order to comfort me. This time, I wanted to be the one to comfort him. So I kept my tears to myself and let him say whatever it was he needed to get out.

"I asked them to leave my crew alone—to interrogate me instead. To do … whatever they were going to do … to me." His voice lost focus, sounding distant though he was speaking right outside of my ear. "They made it twice as bad for my crew instead, leaving me alone to rot. They didn't question or touch me for months. They made what I was willing to sacrifice for my crew a curse upon them instead."

His head fell back, lolling under the stream of the water, his eyes squeezed shut like Keenan's would when he saw something scary. I watched the water roll down his face, wishing it could wash away the demons he carried until they'd all disappeared down the drain at my feet.

"There was one time when one of the guards got lazy. He forgot to double-check my lock after bringing in a meal. I knew the door was unlocked. I knew I could open it and try to escape whenever I wanted, but I waited." He lowered his head but kept his eyes closed. "I didn't know where the rest of my crew was being held, and I couldn't leave without them. So I waited until I heard one of them. The only time I heard them was when they had one of them in the *interrogation* room. It was McVay. Her screams were always the worst because she'd try so hard not to cry, which only made them try harder to get one out of her. When she did finally scream, I swear it rattled the bars in my cell. I can still hear it."

I was holding my breath, afraid a sob would choke out when I opened my mouth. He'd been right. I didn't want to know what had happened. I could imagine the worst, and it still wouldn't feel as crippling as hearing him relive the event, one word at a time.

"I left my cell, heading in her direction. There were two guards inside with her, and I managed to tackle them both, giving her a chance to run. I told her to go, to escape. I gave her as much of a head start as I could. She barely made it out of the room before they caught up to her. Barely out of that room." His words echoed, hollow and faint. "They dragged her in front of me … did awful, terrible things"—his fingers dug deeper into me—"and then they killed her. Five feet in front of my eyes."

My body trembled, but it was at the same time his did, so he didn't notice.

"I tried to help her—to save her—and I got her killed." His eyes opened then, staring at me with something I rarely witnessed in him—fear. "I killed her."

I had to swallow before I could speak. My hand slid around front to settle into the slope where his jaw ran into his neck. "You tried to help her."

"Trying to help turned out to be the opposite of helping her. It doesn't matter that I tried to help her."

"Yes, it does"—I surprised myself with how loud my voice projected—"because she died knowing someone cared. Knowing you did. Knowing you tried to help her. Her last moments, she knew someone was willing to sacrifice himself for her. That matters."

He stood there, eyes locked on mine, like he was trying to determine if I really meant that, if he himself really believed that to be true. In the end, he sighed. "I'm a marine. We only think in terms of the end result, not what went into getting it."

I lifted onto my tiptoes. "You're also a human being."

"Sometimes I wonder if they beat all of that out of me. That maybe it's all scattered in pieces around some bombed out prison half a world away."

I blinked. "For someone I admire so much, who I look up to and respect the hell out of ..." Leaning in, I kissed him until I felt him relax in my arms. "You can say the craziest things."

The corner of his mouth moved. A small success. He'd led me into that dark world with him, let me be a part of it, and now it was my responsibility to lead him out of it. To make sure he didn't stay trapped inside the portal he'd opened for me.

"Hand me the soap." I indicated behind him as I went to adjust the temperature dial. The hot water didn't last long in these "charming" little cabins.

"Why?" he asked, already handing it to me.

"Because we're in a shower. The place one usually comes to clean oneself."

"That was my whole plan until you decided to step in here fully dressed and coerce me into talking."

"I hugged you. And this isn't fully dressed." I stepped back to indicate the nightgown plastered to my body.

"You hugged me *and* said 'it's okay,' which everyone knows is like some secret way to get a person to spill their guts. And now that you mention it ..." Brecken's fingers slid under the straps of my nightgown, tugging it down my arms and off of my body. It hit the shower floor with a wet smack. "There. Now you're naked."

I attempted a stern look, but it only made him smile. Lifting my finger, I swirled it around. When he turned, I smoothed the soap around his slippery back. After hearing his story, the scars on his back were extra obvious, every one seeming bigger than I remembered.

After a minute of washing him, I'd worked up enough of a lather to conceal the span of his back. Brecken stood there, head bent and arms braced against the shower wall in front of him, letting me clean him.

"Did you tell the media all of that today?" I washed a mark on his lower back that was in the shape of an X. I tried not to think about why someone would want to carve those lines into a person's body.

His head twisted against the wall. "No. I told them the *lighter* story. I told them it all happened to me, instead of what I heard ... or what I saw happen to my crew." The muscles banding down his arms burst to the surface as his hands tightened into fists. "Those families have been through enough without knowing what actually happened down there. Whatever they've thought about—whatever they imagined—isn't half as bad as what truly happened. They've been through enough. They don't need to go through the whole nation knowing what their loved ones suffered."

My hands moved lower, washing the curves and cuts of his backside. "You don't think once they hear about what you went through, they'll assume the same things happened to the others?" When he stayed quiet, I assumed my question must have gone too far. "Never mind."

"They died right after we were taken. Were killed at the same time my supposed execution took place." His feet shifted weight.

My hands stopped moving. "But you said—"

"What I just told you is the truth. What I told the reporter today was the truth those families deserve."

"You don't think they deserve to know the real truth?"

"I think some people have been through enough without having to know the details. I think it doesn't change what happened or that three marines aren't coming back home." Brecken straightened and slid under the shower stream, letting the soap rinse off his back. "You don't think I did the right thing?"

Setting down the soap, I watched the suds wash down him, my eyes going to the patchwork of mutilations on his back. "I don't know if there is a right or wrong in this kind of a situation."

"If you had a loved one go missing, then wound up finding out they were dead, would you want to know what happened in between? If it was the worst kind of thing? Would you want to know?" He shoved off of the wall and turned around, waiting.

"I *did* have a loved one go missing." My hand settled on his chest. "I *did* think he died. I *do* know what happened."

"But I came back. I survived it."

The pads of my fingers crested several scars as they moved across his skin. Small, round white ones. Long, uneven purple ones. Would I want to know what went into the creation of them if he was already gone and I'd made my peace with that years ago? Would I want to know what he'd suffered—how much he'd suffered?

"You did the right thing." I kissed his mouth, repeating my words.

He let me kiss him again before he reached for the bottle of shampoo and had me turn. His fingers curled into my scalp, cleaning my hair slowly, methodically.

"You remember when I told you how I was saving up for a little house as close to the beach as we could get?" He worked the shampoo into the long ends of my hair before adjusting the shower so it was angled toward me.

"Of course. I still picture what it might have looked like." I leaned my head back, letting him comb the lather out of my hair with his fingers.

"I bought it." His hands stopped moving. "I'm not sure if it's anything like what you pictured, but I found that little house close to the beach."

My head lifted, twisting over my shoulder to look back at him. "You bought a house? In California?"

He was squeezing some conditioner into his palm. "Yeah. I'm in the process of it, at least. With all of that back pay and money from the interviews, I had to spend it on something, and I keep hearing how real estate's a good investment." His hands combed through my hair again, massaging in the conditioner. "It's ours. When that day comes, sooner, later, we've got a home. Away from here."

It could have been what he'd just told me. It could have been the way he was washing my hair—such an everyday ritual, done with so much care and attention—or it could have been that our time was running out. It could have been any other billion reasons why I had to be close to him right then.

Moving until my chest was against his, I roped my arms behind his neck, rose up onto my toes, and covered his mouth with mine. His hands fell from my hair, scooping under my backside to lift me. We stood like that for a while, kissing under the spray of the shower, before he backed me into the shower wall. His hand moved between us, aligning his body with mine.

"What are you doing?" I smiled against his lips, bowing my back closer.

He moved inside me in a controlled, unhurried way. "Loving you," he rasped when he could go no deeper.

"And what was that up against your truck just now?" I asked.

A brow curved into his forehead. "Taking you."

My body writhed against his as he pulled out. "And the difference is?"

His mouth dropped to my neck, his tongue tasting my skin as he pressed deep in the same deliberate manner. "Let me show you."

# fifteen

He was leaving soon.

It wouldn't be long before I'd have to accept that in a different way. In a more permanent way. That was the thought I awoke to the next morning—the sense of dread and acceptance that he was leaving. Today, for his final interview. In twenty-odd days, forever. Or at least for a very long time.

I was drenched in sweat. The blankets and sheets tangled around me were damp as well. It wasn't until I blinked myself awake and rolled onto my side toward Brecken that I realized I wasn't the one who'd broken into a sweat in my sleep. It was him.

He'd kicked off most of the blankets, but the sheet was a twisted web from his waist down. He was sweating so badly, it was rolling off of him, and his face was drawn into an expression I had yet to witness on him. I didn't have the right emotion in my vocabulary to try to name it either.

"Brecken." I leaned up onto my elbows, whispering his name again.

He was typically a light sleeper, snapping awake at the faintest of noises.

I cuffed my hand around his arm and lightly shook him. "Brecken."

His eyes snapped open, unfocused and feral, then his body went into motion. His arms flew toward me, his hands gluing to my shoulders before his body twisted over mine. I crashed back onto the mattress, Brecken hovering above me, pinning me, that untamed look reflecting down at me.

My chest stopped moving. I had nothing to fear from the man hovering above me, despite every sign indicating otherwise.

"Brecken," I said, my hand sliding down his clammy, quivering arm. "It's okay."

It took a moment for him to crack through whatever dark place he was in, but I watched his eyes go through each stage until they were the ones I knew. His chest was still moving hard, his skin dripping with perspiration, when realization broke across his face.

"Did I hurt you?" His hands snapped away from me as he pulled himself off of me, his eyes running down and around me.

I stayed lying back, still recovering from the shock. "I'm fine. You didn't hurt me."

"Are you sure?" His eyes were still running the expanse of my body.

"I'm sure." I sat up in bed, dropping my hand to his to tie my fingers through his.

"I'm sorry." His head lowered as he slid to the edge of the bed. "It was … I was having …"

"It's okay," I repeated, not wanting him to make a bigger deal of this than it was.

His head shook. "What if I had hurt you?"

"No." My head shook hard. "No what-ifs. This is complicated enough between us without adding in all of the what-ifs. We'll deal with everything as it comes, one day at a time, one moment at a time. Forget the what-ifs." I lowered my head so it was even with his. "I'm okay. You're okay. That's what matters—not what could have happened."

"If I ever hurt you …" His voice was a quiet echo between us.

"You won't—"

"Then I'd be no better than him." His eyes lifted to meet mine. "No different than him."

That was when I got it. When I understood. My hand curved under his jaw, feeling the muscles strain beneath it. "You are so much better than him. So entirely different than him. Whatever happens, whatever might, you and he are nothing alike."

"We both carry demons inside. His might be different than mine, but that doesn't change the way they manifest."

I scooted closer. "You won't hurt me."

We sat like that for a minute, then a few more. We sat there in front of each other, staying twisted in the tangle of the night for as long as we could. When the alarm on my phone chimed later than morning, I was still in the same spot, feeling as though he was being torn away from me all over again. This time, I was losing him to an invisible force I had no name for, an enemy that made no negotiations and took no prisoners. An enemy that was merciless.

Keenan had fallen asleep in the backseat an hour ago, and it had been quiet in the cab of the truck ever since. Like yesterday, Brecken's interview today had run late, which meant he'd gotten back to the cabin late too. When I suggested we just spend the night and leave in the morning since he'd paid for the full three nights, he'd said we needed to get back, a soldier-like authority in his voice. An air of resolve, as if he were preparing to head off to war.

I'd asked how the interview today had gone, and he'd answered my questions in the vaguest possible way, limiting his words to a handful at a time. I guessed he was still upset about what had happened this morning, still letting his guilt get to him. I also knew nothing I said to try to convince him otherwise would work. It would take time, and that was something we didn't have.

After Keenan fell asleep, I'd held my hand out toward Brecken, not sure if he'd take it. I knew he noticed it from the corner of his eye. His fists wrung the steering wheel a few times, like he was fighting to keep them there. Then he let out a breath at the same time his hand fell from the steering wheel to meet mine. He hadn't let go since, and even after he pulled into his driveway a little before midnight, he kept his fingers tied through mine, staring out the windshield after he turned off the engine.

"Let's get some sleep," I whispered, glancing back at Keenan, who'd managed to prop himself against some of the bags in the backseat.

"I'll walk you two in, but I'm going to stay at my place tonight."

My eyebrows came together as I twisted in my seat.

"I think that would be best, after the past three days." He checked the rearview mirror, scanning out his window after. "Let me have a night to decompress or … whatever, before you fall asleep beside me again."

I didn't want to be without him tonight. I didn't want to be alone. I didn't want him to be alone. I didn't want to roll over and find the bed cold where there'd been a warm spot beside me the past few nights. I didn't want to waste what was left of our time together.

More than all of that, I wanted to give him what he needed. Even if that was a night away. Even if that was every night away.

"You want to grab the kid or the bags?" I opened the door and stepped outside. My hand felt cool now that his wasn't around it.

"I've got it all. You just grab the door." Brecken stepped out of the truck and slid his seat forward before reaching in for Keenan. He pulled him from his booster seat without making a sound and cradled him to his chest as he wrapped both arms around Keenan.

I had the door unlocked and open by the time Brecken made it up the steps, moving without making a noise. The porch light wasn't on, but I still found myself scanning the street and sidewalks. Getting in late tonight instead of midday tomorrow so no one would be up or out to see the three of us arrive together was part of Brecken's plan. There was no one to be seen. The whole neighborhood was still. Eerily still. Like the kind that makes a person wonder what's hiding in all that darkness, the reason for all of that hush. Shaking off the feeling creeping up my spine, I moved inside and flipped on a few lights.

Brecken was moving down the stairs, having already tucked Keenan in. His eyes seemed trained on the spot at the bottom of them. "I'll grab the bags and then do a quick check, just to make sure everything looks good before heading to my place." Translation: I'm going to check every nook and cranny to make sure Crew isn't lurking anywhere in the house.

"Are you sure you don't want to stay?" I paused with my finger on the lamp switch I was about to twist on.

He paused in the doorway. "I'm sure." When he glanced back, he'd forced a smile. "Save me a spot tomorrow night, okay?"

My fingers left the lamp switch, leaving it off. "Okay."

After Brecken brought in Keenan's and my bags, he checked around the house, one room at a time, clearing it as he'd been trained. Then he checked once more. Before he left, he pulled me into his arms, holding me like a person might clutch a bird in their hands. Then he let me go and waited just outside the door for the sound of the lock turning over.

I watched him through the same living room window I'd first watched him. He went into his house and not a single light came on. It was strange to realize he was so close when he felt so far away. He was one lawn away, maybe fifty feet total, but he felt like he was totally out of reach.

Knowing I was incapable of falling asleep and looking for any kind of distraction, I went into the kitchen to check the messages. There were none. So I moved on to the fridge, cleaning out a few leftovers and items that were nearing their expiration dates. Then I decided it needed a full-on cleaning. From there, I found distractions everywhere I looked. From the ceiling fans that needed to be dusted despite being cleaned a few weeks ago, to the baseboards that needed to be polished even though they were gleaming.

I couldn't sleep. I didn't want to. I was afraid of the nightmares I'd see if I let myself close my eyes, but mostly, I was afraid of the nightmare I'd wake up to.

A while later, I went up to check on Keenan. He'd kicked off his blankets and was sleeping on his back, as spread out as he could be, taking up as much of his bed as possible. I found myself comparing it to the way I slept, in as small a ball as possible, tucked beneath as many layers of blankets as I could stand.

My mission of protecting my son from what was happening under this roof had worked. For now. He had yet to know the sting of a hit or witness one land on his mother. I wasn't ignorant enough to pretend things would always stay like this. I would try—I would give whatever I could to preserve his innocence—but I couldn't afford to be naïve either.

That was what had me moving toward Keenan's closet, a plan forming. A dangerous one, but a necessary one. A plan I might never need to carry out if I could keep the next thirteen years as much a secret as I had these five.

Digging way into the back, I retrieved a few sets of old clothes, pajamas, socks, and underwear. A pair of shoes that still fit him but he didn't wear as much as the others. Items that wouldn't be easily missed. Then I found myself in the bathroom, rounding up old trial-sized toiletries I'd collected from hotel stays and dentist visits.

Next, I moved into my bedroom and gathered up the same types of items. I added an array of bandages and gauze, knowing that if life ever sent me down this desperate of a path, it would be because something bad had happened. The worst, or whatever stair-step was just above it.

Then I dumped everything I'd collected onto the hall floor just outside of the linen closet. I pulled out a couple of old, seldom-used flat sheets and packed Keenan's stuff into one, mine into the other. I had a different hiding spot for some emergency money I'd stashed away, a few dollars here, a few more there. Once I'd tied everything up, I shoved the two satchels into the far back of the closet, carefully concealing them with folded stacks of sheets and pillowcases. This was the one door Crew never opened, but still, I didn't want to take a chance.

After making sure everything was properly hidden, I closed the door and jogged down the stairs. Other than to clean it, I never went in Crew's office. There was an unspoken rule that it was off-limits, and really, it wasn't a place I wanted to visit. I'd seen Crew enter it as a man only to leave it as a monster too many times.

My pace didn't slow as I went to the desk. The air inside was stale, other than the faintest hint of whiskey. As I tore into each drawer, thumbing through files and paperwork, I found myself getting chills. Almost as though a ghost were lurking in the room, hovering over my shoulder as I searched.

Once I'd gone through everything in his desk, I moved to the filing cabinet and searched it. When nothing came up from that investigation, I started looking in less obvious spots. Beneath the floor rug. Behind the bookshelf. Between the books. I even opened the floor vents and reached down inside. There was nothing. Not that I'd expected there to be, but I'd let myself hope. The stacks of evidence Crew had against me were probably locked away in some private security box, stuffed inside some bank's vault. He wouldn't risk me being able to find them. He wouldn't chance his whole plan of keeping me from running by tucking the proof inside some desk drawer. It was blackmail. Untrue, though not untrue enough for a court of law. He had it stashed away in such a secret spot, I'd never find it.

I was stuck. Not that I didn't already know that. Not that I hadn't accepted that years ago. Until Keenan was grown, I wasn't going anywhere. I couldn't take my son and hope to escape, and I couldn't leave him to make my own run.

As I watched the sun rise that morning, I accepted that I was responsible for all of this. This hadn't happened *to* me; it had happened *because* of me. I'd dug my own grave, and I would lay in it.

# Sixteen

When Keenan and I did some grocery shopping the next day, I didn't miss the media vans and SUVs parked at the nicest hotel in the Medford city limits. Keenan paid them no attention as we walked by. He was too excited by the promise of picking out a treat from the candy bar section to pay attention to much of anything. Some of them were from big news stations, and some were smaller ones I recognized out of Portland. I wondered why they were still here. I didn't wonder who it was they were still here for.

Brecken had given his last interview yesterday, so why were a dozen crews still stationed here in town? When we reached the store, I made myself concentrate on my grocery list to distract myself. Every Monday, Crew gave me a cash allowance to use for everyday items, from groceries to gas. Making it work required budgeting and coupon-clipping, but we always had enough for what we needed. Maybe not what we wanted, but what we needed. I didn't have access to the bank account, nor did I have a credit card, per Crew's rules. It was another way for him to exert control and keep me on a short leash.

Since Crew was away, this Monday, I didn't have new funds to get through the week, so the list was limited to the essentials. After rounding up what I needed, and letting Keenan take as long as he wanted choosing a candy bar, we checked out and I shouldered the few recyclable bags I'd brought along for the walk back.

Crew had taken the only car, leaving his wife and son essentially stranded to wherever our feet could take us. I didn't see the familiar truck parked out front of the grocery store at first. It was Keenan who recognized it and waved at the driver, who was already crawling out.

Brecken smiled at us, coming closer until he could slide the bags off of my shoulders. "Figured you might want a ride." His hand brushed down my arm as he took the bags, then he exchanged high-fives with Keenan as we headed for his truck.

"Thanks," I said, catching myself as I started reaching for his hand. "How are you?"

He bumped his shoulder against mine. "Better now."

After pulling the truck door open, he helped Keenan into the back before setting down the groceries. When he noticed what was, or what *wasn't*, inside, he reached into his back pocket.

"Why don't you go get what you need?" He pulled out a few twenties and stuffed them into my hand. Before I could object, he added, "What you *really* need."

My fist closed around the money as I shifted. Money was power, no matter how people wanted to argue it. Crew had used it as a way to strip me of power, whereas Brecken was using it to give power back. "Do you need anything?"

"Everything I need is standing a foot and a half in front of me. I'm good." He caught himself just in time too, and his hand, which had been reaching for my waist, settled back at his side. "Take your time. Keenan and I will hang out in the air-conditioning, listening to rock 'n roll and eating candy."

Brecken waved at Keenan in the backseat, who already had melted chocolate all over his face and fingers from his candy bar. Crew would have insisted on hosing him off before letting him into the car. Brecken didn't even flinch when Keenan accidently touched the leather with his sticky fingers.

Making the return trip to the store, I grabbed a few fresh items I hadn't had enough for before, as well as some packages of granola bars, jerky, and nuts. Items that wouldn't spoil and didn't take up too much space. Once I got home, I'd stash it deep inside the linen closet. We'd have enough food and supplies to get us by for a couple of days at least, if that was what it came to. I wasn't hoping for a reason to run, because I knew how dangerous it would be, but I needed to be prepared for it.

Brecken and Keenan were rocking out to a classic Pearl Jam song, both of them playing air guitar in the same way.

"Encore," I greeted when I slid inside the truck.

Brecken turned down the radio and set the new bags into the back. "Need to go anywhere else?"

"All set." I grinned back at Keenan, who was still air-guitaring the heck out of "Alive." As we were leaving the parking lot, I pointed at the hotel parking lot. "Any idea what that's about?"

"The world decided they were missing out on the Medford County Fair?" He kept his face aimed forward as we drove by the brigade of news vehicles.

"I thought you gave your last interview?"

"I did." His shoulder lifted. "My media liaison with the marines said giving the interviews would probably draw extra attention. At least for a while. It'll blow over soon. Once everyone figures out I don't have any weird fetishes or dark secrets to unearth."

I stared out the windshield so he wouldn't see the look in my eyes. Our relationship might not have been a dark secret to him, but the world would think otherwise. If anyone found out he'd rekindled an old relationship with the married woman who lived next door, an affair that could last the same amount of time said woman's husband was in rehab, the story would spread so fast, the whole country would know in a matter of a day.

We'd have to be careful. More careful than we'd already been. This might have been a good time to put an end to what was going on between us, but the thought of letting him go so soon after getting him back was too much to bear. Everything came with a degree of risk, and having Brecken in my life was worth this one. I'd do my part to be extra careful, and I knew he would too.

"You can take the truck whenever you want to go somewhere. I'll get you an extra key," Brecken said as we turned down our street.

I was about to reply when I noticed someone on our porch as we pulled into the driveway. My heart stopped, ice forming in my veins. It wasn't until the person rose from the chair they were sitting on that my lungs went back to functioning.

"What's he doing here?" Brecken's voice was low, his eyes checking the rearview.

"He probably heard what happened with Crew. Wanted to check up on us." My hand was trembling, but not so much that Brecken noticed. I'd never realized how similar Crew and his father looked. From a distance, hiding in the shadows … they looked like clones.

"What do you want to tell him?" Brecken turned off the ignition, not letting anything show on his face.

Keenan had barely registered that we were back home.

"That I needed to run to the grocery store and you offered to give us a ride." I shoved the door open, reaching for a few bags in the back. "End of story."

Brecken tipped his head in acknowledgement before stepping out of the truck. "Come on, little man."

He unbuckled Keenan and helped him out of the truck before grabbing the rest of the bags and following me. He caught up to me, keeping his distance but staying close at the same time.

Keenan finally noticed who was waiting for us on the porch. "Hey, Grandpa's here. He never comes here."

*That was just fine with me.*

"Hi, Lester. Have you been waiting long?" I kept my voice as unaffected as my face, acting like it was no big deal that my degenerate father-in-law was waiting for me while I came strolling up the steps with the man I'd once promised to marry. Just like any other day, I told myself. Don't give him anything to suspect.

"Not too long," he answered. The *but long enough* was implied in his expression.

"Can I get you something to drink?" I shuffled the bags to one arm, digging my key out of my purse. *Something of the non percent-by-volume variety?*

"I came to check on you and Keenan. Make sure you were both doing okay." Lester's gaze cut to Brecken coming up the stairs with my groceries in one arm, Keenan hanging off his other like a limp monkey. "Looks like someone already beat me to it though."

"Yeah, you remember Brecken Connolly, right?" I waved between the two after pushing the door open. "He offered to give me a ride to the grocery store since I was out of groceries—and a car."

Lester held out his hand. Brecken held his arms out at his sides, indicating how full they were, followed by a shrug.

"Awfully neighborly of you."

Lester slid his hand into his pocket, looking between the two of us like he was waiting for something. I didn't know what, or maybe I did, but I wasn't going to confirm or deny it. Playing ignorant was my motto where all things Brecken was concerned.

"I heard about Crew. Checking himself into that damn rehab facility."

Before Lester finished speaking, Brecken had stepped inside the house, Keenan still hanging off of him. I could have kissed him for it. I was going to kiss him for it. Later. Behind locked doors. Sealed windows. Motion detectors.

"He's always been weak, taken the easy way out. Been an embarrassment to his mother and me, and now, his wife and son." Lester rolled his fingers, his knuckles popping one by one. "Anyway, I just wanted to check up on you two."

"Thank you." My body relaxed as he started down the stairs, stopped when he'd reached the bottom.

"I stopped by a couple of days ago, but you and Keenan weren't here. Still weren't back later that night," he said.

I made myself take a breath before answering. When dealing with someone like Lester, one must always think first before answering. "I took Keenan out of town for a

couple of days. To try to get his mind off of missing Crew."
I held a smile, holding his stare.

His fingers rolled across the handrail. "Did you head
out of town on your own two feet then?"

My breath caught. For half a second. "We took a bus."

"Ah. Of course." Lester's head bobbed, but he didn't
believe me. I should have known better than to think I could
get a lie past the devil himself. "You will give us a call if
anything comes up? Oh, and do me a favor and thank the
lance corporal for taking care of you two." Lester's gaze
skimmed down me like he could see Brecken's fingerprints
scattered all up and down my body. "Looks like he'd been
doing a mighty fine job of it."

My throat moved, but I couldn't swallow. My lungs
strained, but I couldn't breathe. Lester suspected something,
but he suspected everyone. He wouldn't have given Mother
Teresa the benefit of the doubt, least of all his daughter-in-
law.

"I'll let him know. Say hello to Margaret for me." With
each word, I chased away a smidgeon more fear.

I wasn't talking back to Lester, but in a way, I was. I
was proving I wouldn't be intimidated, I wouldn't be bul-
lied. He knew nothing, had no proof, but even if he did, I
wasn't sure he'd tell his son. Or if he did, it would be to
mock him. It would be to make him feel small and inadequate.

A cycle. A pattern. I recognized it, and I supposed that
was the reason my throat burned when I moved inside the
house and saw Keenan. Was it DNA that spread the monster
from one man to another? Or was it their environment? I
found myself praying it was one instead of the other. I found
myself willing to make a deal with whatever deity was lis-

tening that my son wouldn't grow up to be anything like Crew and his father.

A pattern.

A cycle.

A—

"Hey. You okay?" Brecken emerged from the kitchen, concern furrowing his brow when he noticed me.

When he started toward me, I shook it off. Keenan was nothing like Crew. He never would be.

"Did everything go all right out there?" Brecken followed me into the kitchen.

He'd started putting the groceries away already, but there were still a few left. I didn't miss how he'd left the bag of non-perishable items unpacked, sitting on the edge of the counter.

"Everything's okay. He's gone."

Brecken's arms came around me, his chest pressing into my back as his head tucked over my shoulder. "I missed you," he breathed, his arms winding tighter.

My whole body relaxed, letting me melt into him. There was nothing sexual about his embrace, nothing that suggested he was expecting more. This was nothing more than one person wanting to be close to another. My arms settled above his and I let my head fall against him, closing my eyes.

"I missed you." A tear slipped out the corner of my eye, those few words pertaining to so much more than last night. The six years prior. The countless years to come. Whatever lifetimes were to come where I'd have to exist without him. Here he was, with me, his body draped around mine, and I wasn't sure I'd ever missed him more than I did now.

"I've got some things I need to get done today. I'll be around town, close, but they're important." His lips pressed into my neck. "Are you okay if I leave? I'll keep my phone in my hand, can be here in two minutes if I have to be—"

"I'll be fine," I said, feeling like I really meant it. I was stronger than I was weak. Braver than I was scared. "We'll be fine," I added when the sound of Keenan's action figures smashing together sounded from the living room.

Brecken's gentle laugh vibrated against my back. "You do have the Captain and the Hulk close by if you need them." He pressed one more kiss into the column of my neck, letting it linger just long enough, before letting me go.

"I do have myself too, you know?"

Brecken smiled at me, tipping his chin. "Most badass superhero I've ever known."

# Seventeen

"I miss Brecken," Keenan groaned from where he was sprawled out on the living room floor, his action figures tumbling out of his hands.

"I do too," I said, setting down the book I was pretending to read.

It was getting close to bedtime, but I'd kept Keenan in since I noticed the news vans rolling up to the curb yesterday. It had been shortly after Brecken had left after our grocery shopping excursion, and even though most of them came and went, a couple of them had set up shop outside.

Brecken had sent me a text that he thought it would be best if he didn't chance coming over last night, in case anyone saw. I hated having to agree with him. So now we'd wasted two nights without each other, and with the way the news crews didn't seem in any particular hurry to leave, it didn't look like anything was going to change soon.

"If he can't come over here, why can't we just go over there?" Keenan rolled around on the floor aimlessly.

I slid off the couch to join him on the floor. Being confined indoors in the summer was no fun for a kid. I knew the news crews were here for Brecken, not to document the five-year-old running around in the yard next door, but I didn't know if they knew about Brecken's and my history. I never knew if the random neighbor passing by was dishing dirt to the polished newscasters in pressed suits or if they were just saying hello. I wasn't sure how far they'd dug into Brecken's history, or how much he might have said in his interviews. So I kept Keenan inside.

"Sweetie, I know. I'm sorry." My head turned toward the window that faced Brecken's. The curtain was closed, but I imagined being able to see him. For some reason, I pictured him throwing his arms up as another attempt to scramble eggs resulted in charring them. I found myself smiling at the curtain.

"Why can't they just go away?" Keenan rolled onto his tummy, glaring at the door. I'd told him the reason why he couldn't go outside, and he wasn't thrilled with the media.

"They will. Soon," I said, assuring him and myself. "Do you want to pick out a game to play? Your choice."

Keenan was considering that, as though another board game was as appealing as visiting the dentist, when the lights went out. All of them. In fact, it was pitch black outside too, from what I could see through the beveled rectangular windows on either side of the door.

"Mom?"

"It's okay. I think we just lost power." I rose from the floor and carefully made my way to the front door to peek out through one of the windows. The houses across the street were dark too. Even the streetlights were out. "Yep. Power's out. We better get the flashlights and candles."

"It's not stormy though." Keenan shuffled off the ground, his footsteps moving toward me.

I was already thinking that, wondering what could have caused an outage on such a calm summer night, when I felt my phone vibrate in my back pocket. When I pulled it out, I found a brief text: *The back door.*

Grabbing Keenan's hand, I wove through the house, grabbing a flashlight outside of the coat closet on the way.

"What are we doing?" Keenan whispered.

"Greeting a visitor."

"Don't people normally come to the front door?"

"Except for the ones who come to the back." Flicking on the flashlight, I found Keenan's face drawn up with confusion.

At least until I opened the door and he saw who was standing on the other side.

"Brecken!" he shouted so loudly, I worried it might have actually projected all the way out to the streets.

"Keenan!" Brecken replied with the same amount of excitement, minus the volume.

"I'm going to go get my flashlight so we can play hide-and-seek in the dark!" Keenan lunged into the darkness like he could see in it, his feet scampering up the stairs to his bedroom.

"Be careful!" I shouted to him.

"'Kay, Mom!"

Before I could say anything else, Brecken crashed into me, sending the back door slamming closed. The flashlight dropped out of my hand, and the surprised gasp that followed was silenced by his mouth covering mine. His hands roamed me like they wanted to be everywhere at once, his tongue pushing into my mouth, demanding my submission at the same time giving his own.

As soon as Keenan's footsteps started thumping down the stairs, Brecken let me go, hands, mouth, and body, and stepped away while I focused on not looking like I'd just been pinned against a door, making out.

"Missed me?" I guessed, still feeling the warmth of his lips coating mine.

He crouched to retrieve the flashlight. "I'll show you exactly *how* much I missed you later on. After someone's bedtime."

"I was thinking of showing you the exact same thing." I took the flashlight from him, my fingers brushing along his crotch as I passed.

A breath hissed through his teeth, and what sounded like his head hitting the wall behind him followed.

"Did your power go out too, Brecken?" Keenan's flashlight was on as he flew around the corner, an armful of toys clutched in his hold.

"The whole block's power went out."

"It's not even stormy," Keenan repeated.

"Weird."

My flashlight illuminated Brecken's face as he followed us into the living room. "*So* weird."

When he smirked, I lowered the beam. I didn't know how he'd done it, just that he had. I didn't care how either, because he was here, with us.

When Keenan grabbed Brecken's hand to pull him into a never-ending (at least until he crashed asleep) game of superheroes and building blocks, I headed into the kitchen to grab some candles. I'd stocked up on a bunch of Catholic prayer candles at the dollar store last year after a different power outage. Not because I was the praying kind of person, but because I was the kind of person who liked having a light in the dark.

I arranged some candles in the living room, then I moved upstairs to light up those rooms as well. Before heading back down, I paused at the top of the stairs to check the message I'd missed earlier this morning. The one I'd purposely missed. It was from Crew, and this one was lengthier than his others.

*I'm getting better. I am better. I've given up drinking. I've given up more. Miss you so much it hurts.*

My grip tightened around the phone, unsure what to think of his message. Did he really mean that? Did he believe it? Was he capable of it? Part of me hoped for it, realizing the task of surviving the next thirteen years would be much easier to achieve if Crew dropped the alcohol and what came with it. Part of me knew better than to hope for that though, because expecting the worst was what would keep my guard up when he came home. I'd rather expect the worst and be surprised than hope for the best and be disappointed.

He was either going to come back from rehab recovered, or he was going to come back the same, hitting me when the mood and alcohol turned sour. How much or little time I spent with Brecken wouldn't change that, so I was going to enjoy the time we did have together.

As I made my way down the stairs, I heard the boys talking as they made what sounded like another massive fort.

"Hey, Brecken?" Keenan's voice took on a serious edge. "Sometimes I wish you were my dad. My real dad." He paused for a second while I grabbed the handrail for support. "Don't tell Mom that though."

Like myself, Brecken was silent. I clicked my flashlight off and took the last few stairs.

"If I had my choice of any kid in the whole entire world to be my kid, I'd pick you. No doubt about it." Brecken's voice filled up the dark space, the smile in his voice evident. "Don't tell your mom that though."

Keenan giggled, getting back to making his fort.

When I flicked the flashlight back on, Brecken was already looking at me from across the living room. As though he'd known I was there the whole time. Like he was able to find me no matter how thick the dark was.

**T**hanks to his energy stores, Keenan didn't fall asleep until almost eleven. When he did finally go out, Brecken looked almost as exhausted. At least he did until I whispered something in his ear, took his hand, and led him up the stairs.

Keenan was all tucked into his fort for the night, since he'd made us promise not to carry him up to his bed when he fell asleep. I loved our time together as the three of us, but I also longed for time as just the two of us.

When we reached the top of the stairs, I spun around and worked his belt, feeling as though two days without him had felt more like two decades. My body was reeling with anticipation, knowing I'd come as soon as he pushed inside me. It would be over too soon, but that was what second times were for. And third times. We could take our time later. Right now, I needed him to fulfill a need only he could meet.

"Wait." His eyes clamped closed when my hand slipped inside his jeans, palming his stiff length. He rolled his neck then gently wound his hands around my wrist, removing it from his pants. He winced as he did it though.

"What are we waiting for?" I glanced at where a prominent bulge was pushing against his zipper. My body was just as ready for him.

"I want to show you something first."

"Does this have anything to do with a certain piece of your anatomy? If not, it can wait."

He muttered something about me being impossible, then his face got serious. "I want to show you some self-defense moves. Some basic maneuvers I learned in the military. A few more I picked up from a place in town that teaches women's self-defense classes."

"You want to teach me what?" My mind started to clear the hormones from my system. A little.

"Self-defense."

I blinked at him. "Why?"

"Don't make me answer that question."

"Why not?"

"Because you know why."

My heart was still beating fast, but thanks to a different kind of adrenaline. "And what? I'm supposed to drive my palm into his throat if he starts swinging at me again?" I had to remind myself to keep my voice down. "Is that all I need to do to keep myself from being beaten by my husband? Learn a few simple self-defense techniques so I can keep from 'becoming a victim'?"

Brecken stayed quiet, letting me get it all out. His hands on his hips, his eyes on me, he took everything I gave him.

"Is that why I've been beaten all this time? Because I didn't stand up for myself? Because I didn't know how to defend myself?"

When I waited for his answer, he gave it to me. "No." His jaw worked. "That's not what this is about."

"No, what this is about is you suggesting I actually fight back if he tries hitting me again. You want to know what will happen if I do that?" My hand covered my chest. "He will keep hitting me. Harder. Longer. I've survived, I've made it, because I haven't fought back."

Brecken was quiet once I stopped going off on him. His façade was as calm as mine was not. Then his arm lifted toward the stairs, before rotating toward me. "Don't you want to do more than just survive? More than just 'make it'?"

My anger was crumbling, revealing what it had really been masking—fear. My arms curled around myself as I leaned into the wall behind me. "He's in rehab. He says he's better."

"It hasn't even been a week—"

"He's going to get better. He says he's not going to drink anymore. He says he's not going to hit me anymore —"

"Stop, Camryn. Just fucking stop." Brecken's hands tied around his neck. "You might be content to bet your life on the promises of a piece of shit, but I am not." His arms fell back at his sides, his hands balling and loosening. "I'm not teaching you this to save my conscience. I'm teaching you this to save your life."

I gave myself a minute. The thought of hitting Crew back when he took a swing at me was almost comical. One, because I was half his size. Two, because I could almost picture the look on his face when I did, and it was as funny as it was menacing.

"If I hit him back, Brecken"—my eyes lifted to his— "I'm going to have to run right after."

His head tipped. "*If* he hits you again, I'm going to have to run with you."

"So this is for the worst-case scenario?"

His eyes answered my question.

"Okay." Exhaling, I pushed off the wall. "Teach me how to save my life."

# eighteen

"Parts of the body to aim for."

Brecken circled me in the hallway a couple of nights later. The power had been restored from that "freak" power outage, but the hallway was dark except for the candles burning around us. We needed some light, but I was too paranoid to keep the lights on at night with Brecken in here and the media out there.

"Eyes, ears, nose, mouth, throat, groin, knee, legs," I listed off, rolling my eyes so he'd see he'd sufficiently ground that into me already.

"Parts of your body to use in an attack." He peeked down the stairs where the fort was still standing, a couple of Avenger slippers sticking out from inside it.

Bedtime had come earlier tonight, thankfully, since Brecken had imposed two hours of training every night once Keenan fell asleep before he'd let me get physical with him in a different way.

Another lifting of the eyes. "Elbows, knees, head, knife-edge of the hand, palm of the hand, et cetera."

"Et cetera being?"

I sighed. "Nails, teeth, and pretty much anything else I can use to inflict enough damage to get away."

His brow lifted, giving me an impressed look. Then he reached for his shirt and pulled it over his head. "Next question." He tossed his shirt at my feet, a challenge in his eyes.

"See? Now you're actually motivating me to learn. Good teacher."

His thumb brushed the line of notches on his belt. "Demonstrate how to break out of this hold." His hand circled my wrist, pulling me toward him.

For half a beat, my mind went blank. The surge of adrenaline drowned out what he'd taught me. Then I remembered: take a breath, count to three, then react. Usually the first way we were inclined to react when being attacked was the last way we should.

Taking a deep squat, I bent my elbow, curling it under his forearm until my wrist snapped out of his hand. I bounced up, giving him a victorious look.

"It doesn't help if you stay where you are once you break free, you know?"

My head tipped. "No shit. Now take off your belt already, I owned that break."

Brecken rubbed his mouth in an attempt to hide his smile before lowering his hands to undo his belt. Once it was unclasped, he slid it free, one loop at a time, the smirk on his face making the spot between my legs ache.

"Turn around." He spun his finger, moving toward me.

I did as asked, feeling heady with power. The knowledge of how to defend oneself had an effect that was hard to explain. The trust it took to allow someone to teach you, touching you in vulnerable places, possibly triggering uncomfortable memories, made the reward that much greater once I overcame all of those obstacles. With anyone else besides Brecken, this wouldn't have worked. I knew he'd never hurt me, which made it easier to allow him to pretend otherwise.

His chest pressed into my back as his arms came around me. "Break out of this," he instructed, right before his arms tied around my body.

I went rigid as he wrestled me backward, his hold going tighter. He'd taught me how to break out of this kind of hold, but he'd grabbed me up higher before, so I still had the use of my elbows. I didn't know how to break out of this with my elbows pinned to my sides.

"I don't know how." My voice wobbled, a ribbon of fear creeping inside. "You didn't teach me this one."

"Think, Camryn. *Think*." Instead of easing up, his hold only deepened.

I wanted him to let me go. I wanted him to take it easy on me.

I needed him to hold on to me. I needed him to make it hard on me.

Remembering what he'd told me, I took a breath, cleared my head, and counted to three. He hadn't taught me what to do in this kind of a situation, at least not step-by-step, but he'd taught me how to fight. He'd taught me how to survive.

When the next surge of adrenaline crested, I stomped my foot down on his, throwing my head back against his at the same time. Instantly, his arms fell away as he staggered back. Except he didn't stop staggering like he usually did—he fell to the floor instead.

"Oh shit, Brecken." My smile vanished as I rushed toward where he'd gone down. "I'm sorry. I wasn't thinking. I went full power."

I fell to his side, my hand covering my mouth when I noticed the red mark on his forehead. We'd always trained where I performed the moves but without power behind them. Except for this time. The fear and adrenaline had made me sloppy.

He rubbed his head another second as he shook the foot I'd just stomped on.

"I am so, so sorry." I leaned over him to check his head, feeling terrible.

That was when I heard it. A soft chuckle that was growing with each note.

"Are you laughing?" I leaned back, resting a hand on my hip.

"Of course I'm laughing. I just got knocked on my ass by someone I've got fifty pounds and half a foot on."

I lifted the strap of my tank top back into place. It felt nice not to have to hide when I was with Brecken. Not to be so concerned with covering every mark and scar on my body. The ones from last week had mostly faded, but I had plenty of the permanent kind that would never fade. "Yeah, you kinda did, didn't you?"

He leaned up onto his elbows, his gaze dropping to my neckline. I wasn't wearing a bra either. At the end of the day, I was so tired of all the extra layers, I couldn't wait to get off as many as possible.

"I must be a really great teacher," he said.

I draped my arm across his chest, moving my head above his. "Or else I'm a really great student."

Peaking an eyebrow, I held my chest above his face, feeling my nipples harden from the warmth of his breath seeping through the thin cotton. When his teeth caught one of them, my breath hitched, my thighs squeezing when his tongue tasted me through the material. When he released me, my heart started to beat again.

"Either way, at least I know you can take him down if you need to. That's all I care about."

Swinging my leg over his lap, I reached for the bottom of my tank top. "That's *all* you care about?"

"No." His eyes dropped to where I was working my tank up my body. "That's definitely not all I care about."

I paused, the hem at my chest line. "What else?"

His tongue touched his lips as he pressed up onto his elbows. "I care about you. Giving you what you want. Making you feel good." His hips thrust into me, creating enough friction to draw a moan from me.

I finished pulling my shirt up my body and dropped it on his face once it was off. When he moved to swipe it away, I laid my hand on it, keeping him blindfolded. A grunt ground out of him as my other hand worked his zipper free.

"You are definitely not a good student." His voice caught when my hand formed around him, smoothing up and down. "You're a very bad student. A very *good* bad student."

Leaving the tank over his eyes, I freed myself from my shorts as quickly as I could, yanking his jeans down just enough to free what I needed. So much was charging through my body, from desire to love, power to submission, that I was desperate to feel our connection. Desperate to have his body force from mine what needed to be released.

There wasn't enough time to take off my underwear, so I shoved them aside and joined my body with his, not stopping until I was resting on his lap.

It took him a few breaths before he could speak. The whole time, my tank concealed his eyes, even as I started to ride him. "I wasn't done with my strip tease."

He was smiling, his hands covering my knees as I took control. The feel of his rough jeans rubbed against the insides of my thighs, the fraying seams biting at the sensitive skin. My orgasm was already forming, rising from deep inside.

I leaned down so my chest was bouncing against his with each thrust. "You can finish that once I'm finished with you."

# nineteen

Something reached down into my dream and pulled me out of it. It wasn't the same phenomenon I was used to waking up to in the middle of the night though—depending on his level of intoxication, Crew's hands or fists or the sound of a glass shattering in the office. This was something else.

Blinking awake, nothing but darkness surrounded me. And then I saw him. Standing framed inside the window, staring not out of it but at me.

I rolled onto my side, checking the time. "Can't sleep?"

He was still naked, and with the moonlight spilling in through the window, he stole the air from my lungs. "Don't want to."

"Afraid to?" I said slowly.

"Don't want to miss anything." He lifted his arms, framing me with his fingers for moment. Then his hands fell back at his sides. "And yeah, maybe a little afraid to. You know, after what happened that night."

I sat up in bed. "Back in the cabin? You haven't slept since then?" That had been almost two weeks ago. He'd been awake every morning when I woke up, and now that I was thinking about, I was always the first one to fall asleep after we managed to break our bodies apart.

His shoulders lifted. They were wider every day. "I slept those first couple of nights at my place."

"Brecken, you need to sleep."

"No, I need *you*." His arms crossed. "I don't put sleep and you in the same category."

"Well, that's sweet and romantic and bound to get you laid." I gave him an overdone smile. "At least right up until you kill yourself from it."

His eyes lifted as though I was being dramatic. "I'm having a déjà vu moment here. It's like we've had this conversation before."

"We have. And I won."

He stuck his thumb into his chest. "Which means it's my turn."

Sliding over in bed, I flourished my arm at the open, *warm* space I'd made for him. "You've taught me to how to break out of just about every hold imaginable. I think I can take you if you decide to pin me to the bed again."

His mouth opened and a sigh spilled out before he shoved off the windowsill and approached me. "No more arguing. You—*you* actually need your sleep." He slid into the space beside me, collecting me in his arms, and pulled me to him. His mouth lowered to my head. "Keeping up with a five-year-old all day long, that's no joke."

My arm curled around him, my eyes closing. "And keeping up with a virile twenty-six-year-old all night long's no joke either."

His muffled laugh was the last sound I heard, his kiss the last thing I felt.

"**W**e get to go to the park today *and* stay as long as I want?" Keenan still couldn't believe it, even though I had our bag packed with lunch and we were steps away from the front door.

"Yes. To both." I grabbed his hand before opening the door and sucking in a breath.

This was our first excursion leaving through the front door in broad daylight in days. With the media still lurking around, I'd made it a priority to avoid the ever-ready microphones and cameras as much as possible. Today, I was done hiding. I was done exchanging what might happen for what really could.

Today, we were going to the park.

When we stepped outside, I went through the motions of locking the door and helping Keenan down the stairs, but my heart felt like it had sprouted hummingbird wings.

"Excuse me? Miss?" We'd barely made it down the walkway before one of them noticed us. "Mrs. Graves, can I ask you a few questions?"

Keenan stopped, doing the polite thing I'd taught him to do when adults talked to him. I wasn't concerned with being polite or setting an example at that point though. I was too focused on getting away before any of them could look into my eyes and somehow read the truth I knew was spilling from them no matter how I tried to hide it.

"Mrs. Graves? Have you talked with Lance Corporal Connolly since his return? How would you describe his state of mind? How does it feel to be living next door to a POW who went through so much? Next to a hero?"

Grabbing Keenan's hand, I marched down the sidewalk as fast as our feet would take us. Keenan didn't put up any fight or even mention the encounter, but by the time we'd made it to the park, I still couldn't shake the encounter. How was Brecken supposed to move on when they wouldn't let it go? How could he put the nightmare to rest when people like that kept resurrecting it?

How could we ever hope to keep this a secret when I couldn't step down my front stairs without being noticed?

"Mom?" Keenan's big blue eyes blinked up at me, and he still held my hand despite the fact we were toeing the edge of the playground.

I assembled a smile. "I'm okay. Go have fun."

He stuck beside me for another minute before dashing off toward the swings. He didn't resurface from his endless craze of play until two hours later, when he came back starving and thirsty. After scarfing down his lunch, guzzling a bottle of water, and stretching out in the grass for a whole minute and a half, he took off back to the playground, refreshed and ready to go.

I'd brought a book to read and some kindergarten pamphlets I'd picked up from a few local schools, but I found myself more interested in watching him. His innocence was so unabashed, so infinite-seeming. It was so unfair how quickly that could be taken away. How fleeting it really was.

"Good day for the park." A shadow moved behind me and cut through the sun.

I was familiar enough with the voice that I didn't need to look back. "Every day's a good day for the park." I thought of the day I'd brought Keenan here a couple weeks ago, letting him stay until after dark.

"I haven't seen much of Crew around lately." Gina took a seat beside me on the bench, waving at one of her daughters, who was chasing Keenan. Who looked rightly horrified. Any spawn of Gina Meyers one was wise to avoid.

"He's been gone. For work," I added, not really caring what people in the community knew. The truth. The lie. They'd believe what they wanted no matter what I told them. I knew that from experience.

"How much longer will he be gone?"

"A couple more weeks, I think." The timeframe made my throat constrict. Two weeks could take forever. Two weeks could pass in an instant.

She was quiet for a moment, staring into the park blankly. "Can you believe those bloodsuckers parked out front of Brecken's house like that? You'd think they've gotten enough from him, but I guess there's always more, right?" Gina glanced at her nails. They looked shiny and freshly manicured. She started to pick at the crimson paint, one nail at a time. "Have you talked with any of them yet?"

My forehead creased. "Why would I do that?"

Her youngest daughter was calling for her, asking her to watch before she went down the big slide. Gina never once looked up from her nails. "You know, with you guys being so serious before."

My hands curled in my lap. "No. And I'd prefer if they never find that out."

Gina's head turned toward me. She watched me for a moment, searching. The thing about Gina was that she'd spent her whole life living life in a puddle—she didn't know the first thing about what an ocean looked like.

"Did you see the article that came out today? The one about him and the other POWs?" she asked, still working at her nails.

"No," was all I answered.

"Probably for the best. If I could go back in time and unsee those pictures and unread those words, I would." She gave a shiver. "It's crazy to think how much the human body can endure, you know? Makes me look back on childbirth and wonder why the hell I did all that screaming."

My hands clasped then unclasped in my lap. I'd known the first article would be published today in one of the major national magazines, before the newspaper article, then the television interview would go public. I'd already prepared myself, knowing I had no intention of reading or watching any of them. I knew enough. I didn't need to know it all.

"I have a hell of a lot more respect for Brecken Connolly after reading that than I did before." She pulled her phone from her purse, checking it. Whatever she found made her frown. "That's a man who wouldn't just leave someone behind without telling her he was leaving? He's the one who'd lay down his life for his woman, you know? He sure as hell wouldn't forget to drop her a line to let her know he was thinking about her. Or that he'd left and when he'd be back." Gina combed her chipped nails through her styled hair, raking at it until she'd twisted it into a messy bun on the top of her head.

It should have been more obvious. I should have figured it out before now. But I'd been too busy trying to stay out of Crew's business, rather than trying learn about any more of it.

The wife was sitting next to the mistress. I didn't need to ask her to confirm it—she was confirming it in every other way. When other wives might have let loose on the woman they'd just learned had become an "extracurricular activity" in her husband's life, I felt … nothing. Maybe some curiosity as to how long it had been going on, some wonder if her husband had any idea, even a bit of sadness, though not for myself. For her. Did he hit her too? Would he eventually? Did she know about his drinking? Had she fallen for the man only to be stuck with the monster, as I had?

Watching Keenan run around the playground, healthy, happy, and alive, some of the guilt from the past melted away. Crew didn't deserve my guilt, no matter the offense.

"We'd better head out. I'll have to get dinner started sometime today." Gina stood, blinking to clear her eyes.

My gaze moved to her. My husband's mistress. "Say hello to Jerry for me, will you?"

She slid her purse onto her shoulder, kicking off the wedges she had on. "I sure will." Leaning down to pick up the shoes, she hollered at her girls that they were leaving.

"He's a lucky man. Be sure to tell him that for me."

When Gina glanced at me, I was all smiles, but I thought she could see what was behind it. She yelled for her girls, who were still glued to the monkey bars, before starting to leave.

The park went back to being peaceful after that, and as promised, I didn't push Keenan to leave until he told me he was ready. The kid had days of energy to work off, and he'd made that his mission.

It wasn't dark when we left the park this time, but it was dusk. We'd left because he was hungry and he'd demolished the last of the snacks a few hours ago. A couple of news vans were still staged outside of Brecken's house, but no one noticed us this time. However, I noticed something new in his front lawn. Flowers. Bundles of them laid out, stacked on top of each other, the way you saw on the news when someone famous had died or there'd been some awful tragedy. It took me a moment to realize why the front of

Brecken's yard was covered in flowers—the article. I was probably the only person in the community who hadn't read it, and those who had were moved enough to leave flowers for him. He hadn't died, but there'd been a tragedy. It felt like there was no end to it.

After Keenan ate a grilled cheese sandwich, he started to fall asleep at the dinner table. He'd finally worn himself out. Collecting him in my arms, I carried him up to his bedroom, taking extra care on the stairs. All of my bruising was gone, except for the worst on my side and the marks on my back. With Crew gone, no new ones had been added. Today had been the first time in years I'd been able to wear something short-sleeved. The feel of air moving across my arms, the tickle of my son's hair as his head lolled to the side, I felt free. I'd found freedom even while living in the confines of a cage.

It gave me hope for the future. Hope that I could endure whatever came.

After tucking him in, I waited for the text. Brecken usually waited until nine or ten to sneak over, waiting until it was dark and quiet outside. Most nights, Keenan was still awake, so he could spend time with him too. He'd be upset in the morning when he realized he'd fallen asleep before he could play with his real-life superhero, but there was tomorrow night. And the one after that.

I stopped when I realized I didn't want to count how many we had left. Not many.

The text came in a little after ten. It asked me to meet him in the backyard. That was a first, but I didn't think much of it. Brecken had been doing a lot of things out of the ordinary lately. Leaving his house several times a day, giving vague answers when I asked him what he'd been up to.

He'd been working on something, though I didn't know what.

Turning off the back porch light, I moved out into the yard, letting my eyes adjust. Before they did, his hand formed around mine.

"Do you listen to every man who asks you to meet him in a dark backyard late at night?"

His voice instantly made me smile. "Only the really insane, deranged ones."

His lips pressed into my temple before he led me across the dark yard. "Good to know."

"What are we doing?" I glanced down his driveway toward the street. There were a couple of vans still there, but it was quiet. No reporters milling around the sidewalks.

"I'm showing you what I've been doing during my days when I can't be with you, thanks to them." He gave the vans in the street the side-eye before stopping in front of his garage tucked back at the end of the driveway. He crouched to grab the door handle then lifted it slowly. Even slower when it made a couple of creaks.

I held my breath, checking the street again. Nothing.

Once Brecken had opened the big garage door, he flipped on the lights, grabbed my hand, and pulled me inside. He didn't say anything until he'd closed the big door again.

When he waved at what was taking up most of the space, my forehead creased. "You got a new car?"

His arms fell at his sides. "No. This isn't for me." He came around the front end; he'd backed the car into the garage to make it easier to pull out. "This is for *you*."

"You got me a new car?" My forehead creased deeper.

"It's not exactly new, but yeah, it's for you." He patted the hood and stopped in front of me.

It was a silver Honda four-door. Nothing flashy or fancy, but it had that reliable, I'll-never-let-you-down look. Compared to having no car, it was like being given a Ferrari or something, but I wasn't sure where he was going with this. Brecken was smart—he knew he couldn't just buy me a car.

"What's this for, Brecken?"

Grabbing my hand, he led me around to the trunk. When he popped it open, my hand went to my stomach.

"This is for the worst case. Isn't it?" My eyes ran over the items stuffed in the back: sleeping bags, pillows, bottled water, food, clothes … a first aid kit. My feet slid back. "I don't want to think about that."

He guided me forward again. "That doesn't mean we shouldn't be prepared for it."

I thought about what this car meant, what kind of a hopeless situation I'd have to be in to use it. "If I have to use this car, that means I'm having to run. I can't run. We've talked about this. He'll find us. He'll take Keenan away from me." My voice broke every few words, my eyes fixed on the car seat he'd thought to have buckled into the backseat already.

"He's not taking Keenan away from you. You hear me?" He stepped in front of me, his hands cupping my face. "Whatever worst case it might come to, it will never come to that. I give you my word."

"You can't be sure—"

His eyes lowered directly in front of mine. "I will kill him before I let it come to that." He didn't blink, his voice didn't waver. "I will end him before I let him try to take your son away from you. *That's* how sure I am that no matter what, you're not going to be separated from Keenan."

He didn't let me go. He held my face, his eyes comforting mine, until I felt an overwhelming sense of relief, followed by gratitude. Setting aside what he'd just sworn to me, having this car available and stocked provided a level of peace I hadn't expected to find in the midst of this mess.

"The key will be in this drawer." Brecken led me around to the side of the garage where a few shelves had been built into the wall. He opened the middle drawer of his toolbox to show me where he'd hidden the key. "You'll need to grab that, and this ..." He crouched to pull an old metal coffee container from the bottom shelf, then he popped off the lid. What I saw inside made my breath hitch. "Don't forget it. I stuffed some money into the glove box, but this will get you much farther."

It wasn't a small coffee tin. It was one of the big ones. The kind grandparents used to keep on their kitchen counter. It was stuffed with money. Rolls of it. Mostly tens and twenties, but I'd seen some fives and fifties rolls inside too. There was tens of thousands of dollars in that coffee can.

"Brecken, I couldn't—"

"You better."

It wasn't just the money though. It was the thought of leaving ... him.

"You need to be able to take care of Keenan and yourself. You're going to need this to get away."

"But what about you?" My teeth sank into my lip. "You can come with us."

He snapped the lid back on the tin and shoved it back onto the bottom shelf. "In the event I'm not able to though, you need to be ready."

He didn't say anything else; he didn't have to. I knew what it meant if he couldn't escape with us.

He opened the passenger door and sat down so he could show me the contents of the glove box. Inside was a roll of money, a few maps, a cell phone with its charger, and a couple of passports. One for me and one for Keenan. They weren't real, but they looked real enough. Knowing Brecken, they'd be real enough to get us through airport security too. My eyes welled when I realized that he'd given me back my wings. One man had clipped them—this one had fixed them.

"How did you do all of this? How did you have time for it all?" It had only been a couple of weeks. This sort of plan seemed like it would takes months to put together. "Giving interviews, working out, spending all night with us, being the world's hero?"

Brecken closed the glove box. "I never asked to be the world's hero. All I ever wanted was to be yours."

My heart ached until my hand connected with his. "You are." I gave a little tug, and he moved out of the car. "You always have been."

Tying my other fingers through his, I lifted up to kiss him. He let me set the pace, standing there holding my hands at his sides as I attempted to thank him with the conviction of my lips. When I leaned back a while later, his eyes stayed closed, a peaceful look on his face.

"We've only got a little more time together." The space between his eyebrows slowly creased. "Are you sure you don't want to run away now? We've got plenty of money that could keep us good and invisible for a long time. Keenan, you, and me." His eyes opened, searching mine. "He'd never find us."

If this was a fairy tale, as it so often felt when I was with him, my answer would be yes. But this wasn't a fairy tale, this was the opposite, so my answer could only take one shape. He read the answer in my eyes before I spoke it.

"I'd do it if it was just Crew and me and you, but it's not." His fingers tensed around mine. "Keenan. I have to do what's right for him. Running away isn't. I can't risk what could happen. I *won't* risk it."

If we did what Brecken was suggesting, someone would pay with their life. Whether it was Crew's physical one, the rest of Brecken's spent behind bars, or Keenan's spent on the run or in the clutches of a monster for the next decade and a half, someone would pay a dear price. Staying would cost me, but it was a price I'd already paid. One I was willing to keep paying.

"Staying isn't the right solution either, Camryn." His hand lifted to my hairline, tracing the fading mark from my fall down the stairs.

"Even when you have two bad choices, you still have to make a choice. Staying is the better of the two."

His mouth opened, but he clamped it closed, swallowing whatever he'd been about to say. A storm rolled through his eyes before he let out a long breath. "Thirteen years?"

The corner of my mouth twitched. "It always goes by faster than it seems like it will."

He pulled me to him, one arm tying around me at a time. It felt like the same kind of embrace he used to pull me into when he was about to ship out for a deployment. "I'm not worried about the time. I'm worried about what I'll do if he puts his hands on you again."

I felt his jaw clench beside my head. "Well, don't turn thirteen years into a life sentence please."

His hold tightened before he let me go. Holding hands, we moved toward the front of the garage.

As he opened up the garage door, as slowly and quietly as before, I added, "I can deal with living with Crew for now. I can't handle having to live without you forever."

When the door was open, before we stepped out into the night, he turned to face me. "No matter what, I'll always be with you."

My throat constricted, realizing what he was saying. I'd lost him once. I wasn't losing him again. No matter what, he wasn't sacrificing any more of himself.

My hand settled over his heart. "I know."


It was the middle of the night. The spot beside me was cool, the depression of his body barely noticeable. He was at the window again, but this time he wasn't looking inside; he was staring outside. His whole body was tense, like he was standing guard and expecting the enemy.

"Come to bed. Please." I brushed the hair out of my face and dropped my hand onto the spot on mattress where he'd been when I'd fallen asleep.

After leaving the garage, he'd carried me up to my guest room, took off my clothes one piece at a time, his mouth tasting every part of me as he did, then he'd laid me down and moved inside me in the same restrained, unhurried way. As soon as either one of us got close, he'd stop, wait until the rush had receded, and continue. When I did finally come, it was the most powerful thing I'd ever felt. I'd somehow managed to feel as though I was the single most invincible creature on the planet and, at the same time, the most fragile. I shattered around him at the same time I fused back together.

I could still feel him moving inside me, still hear his breath outside of my ear.

"I trust you. Come to bed."

His body only seemed to further cement to his perch at the window.

I knew I couldn't fall back asleep just as much as I knew he wasn't close to caving to my request, so I slid out of bed and padded out of the room.

"Camryn?"

"Be right back," I said before moving down the hall and into the master bedroom.

I hadn't spent a single night in here since Crew left. The only time I came in here was to grab fresh clothes, and I'd come to dread even those few minutes there. This room, as welcoming as it appeared, was my own private hell. It was saturated with bad memories and feelings. The chamber where Crew used his body to misuse mine, in so many more ways than one.

Rushing through the bedroom, I went into the bathroom and kneeled in front of my sink. I had to reach deep inside the cupboard to find it, but I guessed I'd remember the feel of the plastic soap box in my next life too. After pulling it out, I popped it open and picked up what I kept hidden inside. My hand closed around it, feeling the cool metal warm in my palm.

When I left the master bedroom, I sealed the door behind me, then I made my way back to him. He was still standing at the window, staring out it like he could see things I couldn't. When he heard me coming, he turned away from the window.

"Here. You're going to need these."

His gaze went to the tags hanging from my hand, something sparking in his eyes. "But I'm not leaving."

Lifting the chain, I dropped it around his head. The tags clattered down his chest, swinging into place. "But you're not staying either."

His shoulders tensed when he realized what I was getting at. "I'll be right next door."

"I know." I stared at the window over his shoulder. "But it'll feel like you're on the other side of the world."

His tongue worked into his cheek. "You should keep them. You've had them this long. I want you to."

My head shook as I backed a few steps away when he started to slide off the chain. "The only reason I had those was because I thought you were dead. I'd rather not have them and know you're alive." I wrapped my arms around my body. "Somewhere."

"Somewhere?" I heard the puzzled note in his voice. "I'll be right here. Fifty feet away. I'm not going anywhere. Not without you. Not until you."

My weight shifted. "Thirteen years, Brecken. That's a long time. I don't expect you to wait for me. I don't want you to wait that long for me."

He moved farther away from the window, closer to me. "What do you mean?"

My eyes closed so I could concentrate. "I want you to be happy. I want you to live your life and make up for lost time." My breath was echoing in my ears, my heartbeat sounding far away. "I don't want you to spend the next decade and a half waiting for some damaged girl who's only going to be more broken when she gets to you."

Brecken let out a sharp huff. "I *am* happy. I *am* living my life and making up for lost time. I *am* going to spend the next decade and a half waiting for the woman I love, no matter what condition she comes to me in." My eyes opened to see him stab his finger at the space between us. "I'm staying right here."

"You'll be living next door to the woman you love and the man she married. For years and years. Don't put yourself through that kind of torture, not again."

His finger lifted to land on me. His chest was moving hard, his eyes darker than normal. "Getting to be by you? Getting to catch a glimpse of you? Getting to hear your voice?" He exhaled sharply. "That's fucking paradise."

I'd been prepared to attempt to convince him to live his life, but all of the reasons I'd come up with vanished when I saw the way he was looking at me. There was love, and there was what we had. It was the kind of feeling that couldn't be substituted or faked. It was the kind that spanned time and distance.

"Brecken …" The last of my fight flitted past my lips.

He moved toward me, lifted me in his arms, and carried me back to bed. He held me against him as I fell back asleep, his fingers tracing down the canyon of my spine.

"I'm not going anywhere," he repeated, like a lullaby, until I'd gone under.

# twenty

The sheets were a wet, tangled storm around my body again, but that wasn't what had woken me. The sun was creeping in through the windows, but that wasn't what had woken me either. It was Brecken beside me, writhing in his sleep, his skin shiny with sweat. He was making little gasping noises, like he couldn't get enough air.

He'd fallen asleep, I was thankful for that, and as much as I knew he could benefit from a few more hours, I couldn't stand to watch him suffer. Even if it was only in his sleep.

Sitting up, I said his name at the same time I dropped my hand on his chest.

His eyes flashed open, a roar emanating from his chest as he grabbed hold of me. He had me on my back, pinned to the mattress again, but this time his hands were tied around my throat.

"Brecken." My voice came out more whisper than cry as I squirmed beneath him.

He didn't respond. His fingers only drilled tighter into me, unfamiliar eyes staring down at me.

My hands came around his as I stared at him. "Please, Brecken."

His grip tightened, his body quivering from the force he was exerting.

"I can't breathe." My words were more an enunciated gasp as I struggled for air. My fingers tried braiding through his, but they were zippered shut and searing hot against my throat.

My vision went blurry on the outside edges as my lungs labored for breath. I felt the energy draining from my body, the fight siphoning from my veins. As my fingers fell away from his, the haze started to clear from his eyes.

As soon as he realized what he was waking up to, his eyes widened and his hands instantly released my neck. He rolled off of me, moving away from the bed.

"Christ. What the fuck's the matter with me?" He didn't stop striding away from the bed until he'd put himself as far from me as the room would allow.

I couldn't help but notice the extreme difference between this time and the last time I'd come between him and his nightmares. The first time, he'd pulled me close. This time, he was pushing himself away.

"Brecken—"

His hand flew in the air. "Don't you dare tell me you're okay. Don't you dare."

My throat was throbbing. My airway still felt constricted. I resisted the urge to gasp and rub my neck though. He was punishing himself enough without having to see me struggle.

"I was suffocating you." His elbows closed around his head as he disappeared deeper into the corner. "I could have killed you."

Quietly clearing my throat, I slid to the edge of the bed. His hand extended at me when I swung my feet over the edge, making himself clear.

"You didn't kill me," I said, staying where I was.

His head lifted just enough for his eyes to meet mine. "This time."

Even though he looked away, my eyes stayed leveled on him. "You won't kill me."

A puff of air came from his mouth. "Some hero I am. The woman I love has to look me in the face and lie to me about believing I won't kill her."

Anger pulsed in my blood. "I'm not lying."

Instead of arguing with me, he gathered up his clothes scattered around the floor. "Why didn't you fight me off like I've shown you? Why didn't you drill me in the face with your elbow? Or knee me in the fucking balls? Why didn't you at least try to defend yourself?" He paused with his arms full of his clothes, his eyes already on the door.

"Because I don't have to defend myself against you. Because you won't hurt me."

I glared at him as he slid into his clothes. Not because I was mad at him for what had happened to me, but because I was mad about what had happened to him. Mad about what had been done to him. Mad at the military and the Middle East, God and fate, the guards and his crew. I was mad at every little thing that had gone into the creation of whatever darkness he now carried inside him.

"What are you doing?" I rose out of bed after he'd finished pulling on his boots and moved toward the door.

He didn't look back as he left. "Whatever I have to do to keep you safe."

The rest of the day, I tried my best to distract myself from what had happened early that morning. I figured out pretty quickly that I wouldn't be successful if Keenan and I stayed locked inside all day. Brecken's truck was gone, and I didn't see any news trucks out front, so Keenan and I left the house after breakfast, going wherever our feet decided to take us.

We started at the city pool, which was a bit of a walk, but I didn't mind. The exercise was an effective way to unplug my mind from certain topics.

After spending the rest of the morning and part of the afternoon there, we headed to the library. It was quiet—most people seemed to be of the mind they'd rather be outside enjoying the sun—we spent the rest of the day there. We were the last ones to leave before closing.

On the walk home, Keenan and I stopped by a burger place for dinner, but he had to finish most of my meal too, because I was too distracted to eat. Now that the day was coming to an end, all of the thoughts and worries I'd drowned out during the daylight hours were creeping in.

I couldn't ignore what had happened. I couldn't ignore what was going to happen. Brecken had wrapped his fingers around my neck. My breath had recovered, but the linen scarf tied around my neck was concealing the proof of what had happened. I needed to talk with him. I needed him to be willing to talk with me about it. I needed him to know that even though I took it seriously, I also seriously believed he could never truly hurt me. He'd call it the justification of a victim. I'd inform him it was the truth of a survivor.

I needed to see him. Tonight. I'd already let too much time go by, knowing him and the way he could brood until he'd lowered himself to the level of pond scum. We'd have to be smart about these night terrors of his, I realized that. I probably should have used one of the maneuvers he'd taught me to free myself and snap him awake. This was an obstacle we'd have to overcome. God knew we'd traversed plenty already.

"Hey, Mom? Can I play a game on your phone?" Keenan asked as he downed the last of my fries.

I stirred myself from my thoughts to dig through my purse. "You can," I said, doing another sweep of it. "If I'd brought it with me."

Keenan slumped into his chair.

"Sorry, I must have left it on the charger. You can play one when we get home." Standing, I held out my hand for him.

He still hadn't let go of it a half hour later, when we finally made it to our street. Only six blocks to go. All of the walking today had made my feet ache and the rest of me tired. From the looks of Keenan, he was in the same shape.

"You want me to carry you the rest of the way?"

He looked up at me. "Really?"

"Really." I scooped him up. "It won't be long before I won't be able to lift you at all, so I better enjoy it now."

Keenan wound his arms around my neck and nestled his head onto my shoulder. He was quiet for about a block, and I almost thought he was asleep when he said, "Do you think Dad will come back?"

My feet kept moving, despite my insides momentarily collapsing. "Yeah, I think so. He said he will."

Keenan's fingers played with the back of my scarf. "But he's broken lots of promises. Like when he said he'd take me fishing. And never did. Or when he said he'd be home for dinner and never showed up ... he breaks lots of promises."

I didn't want to lie to my son. Just as much as I didn't want to tell him the truth. So I stayed quiet, letting him believe whatever he wanted to.

"I hope he doesn't keep this promise."

My head tipped toward him. "What promise?"

"His promise to come back." Keenan burrowed his head under my neck a little deeper.

"Keenan …"

"I'm sorry, Mom. I know that's a bad thing to say. Don't be mad at me." His arms worked around me a bit tighter.

"It's okay, baby." I patted his back, biting my cheek to keep from crying. "Just get some rest. Just fall asleep. It's been a long day."

I made a few shushing noises, rubbing his back until I knew he'd fallen asleep. I managed to hold my tears inside as I carried my sleeping child the last few blocks home.

By the time I made it up the porch, my arms were burning and my legs felt the same. I managed to maneuver Keenan onto my hip to get the door unlocked and opened, then I closed it and started toward the stairs to get him tucked in. I needed to see Brecken.

As I passed the hall table, where I'd left my cell phone on the charger, my cell phone started to ring. I had an idea who the caller would be before I saw his number on the screen. Arranging Keenan in one arm, I unplugged the phone and answered it.

"Camryn." From his voice alone, I knew something wasn't right. "Where are you? I've been trying to get a hold of you all day." Brecken sounded out of breath, like he was running.

I felt chills winding up my spine. "I was out with Keenan. I forgot my phone here. What's the matter?"

"Here? Where's *here*?" Brecken was definitely running, I could hear his footsteps pounding in the background. "Where are you?"

I turned around, putting my back to the wall. "Home. We just got home."

He cursed under his breath, nothing but the echo of footsteps moving quickly coming through the phone.

"Brecken? What's going on?" The anxious tone in my voice had returned.

"You haven't heard? You didn't see? There was an article that ran in the papers today. The big ones, the little ones. All of them."

Putting the phone on speaker, I reached for the newspaper still rolled up on the table where Keenan had set it that morning. My heart drifted into my throat when I saw the front page.

There were two pictures, both of them showing Brecken and me taken last night. One was snapped as we were entering the garage, our hands connected, him grinning back at me. The other was us leaving the garage, his hand still clutching mine, my other hand smoothing down the front of my skirt. The headline read: **The Hero and The Housewife Next Door: An All-American Affair.**

The paper fell from my hand, my hand covering my mouth. The whole world. The entire neighborhood. Everyone knew. Or would know soon. We might not have been getting it on in his garage as the before-and-after photos suggested, but that didn't matter. Because Brecken and I did love each other. We were having a relationship. Everyone knew.

*Everyone.*

"You need to leave, Camryn. You hear me? Don't wait. Just grab Keenan, get to the car, and get out of there." Brecken's words were strong, but I heard the worry in his voice. I read it in the way his footsteps only seemed to come faster.

"We'll wait for you. We're leaving together." My heart and head were racing as I caught up to what this meant. As I realized my whole plan had just gone to shit and I had to construct a new one on the fly.

"No! Leave now!" he shouted. "I've been out looking for you ever since I found out. I'm still a good twenty minutes away … please, just leave now. I'll meet up with you later, but get you and Keenan out of that house."

That chilling sensation wove down my spine again. "It's twenty minutes, Brecken. Nothing's going to change in twenty minutes. It'll give me some time to gather a few things—"

"He checked out of the rehab center."

My veins turned to ice.

"Camryn? Did you hear me?"

"I heard." My hand was shaking as I reached for the phone.

"They wouldn't tell me over the phone, so I drove my ass down here, and sure enough, he's gone. He checked out." He took a breath. "You know where he's going."

Fear. I felt it then. That living, breathing phantom. I'd known its sting before, but never like this—never like it was cutting off my oxygen at the same time it had sliced across my Achilles' heel.

"Where are you now?" My voice was small and weak, both arms winding around Keenan to keep him from falling.

"At the park just outside of town. I'm running to my truck now, but don't wait. Get in the car and go. Call me once you're driving, and we'll figure out a place to meet. Leave." The sound of his feet beating the ground stopped, the screech of his truck door opening following.

"Brecken?" My voice sounded as small as I felt. I couldn't do this.

"You're strong," he rasped, the engine firing to life. "You are so fucking strong. Don't forget that."

My eyes closed as I concentrated on that. I was strong enough to stop trembling and move toward the front door. "I'm leaving," I whispered, ending the call and shoving the phone into my back pocket.

A few more steps and I'd made it to the door. Keenan was still breathing evenly, his arms flopped over my back. I hadn't wanted to run away, but I had no choice left. Crew knew about Brecken and me. If I didn't leave, the next time I came face to face with him, he'd kill me.

Throwing the door open, I froze mid-step.

The look on his face confirmed my theory.

Crew's foreboding frame was blocking the doorway, his brow curved into his forehead. His eyes took me in, clutching Keenan, my composure crumbling one brick at a time.

"Here to greet me at the door and everything?" He motioned at me, one side of his mouth carving into his cheek. "You really must have missed me."

The whiskey vapors rolling off of him perfumed the air around me. When he moved inside, he closed the door behind him and fastened both locks.

"Crew ..." As he moved closer, I backed up, scanning the dark house like I was looking for a magical escape route to show itself.

"You *do* remember your husband's name. I wasn't sure when I opened the paper today and read the front-page article." His foot came down on the newspaper scattered on the floor. "I didn't realize I'd married such a vulgar little slut. I mean, I was barely gone three weeks and you couldn't keep that pussy of yours closed up?"

"Crew, stop," I whispered, praying Keenan didn't wake. Praying this wasn't the one night he slept lightly.

"You made a fool out of me. Everybody knows. Everybody will know that my wife was getting plowed by the cripple next door." His eyes flashed as he threw his arms in my direction. Then he stopped, looking like he was composing himself. The look, or lack thereof, on his face was far more worrisome than the anger.

"Might I suggest putting our son to bed?" Crew's eyes lifted up the stairs to the second floor. "We've got to have a talk. A long one."

I eyed the front door behind him. His brow lifted, a challenge in his eyes. Even with the full use of my body, I'd be lucky to make it past him to get out the door. I wouldn't make it two steps with Keenan in my arms.

When I turned to move up the stairs, Crew followed me, pulling my phone out of my back pocket. "You're smarter than you look."

Keeping myself angled so I could keep one eye on Crew and one on the stairs, I took them one step at a time. I had so much adrenaline in my system when I reached the top, I could taste it in the back of my throat.

Crew stayed a few steps behind, stalking me the entire way up. He stayed at the door of Keenan's room when I carried him inside. Laying him down and letting go was one of the hardest things I'd ever had to do, because I wasn't sure if this was the last time I would get to hold my son. I wasn't sure if this was the last time I'd get to see him.

Sliding the headphones over his head for the first time in weeks, I kissed his cheek. I silently said a few words to him in my mind, then I turned to face whatever awaited me. Crew stood in the hallway when I stepped out of the bedroom, closing the door.

His hand went behind my head, his fingers lacing through my hair, as he pushed me into our bedroom. "We're going to have a discussion. About loyalty."

When we were inside, he shoved me away, hard enough that my feet tangled and I hit the floor. He hadn't even hit me, and I'd already fallen. The beating hadn't even started, and I felt broken.

"Your definition of loyalty?" I curled my legs beneath me to stand. "Does this include or exclude you screwing Gina Meyers behind my back?"

Crew stopped in the middle of rolling up his shirt-sleeves. "You caught me. Good for you," he said, dripping condescension. "And you know what? It isn't really a *discussion* I want to have about loyalty."

Crew's arm swung around, his fist connecting with my cheek. It was so powerful, my vision blacked out for a moment as I spilled to the floor again.

"It's more of a *lesson* on loyalty."

It took a moment for my vision to clear, the taste of blood mixing with saliva in my mouth. My head was ringing, and he sounded like he was speaking in a tunnel. The pain was searing, but the anger crawling out from deep inside me was stronger. He had taken so much from me, the smallest of those robberies being my sense of safety. I'd lost so much to him, given him too much—I wasn't handing over one more fucking thing.

Forcing my hands beneath me, I lifted my upper half. Doing the same with my feet, I forced the rest up.

Crew laughed a dark note as he watched me try to stand. His eyes played that dark note next when he saw me succeed.

"Stay down." This time it was his other arm, the other fist, my other cheek, that sent me crashing back to the floor.

More blood. More ringing. More pain. More anger.

*Fight back.* Brecken's voice echoed in my head. *You don't play dead with the devil. You fight back.*

I focused on my breath as I pushed myself up again, counting to three to clear my mind.

*What parts of his body do you want to target? What parts of your body do you want to use?*

It was as if he was with me, right now, in this room. It was as though this were just another training session, this one with blood and bruised knuckles.

When Crew's arm came around this time, I managed to step out of the way. From the look on his face, I wasn't sure he'd ever been so surprised by anything in his life.

"You think because you know a few self-defense tricks, it's going to save you?"

As he circled around me, I circled with him. *Never take your eyes off of the attacker. Never let them take you by surprise.*

"No," I answered, having to move my jaw to finish my sentence. "But I'm not going to be the only one bruised and bloodied this time."

Crew stopped moving, his expression faltering. He recovered quickly, but I knew he was reeling. I knew he was trying to figure out what had happened to me and why I wasn't curling into a ball on the floor while he beat the shit out of me like before.

When he moved, it was like lightning, a flash of movement before the crack echoed through the room. He was shaking his fist from this hit, my eye already swelling shut.

"Stay. Down." Crew hovered over me, thrusting his finger at where I was spread out beneath him. A couple of his knuckles were split open, thin red slits smirking down at me.

As soon as I started to try to get up, he moved to hit me again. This time, I was ready. This time, it wasn't the voice of my teacher in my head guiding me; it was my intuition and instincts. Brecken had managed to work his lessons deep enough into my subconscious that my actions had become automatic.

Kicking, I smashed my foot into the side of his knee. As hard as I could. I kicked the same spot again when it didn't send him spilling over. He went down this time, and I used his temporary immobilization to put some distance between us.

For the first time in my life, I was thankful for the whiskey. I was thankful he'd downed enough of it to put a lesser man into a coma. His weakness became my strength. His downfall my foothold.

"Stay the fuck down." His lip curled over his teeth as he clutched at his knee.

Bracing my hand against the wall, I crawled up it, one hand at a time, until I was standing. Above him. Over him. It was the first time I'd been on two feet while he'd been collapsed below me.

"No." My voice didn't shake as I stared down at him. "You're never going to stop trying to knock me down. And I'm never going to let you keep me down again. So where does that leave us? Stuck on this twisted carousel ride?"

Crew grabbed hold of the footboard and used it to pull himself up. I could have used the time it took him to stand up to run. To grab Keenan and run. But I didn't want to spend my life running from him. Not when I'd already spent so much of it cowering beneath him.

Limping on his injured knee, he shuffled a couple of small steps toward me. It wasn't until he started lunging that I realized he'd been faking the extent of the damage to his knee.

Before I could shove away from the wall, he was on me, pinning me to it by driving his forearm into my throat. His eyes were unrecognizable, his expression an eerie calm as he punched me in the stomach. My cough caught in my throat due to the way his forearm was rammed into it, restricting my airway until I felt like my eyes were going to burst.

"There's nothing more pathetic than a bitch who thinks she's tough enough to fight back." Crew put his face in front of mine, pressing into my throat harder when it didn't result in the typical brand of fear he was used to seeing in my eyes. "If you were meant to have a pair of balls, they would have dropped when you were still in the womb. Get back in line already, woman."

Harnessing every last bit of strength I had left, I drove my knee into his groin. He instantly fell back, his forearm releasing me as he covered himself like he was shielding himself from any further attack.

"Thanks for the reminder." My voice was raspy from having a forearm smashing into my vocal chords, but I'd never felt so outspoken.

When Crew charged this time, I was expecting him. Leaning to the side, I drove my foot into the front of his other knee, causing a cry to spill from his mouth as he dropped to the floor.

"You bitch. Who in the hell do you think you are?" When he tried to stand, his knee gave out. His fist drove into the floor, a frustrated bellow coming from him at the same time.

"The woman you married." I shoved off of the wall, sliding the ring off my finger. I threw it on the floor in front of him as the blood dripping from my face splattered around it. "Who in the hell do you think *you* are?"

At first he chuckled, like this was an amusing game. Then he fell forward, grabbing for my legs as I backed away. I'd almost put enough distance between us, but I felt his hand snag one of my feet. Just enough to trip me up. When I hit the floor, the air rushed out of my lungs, but I knew I had to move.

He got a hand around my ankle before I could, and he used his strength to pull me back far enough that he could get his other hand around my other leg. "Come here, wife. I want to show you who in the hell I think I am."

He twisted me around, getting both of my legs pinned beneath him so I couldn't kick him. He kept his head just out of reach from my arms too, leaving me feeling powerless. He crawled up my body, sitting over me once he'd pinned my hips. When I moved to drive my palm into his throat, he blocked it, immediately following it with his own thrust to my throat.

I coughed, curling up off the floor as I reached for my throat. His fist came around to send me back down.

Trying to overpower him wouldn't work. I had to be smarter. Flattening my hand, I moved to drive the knife-edge of it into the side of his throat. He grabbed my wrist and squeezed until I cried out from the pain. That only made him squeeze harder, clamping down until I felt like my wrist was going to snap off.

Right before I felt myself about to pass out, he let go. My arm fell like a piece of yarn to my chest, my wrist feeling as though it were burning from the inside out.

"What else have you got? What else did that soldier hero try to teach you to protect yourself?" Crew was smirking at me as he held his hands at his sides. "Because this is kind of fun. It's turning me on when you fight back."

When he rocked his hips into my stomach, I felt his erection straining against his pants. Bile rose up in my throat, churning my insides when I realized how there was no end to the sickness that ran in this man's blood. When he rubbed himself against me again, I thrust both of my fists into him as hard as I could. He barely seemed to notice. Another chuckle was followed by his fists hitting their own mark.

My head lurched to the left from the second fist, my right ear ringing from where he'd hit me. I felt fresh rivers of warmth flowing out of me, my head throbbing so hard I felt sure my brain would dissolve. I'd never been in such a dire situation, but somehow, I felt indestructible.

I heard my phone ringing downstairs. The sound of my son breathing a room away. The beat of my heart drumming. The flutter of the moth's wings beating against the window outside. I could hear every little sound except for the sound of the man still laughing above me. I'd become immune to him. Absolved of my monster.

That was when I saw what had been left under the bed. A belt. Crew's. The same one he'd used to beat the shit out of me the night before he left in search of "help."

Help was on its way.

My arm stretched under the bed. My fingers curled around the metal buckle.

Brecken's voice was back in my head, his words and lessons playing on a loop. *Use what you've got. A bottle. A shoe. A key.*

The metal prong of a belt buckle.

Shoving the prong between my fingers, I swung my hand into him again.

He wasn't laughing anymore.

When I pulled my hand back, a red dot started to bleed through his shirt.

He stared at his side, blinking like what he was seeing wasn't real. The instant his body tensed, I slammed my hand back into his side, the prong piercing him again. He wailed, teetering to the side enough for me to crawl away. I kept the belt in my hand, primed and ready for when he came at me again.

But Crew continued to scoot away from me, keeping his hand pressed into his side as he moved toward the opposite side of the room.

*Get up. Get out.*

I could do this. I could find the strength I needed to push myself up, grab Keenan, and get out of here.

A floor below, there was a crash, followed by a shattering sound that echoed up the stairs, but I kept moving toward the door. Away from Crew. Away from this house of horrors.

In the back of my mind, I heard Brecken's voice calling my name. It wasn't in the same calm tenor as his instructions. It wasn't until I saw the flash of movement in the doorway, followed by a bellow as he took in the room, that I realized I wasn't hearing him in my head anymore. He was here.

Brecken flew in front of me, putting himself between Crew and me, and slid to his knees. "Oh Christ." He was staring at me, looking lost as he scanned me spread out on the carpet. "What did he do to you, baby? What did he fucking do?"

The lost look left his face, something dark taking its place as his head twisted toward where Crew was still drifting into the corner.

"Brecken, I'm okay." My free hand covered his, which was balling into a fist.

Hearing my words, followed by another inspection of my body, made him go rigid. His glare landed on Crew as Brecken's body quivered from the emotions he was barely managing to keep control of.

"I'm going to kill you." Brecken started to rise, his voice sinister. "But first, you're going to suffer."

My hand held on to his, winding around it tighter as he started to move away. "Brecken, look at me." I waited for him to take another look. A different kind. Sitting up, I ran my hands down my body, my one hand still clutching the metal buckle. "Look at him."

Brecken followed my eyes to the man slithering away.

"I did it. I fought back." I got my feet below me to stand, using Brecken to guide me up. Standing beside him, I stared across the room, not missing the difference in the current shape or position of our bodies. "I won."

Brecken's hand lifted to my face, like he wanted to touch me but was afraid it would hurt. "Damn straight you did. And now I'm going to finish it."

Crew's gravelly chuckle came from his body on the other side of the room, now tucked between a window and the dresser. "Come on, hero. Hit a guy when he's on the ground. Prove the kind of man you are." Crew lifted his hand, inviting Brecken over in a mocking fashion. "Show her what you're going to do to me."

The first step Brecken took toward Crew, I cut in front of him. My hand molded onto his chest, my swollen eyes lifting to his. He was too focused on Crew to notice.

"Worst case, Brecken. This is it. I'm ready. Leave with us."

That was when his gaze lowered. His face drew up when he saw my face up close. "I can't let him get away with doing this to you. I can't let him get away with everything he's ever done to you."

When Brecken slid me aside to pass, I moved in front of him again. "No matter what you do to him, it won't change what he's done to me."

"No. But it will make me feel better." Brecken's lip curled when Crew's chuckle continued to roll across the room.

"Come on, tough guy. I know you want to. I know you want to beat my ass for being the guy who fucked your girl for six years."

"That's not the reason I want to beat your ass, you son of a bitch." Brecken's finger stabbed in Crew's direction. "I want to make you hurt because you beat the woman I loved for six years. You fucking tortured her."

My hand lifted to his face, feeling the way his whole body was shaking. I gently tipped his head down so it was aligned with mine. "Leave with us. Don't stay because of him."

For a minute, the room was quiet. Then Brecken's chest rattled as he blew out a breath like he was trying to purge himself of something evil.

"Camryn?" He swallowed, still fighting himself. "Go get Keenan and get in the car. When you're both inside, honk once you make it into the street. I'll meet you then." He slid me behind him after that, blocking me entirely from Crew.

"I'm a beaten man." Crew coughed. "What do you think I'm going to do? Spit on her?"

Brecken stepped toward him before stopping. "You try, and you'll be spitting into a tube for the rest of your life." When he noticed me still behind him, lingering, he pointed at the door. "Get Keenan. I'll meet you both outside."

A smile started to move across my mouth. He tried his hardest to mirror it.

"If you think I'm letting you run away with my wife *and* my boy, you are one dumb fuck." All notes of laughter were gone from Crew's voice. "You aren't putting a finger on my son."

My body moved before my head had made up its mind. The moment my eyes reached the monster across from me, my decision was made.

"He's not your son."

Silence.

From Crew.

From Brecken.

They were so quiet, I wondered if I'd said out loud what I'd been trying to. God knew I'd been trying to vocalize it for years.

"He's not your son." This time, my voice filled the whole room, no mistake.

It was Brecken who responded first, his head turning toward me. His chest was rising and falling hard, his brows drawn together. "Keenan? He's …"

"Yours," I said. "He's your son."

More lines creased into Brecken's expression, his throat moving as he tried to accept what I'd just told him.

My eyes were practically swollen shut, but tears fell from them. "Now you know why. Now you know why I did what I did." I had to stop to keep from choking on the sob I felt rising from deep within. "My dad, if he found out, when he found out, he would have …" My eyes closed when I put myself back into the hopelessness of that period in my life. "I didn't realize I'd only exchanged one monster for another until it was too late."

Something caught in Brecken's throat. "I have a son?" he whispered to himself. "I have a son." This time he was saying it to me.

The belt fell from my hand so I could grab his. "You have a son. Keenan's yours."

As the reality started to set in on Brecken's face, little by little, Crew let out a grunt. "Premature, wasn't that how you explained it to me?" His eyes narrowed on me. "That kid was always a bit of a disappointment. I guess this explains it." He waved her finger between Brecken and me. "He was mothered by a whore, and fathered by a guy who was dumb enough to get caught by the enemy."

When Brecken lunged toward him, I was already there. "This is what he wants." I planted my hands on his chest and pushed. "Don't give it to him."

Brecken didn't take his eyes off of Crew, the exchange between them in that look more impactful than any brawl could have been.

"Get Keenan." A tremor reverberated down Brecken's back from holding himself back. "We're leaving."

I didn't wait. The more time those two spent inside this room, the more dangerous it became. I was a few steps away from the door when I heard it. The metallic ring of a bullet being loaded into a chamber.

Spinning around, I found Crew in the same spot he'd been on the floor, but the bottom drawer of the dresser was open now and a pistol was in his hand. His eyes were on me, but the barrel was aimed at Brecken.

"What did you teach her to save her from this, hotshot?" When Crew aimed the gun at me, Brecken went to lunge in front of me. "Make another move and I'll put one in your spawn after I put one in her."

Brecken froze. "What are you going to do, Crew? Huh? Shoot her? Shoot me?" His voice walked the blade's edge of controlled and crazed. "You know what they do to cops in jails? Do you really want to find out?"

Crew sat up, still grabbing at his side with his other hand. He blinked at Brecken across the room. "You lost it. After all of the interviews, the article in the paper today, your secret lover calling it off when she realized it was wrong. You lost it." Crew's face remained flat, his expression the same as he kept the gun aimed at my chest. "You went crazy. Started attacking my wife, your ex-lover." Crew's gaze circled the bedroom, a disturbed, bloody scene. "I had to kill you," he said matter-of-factly around a shrug. "Unfortunately, my beloved wife died of the injuries you gave her."

He'd worked this all out already. With his connections in the department, I didn't doubt he could find a way to bend the evidence to prove just that.

"Keenan …" That was where every worry led to. My child. The life I'd sacrificed everything to preserve.

"Oh, don't you worry. I'll look after him." Crew smirked at me, his teeth stained with blood. "I'll raise him to grow up to be just like me."

When my body responded by lunging toward Crew, he shoved off the wall, his finger on the trigger. "Show me what you've got now, bitch."

A blast.

A bullet.

A blur of movement.

"Run!" Brecken's voice booming back at me.

A body falling to the floor.

A scream was rising from my chest, but it never surfaced. I couldn't scream. I couldn't cry. I couldn't linger.

I had to run.

I had to save my son. I had to save *his* son.

As soon as I spun around and started for the door, another blast went off. I didn't know where the second bullet settled, if it was in my arm or in the wall beside me. I just kept running.

As I rounded into the hall, I saw Crew shove himself off the wall and follow me. I saw the other body on the floor, facedown, still. I ran. When I wanted to stay, I ran. Because I knew it was what he wanted. Because I knew part of him was inside the five-year-old boy I was running toward.

Crew was shouting after me, his footsteps coming faster. When I reached Keenan's bedroom door, I realized I wouldn't make it. There wasn't time for me to grab him and get out. Crew was steps behind me and had been firing ten thousand rounds at the shooting range every year for years. He wouldn't miss again.

I'd left the body of the man I loved. And now I was moving away from the child I'd brought into the world. My whole life. All of it felt like it just had been or was about to be taken away from me.

As Crew's shadow moved out of the bedroom, I sprinted down the hall and disappeared right before he stepped out into the darkness. I was too scared to breathe for fear he'd hear it, so I stayed silent and still, letting the dark conceal me. He paused outside of Keenan's room, listening for a moment. He kept his gun high as he limped by it.

"Camryn." He sang my name in a way that had my skin prickling. "Come out, come out, wherever you are."

I crouched into as small of a ball as I could as he crept closer, looking over the edge of the stairway downstairs.

"Come out. I know you're in here, and you can't hide forever." He moved toward the stairs, paused at the top, and listened again. "I put a bullet in your boyfriend. He can't save you this time."

I pictured their faces. The sound of their laughter.

I found my strength.

Slipping out from behind the guest room door, I rushed toward him. Full sprint, arms out, hands spread, I channeled everything I was feeling into that charge.

He heard me before he saw me. As he started to spin around, my hands planted into his back and the inertia of my body discharged into his. His body teetered at the top of the stairs. The gun fell from his hands as he spilled down them. Head over feet, the sickening symphony of noise created by flesh on wood, the gasp of air expunged from one's lungs from each impact.

I felt like I was watching my own fall down those same stairs. I felt like I was reliving it. But this time, I was walking away unbroken.

When Crew's body crashed to the floor below, he didn't move. A pathetic whimper crept from his mouth, but there was nothing else.

After walking down a couple of steps to retrieve his gun, I went back up and stared down at his broken body. "I can save myself." I said it to him, but really, I think I was saying it to myself.

I hadn't realized it until now, but it was true. I could save myself.

Once I was certain Crew wasn't going to be getting up any time soon, I rushed down the hall and paused outside of Keenan's room. Opening his door, I sagged with relief when I saw that he was still out, the headphones secure on his head, his superhero stuffie clutched in his arms. I whispered the door closed, then I raced toward the master bedroom.

The sound of that first bullet firing. The noise he'd made when it hit him. The thud his body had made when striking the floor. I didn't know what I'd find when I rounded into the bedroom, but I told myself I would be strong no matter what.

Brecken's body was in the same position on the floor, motionless. My heart throbbed as I moved toward him, falling to my knees when I reached his head. A pool of blood spread across the carpet, coming from his chest.

Reaching into his back pocket, I pulled out his phone. My finger was shaking as I punched in three numbers.

The other end clicked. "Nine, one, one. Where is your emergency."

My hand dropped to Brecken's neck, searching for a pulse. That was when I noticed the dog tags. They were stained with blood all over again.

"I lost him," I said, finally letting myself cry. "I lost him again."

# twenty-one

His death the first time around had been staged.

This time it was real.

Those two instances shared one common thread—he came back from both.

It had been almost six months since that night. Some days, it felt like it had just happened yesterday, and others, it felt like a lifetime ago. Life was like that though, ever-changing, keeping one on their toes.

God knew it had kept me on mine for the past half a year. My life had changed so much that I still woke up some mornings feeling like I was living a stranger's life. The house, the sounds, the peace, the landscape, the people. I didn't wake up feeling like that every morning, but I did awake each morning with a profound sense of gratitude.

An arm lolled across the beach blanket toward mine, his hand braiding through mine. "Stay or go?"

I checked the general position of the sun on the horizon. It was close to dinnertime and would be dark soon. My head turned toward the sound of Keenan cheering after making a goal through a couple of laid out beach toys with the friends he'd made today at the beach.

Then I looked at the man stretched out beside me, broken and whole. Perfect and imperfect. Scarred and healed.

The man who'd jumped in front of a bullet for me.

"Stay." My hand squeezed his as I rolled onto my side. "Did you have a nice nap?"

"I did. And I didn't wake up in a sweating mess, so it was an extra nice nap." Brecken stretched his free arm above his head, tipping his glasses back to search for Keenan. When he found him, he smiled.

"No nightmares?" I asked.

"No nightmares." He took off his glasses, letting me see his eyes wander my body. "But I might have been dreaming about something else that got my heart racing."

My hand went to his chest. Sure enough, it was beating good and fast.

"Later. Just as long as you're tucked in and asleep by eleven." I examined the permanent shadows under his eyes.

He still didn't sleep much at night—he didn't trust himself to not wake up in some crazed fit—but each morning, he seemed to trust himself a little more. We were figuring out this new life together, one day at a time.

"Then we'd better get the boy to bed right about now." He checked his wrist, where he wasn't wearing a watch. "Because I've got a big night planned for us."

I tipped my sunhat back so he could see my eyebrows. "What 'big plans' do you have for us tonight?"

His shoulder lifted as he rolled onto his side to face me. "Making love to pretty much every square inch of your body. For starters."

My teeth bit into my lip to keep from laughing. "Anything else?"

"Just begging you to marry me until you finally agree."

"So pretty much the same plans as every other night?" I played along.

"Basically, yeah."

His hand dropped to the bend of my waist, smoothing the material of my cover-up. Even though I usually kept my cover-up on whenever we came to the beach, I no longer had the need, or felt the need to cover myself up from head to toe. Some scars had faded, some never would, but they were all a part of me. There was nothing to hide.

"First, and I don't know why I need to keep repeating this," I said, lifting my left hand. The platinum band was gone. In its place was the old birthstone ring he'd won me a lifetime ago. "I agreed to marry you a good ten years ago."

"But we're not married." Brecken lifted his bare left hand. "I'm not going to stop begging you to marry me until you actually do."

"Yeah, I think I'm starting to figure that out." I sat up so I could grab the sunscreen. Brecken used to have skin that would tan at the first hint of sun, but now he burned if we didn't keep to a sunscreen schedule. Six years in the dark had a way of changing a person, from the surface layer of skin to what went much deeper.

"Second, I can't marry you until everything's finalized from before."

I distracted myself with the sunscreen so he didn't have to see the look in my eye whenever I thought about Crew. His hand found mine, not caring that it was wet and goopy with sunscreen.

"I know," he said, our hands slippery together. "I'm not going anywhere. My whole life is here, with you and Keenan."

I scooted toward him so I could rub the SPF Albino in-to his chest and shoulders first. He sat up in front of me, giv-ing me a goofy grin as I started to rub it onto his body.

I hadn't seen Crew since the night he'd shot Brecken. He'd spent the first month in a hospital and rehab center, recovering from the injuries sustained from his fall. He'd broken in far more places than I had taking the same fall, leading me to wonder who'd truly been the weaker of us. Since then, he'd been living it up in the county jail, going between court hearings, where he'd been found guilty of attempted murder and repeated offenses of domestic assault, thanks to the photos Brecken had thought to take and I'd been brave enough to bring forward.

Crew was going to spend a lot of time in prison. A lot more than most men in his situation probably, given the fact that the person he'd attempted to murder was an American hero. Crew might have been a cop with connections, but all of that clout bled back into the woodwork when who'd he shot made national headlines. He was lucky he'd made it from the courthouse to the armored van without being shot.

After he'd been sentenced, Crew's chief cleared out his desk and sent me all of the contents. That was where I found the key. The one that went to a security box at one of the banks in town. The one where he'd stashed all of the "evi-dence" that I was an unfit mother.

Brecken and I had burned it all that night, not leaving until the last ash had smoldered out.

Crew was gone from our lives. Exorcised. For good.

After squeezing another dime of sunscreen onto my palm, I smoothed it into the freshest mark on his skin. A puckered circular one, right to the side of his breastplate.

"More scars to add to the collection?" My fingers smoothed over the bullet mark.

He glanced down at it like it was an old scratch. "At least when people look at me, they'll know."

"What will they know?"

He glanced down at himself again, eyeing a few of the many scars that marred him. "That I lived. That I bled for what I believed in. That I fought for the people I loved." He leaned forward to kiss my forehead, then he spun around when I twirled my finger at him. "I told you I'd die for you." He glanced over his shoulder as I sunscreened his back.

"You didn't die," I said, sounding more stubborn than I'd intended. It was a touchy subject for me.

"Pretty sure coding counts as dying." His hands dropped to my feet, and he pulled me against him. "Give me a break."

Smiling at his back, I finished my sunscreening project just in time. The soccer game over, Keenan came jogging back. Brecken's old dog tags were swinging from his neck.

"Hey, Dad?" he called from a ways back. "Dad?"

I nudged Brecken. "Dad."

"Oh, yeah. Still getting used to that." He turned toward Keenan, unable to hide the grin on his face.

A few months ago, we'd sat down and told Keenan the truth. Who his father really was. It had been hard and there'd been tears and questions, but in the end, it had been the right decision. Keenan should grow up knowing his father was a great man, instead of the opposite kind. Brecken had told him he didn't have to call him dad if he didn't want to, and at first, Keenan hadn't. But now, it was coming more frequently. More Dads than Breckens. Both of them were still getting used to it, I guessed.

Having to explain Crew's situation to Keenan had been the hardest part, mainly because I had to say why he was spending the next couple of decades in jail—for hurting me and shooting Brecken. I'd been worried everything would leave Keenan with all of the emotional scars I'd worked so hard to keep from him, but in reality, he was far stronger and more resilient than I'd given him credit for. Brecken said Keenan got that from me. I said Keenan got it from him.

In the end, I supposed he got it from us both.

"What can I do for you, little man?" Brecken asked when Keenan broke to a stop just beside the blanket, grabbed a bottle of water, and chugged most of it.

"Will you go boogie boarding with me?" Keenan pointed out at the waves.

"Let's see, I was really comfortable just sitting here doing nothing, and the sun's going to be right in our eyes, and that water's freezing cold …" Brecken lifted his brows as he bounced to his feet. "Let's do it."

Keenan let out a little whoop, snagging one boogie board while Brecken grabbed another. They both jogged down to the water, looking like a couple of people who'd grown up accustomed to beach life.

That little house as close to the beach as he could get was now our home. I loved it. It felt like it had always been my home, even though we'd just moved in. Good neighborhood, amazing school district, a ten-block walk to the beach, it was the perfect spot to raise a child. Better than all of that, it was a fresh start.

"Hey, Mom!" Keenan came to a sudden stop, hollering back at me. "Want to come with us?"

Without answering him, I stood, slid the cover-up over my head, and grabbed the last boogie board resting in the sand.

I didn't want to be anywhere without them.

They were my peace.

In the way a person wouldn't know light without the darkness, I wouldn't know peace without the pain. I was a survivor. Of life. Of torture. Of abuse.

I must have been taking too long, because Brecken came jogging back with a grin on his face. His arms roped around me before he slung me over his shoulder.

A laugh welled up from inside me as he jogged back toward Keenan. "Can't a girl have a second to herself?"

Brecken's head shook, his arms tightening. "I missed out on six years. I'm not missing one more second. It's torture without you."

*the end*

Thank you for reading TORTURED
by NEW YORK TIMES and USATODAY
bestselling author, Nicole Williams.

Nicole loves to hear from her readers.
You can connect with her on:

Facebook: Nicole Williams (Official Author Page)
Twitter: nwilliamsbooks
Blog: nicoleawilliams.blogspot.com

## Other Works by Nicole:

MISTER WRONG

HATE STORY

CRASH, CLASH, and CRUSH (HarperCollins)

UP IN FLAMES (Simon & Schuster UK)

LOST & FOUND, NEAR & FAR, HEART & SOUL

FINDERS KEEPERS, LOSERS WEEPERS

STEALING HOME, TOUCHING DOWN

COLLARED

THE FABLE OF US

THREE BROTHERS

HARD KNOX, DAMAGED GOODS

CROSSING STARS

GREAT EXPLOITATIONS

THE EDEN TRILOGY

THE PATRICK CHRONICLES

Made in the USA
Lexington, KY
18 July 2017